BLACK BIRD

MARK PAWLOSKY

BLACK BIRD

— A —

NIK BYRON

INVESTIGATION

Ramblin' House
P·R·E·S·S

This is a work of fiction. Names, characters, organizations, places, events, and incidents are either products of the author's imagination or are used fictitiously.

Published by Ramblin' House Press, Kansas City, MO
www.markpawlosky.com

GIRL FRIDAY PRODUCTIONS

Edited and designed by Girl Friday Productions
www.girlfridayproductions.com

Design: Paul Barrett
Project management: Sara Spees Addicott
Editorial: Laura Dailey

Image credits: cover © Shutterstock/Doubletree Studio

ISBN (paperback): 979-8-218-33003-3
ISBN (ebook): 979-8-218-33004-0

Library of Congress Control Number: 2024902998

First Edition

To ForbiddenStories.org's Safebox Network
for reporters.

PROLOGUE

The snowstorm rolled in a little after noontime and continued throughout the evening and into the small hours, turning the Methow Valley into a deep, powdered-sugar landscape. It was the first major storm of the season, and Anne was determined to cut a track in the virgin snow before anyone else had a chance to spoil it. She had waxed her telemarks the night before and was up early now, brewing coffee and making a fried-egg sandwich to pack for lunch. Leza Burdock, her partner, wasn't a skier, and Anne was careful not to wake her when she slipped out of bed. The sky was beginning to lighten, and Anne could see the outline of Goat Mountain from her kitchen window, off in the distance. That was her destination this morning, a fourteen-mile round trip from the cabin. Otto, Leza's portly Dalmatian, sat patiently by the front door, tail rhythmically slapping the pine floor.

Anne had arrived in the Methow Valley in the Pacific Northwest nine months earlier after she was dismissed from Xion Labs, a biotech and life sciences company located outside of Washington, DC, in Rockville, Maryland. The company informed her that it had lost its government contract and could no longer fund her virology department, firing her core team of research scientists and scattering other associates across the company.

Anne secured severance packages for herself and the three other dismissed colleagues, and after cashing in her settlement and selling a condo she owned in Alexandria, Virginia, she packed up her late-model Subaru and headed west, searching for a spot to set down roots. She found what she was looking for in the remote North Cascade mountain range in Washington State.

Her former colleagues, Thom Berg and Deidre Steward, also fled to out-of-the-way places, Berg to Bokeelia Island in Florida, and Steward to the Outer Banks in North Carolina. Based on a postcard Anne had happily discovered one day in her mailbox, Puck Hall, the youngest member of the research group, was making plans to hike the Appalachian Trail.

Anne had immediately fallen in love with both the Methow Valley and Leza, a large-animal veterinarian, whom she met one morning while browsing at the local farmers' market in Twisp. On the surface, the two didn't have much in common: Anne was athletic where Leza was bookish; Anne was a vegetarian, and Leza loved nothing better than a medium-rare T-bone steak; Anne was outspoken, while Leza was quiet. Anne was a Democrat, and Leza a Libertarian; Anne was urban, Leza was rural.

Nonetheless, they found common ground in their shared love of nature, cheesy eighties movies, road trips, inexpensive wine, and yard sales, and five weeks after meeting, Anne moved in with Leza and Otto.

If there was one area of her life Anne was reluctant to share with Leza, it was her past work in the Washington, DC, area. At first, this reticence troubled Leza—she felt Anne was trying to hide something from her—but as kindred spirits, they had a thousand and one other things to talk about, and Leza didn't dwell on it.

Anne filled her CamelBak with water, wrapped the sandwich in waxed paper, poured trail mix into a brown bag, and dropped it into her backpack. At the last minute, she grabbed the GoPro from the hallway closet and crammed it in the bottom of her pack. She hated the damn thing, thought it intrusive and a pain to operate, but felt she at least needed to make a show of using it since it was a birthday gift from Leza. She debated whether to take Otto but, in the end, decided against it, fearing he would sink into the fluffy snow and only slow her down. As it was, she'd be doing well to be back home before nightfall, and that was if she hustled.

"I'll take you out tomorrow for a long run," she promised the sad-eyed animal and poured a scoop of kibble in his bowl. "The cross-country trails will be groomed by then." She could hear Otto pawing at the door as she stepped outside and closed it behind her.

Anne clicked into her skis and, with a powerful thrust of the long poles, was quickly skating down their drive and in no time was whistling through a stand of ponderosa pines. She crested a slight hill and nearly toppled over when she stopped suddenly to avoid hitting a porcupine that meandered across her path. She shoved off again and was instantly lost in the serenity of her surroundings.

After heavy poling over a long, flat expanse, Anne rounded a bend and broke out of the tree line, the base of Goat Mountain coming into view. She calculated she could reach the mountain in less than an hour and, from there, slip the skins over the skis and climb a quarter of the way up, maybe farther, depending on how tired she was, and then ski down.

It started snowing again, lightly at first. By the time Anne reached the mountain, the snow was coming down harder, dry flakes the size of small clamshells covering her head and upper body. She unsnapped her skis, slung the backpack off her shoulders, and sat on a deadfall to eat her sandwich and hydrate before making the ascent.

She had written Leza a short note that morning before leaving but hadn't told her the route she intended to take and now mildly regretted the oversight. Anne finished her sandwich, begrudgingly attached the GoPro to the handle of her ski pole, activated the avalanche beacon she carried, affixed the skins to the skis, and started to climb.

She was surprised at how swiftly she moved up the mountainside. The yoga and running had actually paid off, and seventy-five minutes after starting the climb, she reached the quarter-way point. She was tempted to continue on, but the snow showed no signs of letting up, and she didn't want to press her luck this early in the season by herself.

She activated the GoPro camera and looked around in awe. "I have Goat Mountain all to myself. It's a glorious day."

Anne had not seen a single soul on her way out that morning, but now, as she looked over her shoulder, another skier was clawing up the mountainside. "Who can that be?" she said under her breath as she turned around to face down the mountain.

She considered skiing downhill, but whoever was coming toward her was directly in the fall line she intended to take off the mountain. Anne shrugged off her backpack again, grabbed a handful of trail mix, and leaned against her poles to watch and, in so doing, knocked the camera loose and into the snow. "Ah, shit. The hell with it," she muttered as she shoved the GoPro back into her pack.

Anne didn't have long to wait. The climber was fit and chewed up the terrain in long, powerful strides.

"Congratulations," the skier said, huffing, when she reached Anne. "You beat me. Doesn't happen often. It's a personal point of pride with me to be first on the mountain after a major dump. Name's Narda."

Narda slid her sunglasses off her nose and perched them on the top of her candy-cane-striped knit cap, a red pom-pom on top, revealing pale-gray eyes the color of cement and skin as shiny as a copper kettle from the sun.

She had an angular face and wide, muscular shoulders. Anne smiled victoriously and reached out her gloved hand. "Anne, Anne Paxton. Nice to meet you," she said.

"Nice to meet you as well," Narda said, releasing Anne's hand. She tugged down the sunglasses and started to climb again.

"You're not skiing down?" Anne asked.

Narda shook her head. "Aiming for the ridge," she said and motioned across the face of the mountain with a pole to a spot about three hundred yards above them. "It's my favorite run. The powder is sublime."

"Never been up there," Anne said.

"Not many people have. That's why I love it. Come on. I'll break a trail and you can follow."

"I don't know." Anne hesitated. "It looks awfully steep."

Narda laughed. "Steep? It's a sheer cliff, but there's a switchback on the far side that winds around through a stand of birch trees to a nice gradual descent. You can't see that from here, but suit yourself."

Anne checked the time on her smart watch. She might be able to make the ridge, ski down, and still be home in time for dinner if she didn't loiter. It'd be tight, but she could do it, and she'd text Leza when she reestablished cell coverage and let her know she was on her way.

What the hell, you only live once, she thought and tucked her chin against her chest and plunged forward. The snow was as light as goose down, and she practically floated in the track Narda cut.

By the time they reached the ridge, though, Anne had a dull ache in her thighs from skating up the vertical incline and decided to rest briefly, drink some water, and eat a couple more handfuls of trail mix before starting down. Both skiers stripped the skins off their skis while they caught their breath.

"You ready?" Narda asked.

"Lead on," Anne said and wrapped the pole straps tightly around her gloved hands.

Narda dug her poles into the snow and, with a heave, disappeared around a sharp downhill curve. Anne followed but soon lost sight of Narda as she zigged and zagged down the steep switchback.

Darkness was beginning to seep in around the edges of the sky, and Anne now cursed herself for following Narda in the first place. It was foolish of her, and the terrain was nowhere near as gentle as she had been led to believe. She was becoming exhausted, and her legs were turning rubbery from the exertion.

Anne shot around a hairpin turn and pulled up abruptly, the mountain dropping off below her, thousands of feet of nothingness beyond the tips of her skis.

Her heart was hammering so hard, it felt like it was going to burst from her chest. She closed her eyes and forced herself to inhale deep gulps of cold air to steady her shaking limbs.

Anne finally collected herself, planted her poles to push back from the abyss, but stopped when she heard a soft cough from behind her.

Narda appeared out of nowhere, skis off, in boots. "You need to be more careful, Anne," she said. "You're lucky you didn't sail right off the edge."

Anne twisted her head around. "Narda, thank goodness. I thought I'd lost you. You should have warned me about this turn. I might have killed myself," she scolded.

"You got a helluva set of brakes on those skis, I'll give you that. What's the brand?" Narda said, smiling. "I need to get me a pair."

"Don't joke. It's not funny, goddamn it," Anne said and attempted to back away.

"Sorry, you're right," Narda said, advancing, straddling Anne's skis, blocking her retreat.

"Narda, what are you doing?"

Narda pushed her sunglasses to the top of her head, her eyes like two cold gray spikes now, the smile gone.

Anne, unable to maneuver, panicked, and then it came to her. "No," she begged, ashen-faced. "I swear to God, no one knows anything. I haven't told a soul."

Narda drew closer.

"Please, don't do this," Anne pleaded. "I'll disappear. For good, this time. I promise."

"You got that right, sister," Narda said and shoved her in the back. She watched as Anne pitched forward, arms and legs helicoptering, fighting, unsuccessfully, to arrest her descent, until she was swallowed up by the darkness.

CHAPTER 1

Nik Byron caught a glimpse of himself in the hallway mirror as he strolled past, a bundle on his shoulder, and grimaced as if someone had stubbed a cigarette out on his arm. His reflection depressed him. Unshaven, disheveled, red-eyed, irritable, Nik easily had packed on a dozen pounds over the past several months, love handles like sandbags spilling over his waistline. He couldn't remember the last time he had been dressed in anything but sweatpants and hoodies.

He sighed, gently shifted the bundle, careful not to jostle it, and continued to pace. Nik had not slept for more than three hours at a stretch in the past week. Isobel, his newborn, was colicky and unsympathetic to his needs.

The child's mother, Samantha Whyte, was expected home that evening after completing a five-day swing through the Midwest with her new boss and potential presidential candidate, US Senator Eva Summers. She couldn't walk through their front door fast enough to suit Nik. He loved Isobel, but, so far, fatherhood had been a living hell.

It'd been months since Nik had taken his scheduled leave from *Newshound,* the online media organization where he worked as an editor, investigative reporter, and podcast host, intending to marry, honeymoon in Spain and Portugal with Sam, and then return home to oversee work converting a spare bedroom in his Washington, DC, condo into a nursery for the baby.

At least that was the plan, until the novel coronavirus had crushed their dreams like stampeding bulls in Pamplona. The wedding was postponed, the trip to Spain scrapped, the nursery conversion delayed. The only event that had come off as scheduled was the baby's birth. Isobel showed up right on time and now slept—when she slept—in a secondhand crib tucked in a corner of Sam and Nik's bedroom.

With the coronavirus now a fading memory and life returning to normal, Nik was looking forward to this day. It had been circled on his calendar for weeks. He was scheduled to return to work at *Newshound* as night editor, not the most glamorous job, but still, he was grateful for the opportunity to reboot his career and to actually have a life once again after having been cooped up first by the virus and then by childcare duties.

Isobel had finally stopped fussing in his arms, and when Nik looked down, he saw her eyelids slowly close. He didn't dare attempt to lay the baby in the crib and risk jarring her. Instead, he eased himself gently into an overstuffed chair in the living room and started softly humming. Within minutes, both father and daughter were fast asleep.

When he woke, the room was dark and Sam was smiling kindly down at them, a bag of groceries in one arm, a stuffed giraffe in the other. Nik blinked rapidly, three or four times, and looked around, confused.

"Shhhh," Sam said when he was about to speak.

"What time is it?" Nik whispered, his mouth dry, a kink in his neck from sleeping awkwardly.

"A little past seven. How long has she been out?"

Nik thought for a moment. "Almost six hours," he said, astonished and, for the first time in days, feeling rested. He rubbed a hand across his face to revive himself.

"I think you cured her of her colic, Nik Byron," Sam said and set the groceries and stuffed animal down on a coffee table before bending low to give him a kiss, her bangle earrings clanging like small wind chimes, and gingerly prying the baby from his arms. "Why don't you shower. I'll lay her down and then fix us some dinner."

Nik staggered to his feet and wandered off to the bathroom. "I want to hear all about your trip," he said over his shoulder, but Sam didn't hear him. She had already walked into their bedroom and closed the door.

Privately, Nik fretted about his return to the newsroom. He worried he had accumulated too much rust, to say nothing of fat, sitting at home all those months not working, but to his relief, the overnight desk proved to be the perfect reentry vehicle to the office. After a couple of back-to-back shifts, he felt like he had never left.

True, it had been fairly calm, news-wise, and managing the spartan staff wasn't a heavy lift. The usually bustling newsroom, with its warren of cubicles, was as quiet as a monastery at night. In addition to Nik, the night crew consisted of a copy editor, a sports reporter, a news clerk, and an intern.

Nik was chatting up the overly caffeinated sports reporter about possible Super Bowl matchups when the copy editor, a dark-haired, thick-waisted woman with smudged glasses, approached, the intern in tow.

"You see this?" Doria Miller asked, waving a printout in front of Nik's nose like a matador's cape. Nik considered Miller one of *Newshound*'s better copy editors. She was fast, exacting, and a strong wordsmith, but she could be officious and didn't hide her contempt for reporters, or editors, for that matter. It was a mystery to Nik why she had ever chosen a career in journalism in the first place.

"It's impossible for me to read if you keep flashing it in front of my eyes like that, Doria," Nik said. "What is it?"

"A story Zach wrote," she said and gestured toward the intern, who was hidden behind Miller's bulk. Nik craned his neck to look at Zach, a lanky, unkempt twentysomething with a mop of brown hair. "It's an obit or, more accurately, obits," Miller said.

"If it isn't the president, the vice president, a Supreme Court justice, or a Nobel Prize winner, I ain't interested," Nik said dismissively. "We don't handle run-of-the-mill obits. You know the policy, Doria. That's what newspapers are for. Zach shouldn't be wasting his time chasing them down."

"Yeah, I know the policy," Doria parroted Nik, "but it's been pretty slow around here lately, and the kid could use the practice. Story needs more reporting and better organization but makes for interesting reading. Raises a number of questions, you ask me," Miller said and handed the hard copy to Nik.

Nik tilted his wire-rimmed glasses back on his forehead and began to read the printout. After a couple minutes, he turned to Zach and asked, "All three of the deceased are former DC-area residents who worked for the same biotech company in Rockville and died in a relatively short span of one another?"

"That's my understanding, Mr. Byron," Zach said.

"I see," Nik said and continued scanning the story. "And you say here a fishing guide found Thom Berg's drowned body, neck snapped, floating in a capsized kayak in Florida, and Deidre Steward washed up on a beach in North Carolina, skull caved in by a boat propeller. The Paxton woman skied off the side of a mountain in Washington. I got all that right?"

"That's what I was told, Mr. Byron. I talked to the sheriff's departments in each county, and it appears the guy in Florida died first, then Paxton. They're not exactly sure when Steward died. She was nearly decapitated and her body partially decomposed."

"Name's Nik. How did you tie the three individuals to the lab in Rockville?"

"I didn't at first, but then I looked at Steward's Facebook feed and saw that Paxton and her were friends. After some more digging, that eventually led me to the company's website. I used the internet's Wayback Machine and found archived pages where all three were listed as researchers."

"And their deaths have been declared accidental?"

"That's the preliminary findings. Boating accident, skiing accident, drowning."

"Helluva coincidence."

"That's what I thought," Zach mumbled.

Nik started reading again, and when he finished, he looked up from his desk. "You talk to anybody at the company?"

"Uh-huh. A spokesperson."

"And what did they say."

"Said those folks left the company almost a year ago and that's the last they heard from them."

"That it? They say anything else?"

"Yes. When I asked what they did at Xion, the spokesperson said it was a matter of national security and she refused to answer any other questions."

"'A matter of national security'?" Nik said. "Those were their exact words?"

"Yup."

"See. Told ya," Doria said.

CHAPTER 2

"It's on my bucket list, that's why," an exasperated Puck Hall had explained to her mother when she had objected to her daughter's plan to solo a section of the Appalachian Trail after she was laid off from her research position at Xion Labs, the first job she'd had after graduating from the University of North Carolina at Chapel Hill with a dual degree in plant biology and bioinformatics.

"I'm twenty years older than you, and I don't have a bucket list," her mother had protested. "You're too young for a bucket list. And besides, it's dangerous."

"You're twenty-*five* years older than me, and I don't want to wait until I'm an old woman to start living my life," Puck shot back, "and I can take care of myself."

Puck was compact with powerful hands and legs, the result of having taken dressage riding lessons ever since she was eight years old. She was also fiercely competitive. She excelled at every sport she played in high school and walked on to the women's Tar Heel volleyball team as a freshman. After watching Puck sacrifice her body with reckless abandon time and time again to save a point, her teammates had admiringly started calling her "Fuck All" instead of Puck Hall.

"I'm not an old lady, thank you very much. I'm your mother, and I'd kindly ask that you remember that. And while you're at it, you'd do well to also remember who paid for your college, not to mention a gap year so you could 'find yourself.' What you need to find, young lady, is another job."

"They gave me severance and benefits. I'll be fine for six months. Everything's always money with you. I want experiences."

Lying on her back now, staring up at the Milky Way on a gin-clear evening, 144 miles of dusty Appalachian Trail behind her, Puck rubbed her sore feet and lamented the argument. Her mother was only thinking about her daughter's safety, after all, Puck knew. Her mother would be happy to hear that, up to this point, the journey had been inspiring but uneventful, the weather cooperative, and fellow hikers friendly.

Puck's mother had Googled "crimes on the Appalachian Trail" before her daughter had departed, and there had been a fair number over the years, mainly garden variety. But she was distressed to discover there were at least a half dozen homicides, the most recent in 2019, when a thirty-year-old Massachusetts man had hacked a hiker to death with a machete.

To reassure her mother, Puck had purchased a satellite phone for emergencies; a handheld GPS device; and installed the location app, What3words, on both their mobile phones so she could keep her mother up to date on her whereabouts when she had cell coverage or Wi-Fi access.

She had also promised to meticulously record her name, destination, and date on the numerous shelter logs that volunteers maintained along the trail. She had packed bear spray, a folding knife, and a small hatchet for personal protection and felt confident of her outdoor skills after having completed a grueling Outward Bound wilderness survival camp during her gap year.

"And I'll cut my hair so I look more like a boy," Puck had said one morning while standing in front of the bathroom mirror at home, shears in one hand and thick tresses of chestnut-colored hair bunched up in the other, and started chopping away.

Most injuries on the Appalachian Trail were self-inflicted, and so far, Puck's biggest health concern was an ugly blister the size of a hickory nut on the heel of her right foot. She covered the blister in moleskin and hoped it would fade while she rested up at her next way station, the Fontana Dam Shelter in North Carolina, the entrance to the Great Smoky Mountains National Park, which, according to her calculations, was about twenty miles north of her current location at Sassafras Gap.

Puck had written her mother a long letter to, if not exactly apologize, at least explain the blowup: "I feel like Dad, if he were still alive, would encourage me to do this. He was always pushing me to be independent."

She had mailed the letter before she entered the southern gateway to the Appalachian Trail at Springer Mountain, Georgia, twelve days prior. Puck was hoping to find a reply waiting for her at the postal drop at Fontana.

Sassafras sat at 4,300 feet elevation. From there, the trail climbed another 1,000 feet before starting a gradual descent to Fontana Dam, where it leveled out at 1,800 feet. Sassafras was a popular overnight stop with hikers and, therefore, safe. Puck had counted at least seven other tents scattered around when she arrived.

She planned to break camp and be back on the trail at sunup and, weather permitting, should arrive in Fontana sometime in the afternoon.

Puck yawned, stood, stretched, and headed for her tent, intending to turn in for the evening, when another hiker staggered into the Sassafras campsite. It wasn't unusual for hikers to show up at all hours of the night off the trail, and it was customary for those already in camp, if they were up, to offer assistance to new arrivals.

Puck wandered over and greeted the newcomer. "Where'd you set out from this morning?" she asked when the hiker knelt and started to wrestle a heavy backpack to the ground.

"Licklog Gap. Got a late start. Picked up giardia somewhere along the trail, and it made for a rough night, but I'm feeling better now."

"That's a good day's hike if you're under the weather. You must be exhausted. I have some beef stew left over from dinner if you've got an appetite," Puck offered.

"Are you kidding, I'm starving and I really don't have the energy to cook dinner for myself. I was just going to eat a fistful of GORP and hit the hay. Stew sounds wonderful."

Puck lit her single-burner stove, reheated the stew, and boiled water for two cups of instant cocoa while the new arrival pitched a tent. "Sorry I don't have anything stronger to offer you to drink," she said and handed the cocoa to the hiker.

"This is perfect, thank you. I'll return the favor and fix breakfast in the morning. You like strong coffee?"

"Couldn't live without it," Puck said.

"What's your destination?" the hiker asked between mouthfuls of stew.

"Headed to Fontana tomorrow. Plan to rest up for a few days, take a long, hot shower, and resupply."

"That's where I'm headed. You care for company?"

"Would love some. Name's Puck, by the way. Pleased to meet you."

The hiker wiped the back of her mouth on her sleeve and thrust out her hand. "Narda," she said. "Nice to meet you, Puck. Pleasure's all mine."

CHAPTER 3

Nik quietly inserted his key into the lock of his condominium, slowly turned the doorknob, gently eased the door open with his toe, and stepped stealthily inside. It was six a.m. and he didn't want to disturb the household. He'd taken two steps down the hallway when Gyp, the Hungarian vizsla he'd had since it was a puppy, erupted with a howl from the back of the apartment, followed immediately by a baby's wail.

"That you, honey?" Sam's voice came from the kitchen.

"Yeah, sorry," Nik apologized. "I was trying to be quiet."

"That's okay. I've been up for a while," Sam said and appeared around the corner, a cup of coffee in one hand, a baby's bottle filled with formula in the other. "I have an early-morning meeting, and Karsen, the new nanny, is on her way now. I wanted to go over Isobel's schedule with her one more time before I had to leave for the office."

Sam was dressed in a gray skirt and black sweater, her strawberry-blond hair in a French twist. She was in her late thirties and a first-time mother. Sam walked over, gave Nik a kiss, and handed him the coffee. Her hair was still damp from the shower, and she smelled like lilacs. "How was work?"

"Thanks," he said and took the coffee. He removed his shoulder bag and set it on the hallway table. Nik, as usual, was dressed in pressed khakis from the Gap, a white button-down shirt, a sport coat, and loafers. "Interesting."

The baby let out another long, loud cry. "She's hungry. Let me give her this bottle, then you can tell me all about it. There are eggs on the stove," Sam said and hurried down the hallway in stocking feet.

The condo's galley kitchen was covered in shades of gray and white tile and set in a sea of stainless-steel appliances that Nik had seldom used when he was a bachelor but now found impossible to live without. Sam had closed up her charming but small Craftsman in Foxhall that she'd inherited from her aunt and moved in with Nik after they got engaged. She had thought about listing the house on Airbnb but couldn't bear the idea of renting it to strangers.

Nik lifted the lid of the frying pan, scooped scrambled eggs onto a plate, added a pinch of salt and a twist of black pepper. He eyed a half dozen strips of crispy bacon on the side burner but resisted. He was determined to get back to pre-baby weight and was puzzled by how Sam had managed to so quickly snap back into shape after the birth of Isobel.

He had just sat down at the counter and opened the *Washington Post*'s sports section when Sam returned, Isobel cradled in her arms, the baby purring like a kitten, a bottle to her lips.

"She slept the whole night through," Sam boasted.

"Lucky you," Nik said with a tired smile. His body clock had not fully adjusted to the overnight shift at *Newshound*, and he was equal parts fatigued and wired. He shoveled a forkful of eggs into his mouth and washed it down with the coffee.

"Tell me about work," Sam said as she paced around the kitchen.

"You ever hear of Xion Labs?" Nik asked and got up to refill his coffee. He stole a look at the bacon again.

"How do you spell that?" Sam asked.

"X-I-O-N."

"I don't think so. What do they do?"

"They're over in Maryland, somewhere near the National Institutes of Health, I think. According to their website, they're a biotech and life sciences company. They conduct work for the federal government, among other things."

"Sounds fairly standard. Most of the biotech companies around here depend on the government for their survival." Isobel finished her bottle, and Sam was now rocking her back and forth and cooing at her.

"True, but three former researchers who worked at Xion recently died under suspicious circumstances within days of one another. When we called to ask about what the employees did at the company, a Xion official claimed they couldn't discuss it because of national security. That's a little unusual, wouldn't you say?"

"Hmm, certainly not typical, but not totally unheard of, either. You know Senator Summers sits on the Homeland Security and Intelligence Committees. I could ask around."

"Really? That would be a big help, but I don't want you to get in trouble, or us to get in a knockdown fight over this."

"Same rules apply?" Sam asked.

"Of course," Nik said.

Before joining Eva Summers's staff as press secretary, Sam had been lead investigator and chief spokesperson for the Northern Virginia sheriff's department, and she and Nik had often butted heads over stories he was covering for *Newshound.*

They had eventually arrived at a workable solution—Sam would confirm information Nik learned elsewhere, and if Sam provided him a tip, he had to get two other sources on the record before he could use it and never attribute it to her.

There had been no need to put their accord to the test with Sam in her new role, largely because Nik was officially on paternity leave and not working, and, as a rule, he didn't cover national politics.

There was a knock on the door. "That's the nanny now," Sam said. "I know you're tired, but can you stick around for a bit? I want you to hear this."

"Sure," Nik said, and when Sam disappeared down the hallway, he dashed back over to the stove. He stabbed three thick pieces of bacon and laid them between bread Sam had toasted. He was just about to take a bite when his cell phone vibrated.

It was an incoming text message from Zach, the intern, and it included a picture of four people, one man, three women, standing in front of a sculpture of the human genome, squinting into the sun.

The man was short and balding and looked to be around sixty, while two of the women appeared to be in their forties, both with close-cropped hair. These three looked straight ahead, half smiles on their faces. The third woman, younger by at least twenty years, with shoulder-length hair, was beaming, teeth as white as porcelain, and judging from the angle of the shot, taking the group selfie.

"I pulled this image from Anne Paxton's LinkedIn page. The woman on the far left is Paxton. She was the head of the Virology Department at Xion. The others worked for her. The woman next to Paxton is Deidre Steward. The man is Thom Berg, and the young woman is Puck Hall, a junior researcher at Xion. I was able to grab Hall's bio and contact info from her social media accounts. I reached her mother. She said her daughter is hiking the Appalachian Trail and checks in periodically. She hasn't heard from her in a few days. She said that wasn't unusual, but she sounded worried to me."

Nik texted his reply. "Need to grab a couple hours of sleep, shower, and then head back to the office. Meet me there at noon. Good work."

Sam reappeared with the nanny, a twenty-three-year-old, apple-cheeked woman from Brazil, and began going over her instructions. When she finished, Nik got up to leave, stopped, and turned back to Sam.

"You know that thing we were discussing," he said, concealing the sandwich down by his side. "I'd appreciate any help you could offer." Nik stepped toward the hallway, and that's when Gyp ripped the sandwich from his hand and ran under the kitchen table, where he greedily devoured it.

CHAPTER 4

"Hey, look who's back. It's the proud papa," Patrick "Mo" Morgan sang out and clapped Nik on the shoulder when he spied him sitting in *Newshound*'s offices. "I thought that was you I saw waddle off the elevator earlier today. Packed on a few extra while we were away, didn't we, Pops?" Mo said and patted his stomach.

"Hey, Mo," Nik said unenthusiastically. "Nice of you to notice. Now go fuck yourself."

Mo, a sandy-haired bruin of a man and a former bodybuilder, was one of Nik's closest and oldest colleagues. Together, along with Mia Landry and Frank Rath, they had relocated to DC from the Midwest to help establish *Newshound*'s Washington operation a couple of years earlier.

"How's fatherhood treating you?" Mo asked. "I thought it was the woman who was supposed to gain weight during pregnancy."

"Good. How's rehab treating you?" Nik replied, sleep deprived, cranky, and in no mood for Mo's ribbing.

"Ah, you know, once you've seen the inside of one rehab clinic, you've seen 'em all," Mo said with a shit-eating grin. Mo had struggled with his drinking for years, periodically drying out before eventually going on another bender. He was currently sober.

"I thought you were on the night shift," Mo said, pulling out a chair and taking a seat next to Nik.

"I was," Nik said. "I mean, I am. I just came in to work on this story with Zach here," he said and chinned toward the intern as a way of introduction to Mo. "Hard to reach people at midnight."

"Whatcha working on?" Mo asked and leaned in to look at the open laptop on the desk in front of Nik. Mo had assumed Nik's old job as *Newshound*'s deputy editor after Nik had been pushed out of the role by then chief editor Richard Whetstone, Nik's nemesis, who had recently left the company under a cloud.

Whetstone's departure had opened the door for Nik's return to the newsroom after having been banished to Mia's small but accomplished podcast team that operated out of dank offices in the basement of the building. A search was underway for Whetstone's replacement, and both Mo and Mia were leading candidates to fill the slot.

After Nik secured a promise from Mo that he would not attempt to steal the story from the night crew, Nik explained what little they knew about Xion Labs and its former employees.

"So you got three dead people, all former researchers for this biotech company, and a missing girl," Mo said.

"And a company that refuses to talk, claiming it would violate national security statutes," Nik added.

"Huh," Mo said. "Sounds like you're stumped, but maybe I can help."

"How's that?" Nik asked.

"Well, I just might know somethin' you don't know, Nik," Mo said.

"Oh, yeah?" Nik said skeptically. "That would be a first. What is it?"

"Name Bernard Rothschild mean anything to you?"

Nik thought for a moment, then shrugged his shoulders. "Not really," he said and looked at Zach, who was nodding his head yes.

"Zach?" Nik said.

"He's Xion's chief scientific officer," Zach said.

"That's right, Zach," Mo said. "Or, more accurately, was."

"What about him?" Nik said.

"He's dead."

"Fuck you say," Nik replied.

"It's true."

"When did it happen?" Nik asked.

Mo twisted around to look at the clock hanging on the far wall. "Couple hours ago. Housekeeping staff at a motel in Anacostia discovered his body. One of our reporters called it in. Sounds like it was suicide, and you know the rules. We don't cover suicides unless they're committed in a very public setting. But if it were me, I'd get over there and poke around, see what I could learn."

Nik took the Frederick Douglass Memorial Bridge across the Anacostia River to the Suitland Parkway and exited at Alabama Avenue, southeast, and followed that to a throwback motor lodge with a massive ship's anchor planted on a wedge of lawn next to the front entrance. The Anchor Inn was a low-slung, two-story cinder-block motel painted the color of pale putty with a concrete stairway near the front office that led to the upper floor. Ice and soda machines were on the ground floor, and all the rooms faced the parking lot, which had about a dozen vehicles scattered around, not counting the cop cars.

Nik parked and told Zach to go to the front desk and see what he could find out. Then he walked over to the far end of the lot where a squadron of police cars was parked.

He strolled up to the cops nearest him, who were leaning on the hood of their cruiser: one, a Black cop, scrolling through his phone; the other, white, sucking on a plastic coffee stirrer.

"Officers," Nik said and nodded at the cops.

The Black patrol officer picked his head up slightly, gave Nik a suspicious up-and-down glance, then went back to scrolling. The white cop gave Nik an indifferent look.

"Pretty heavy presence for a suicide," Nik suggested.

"What's your interest?" the Black cop asked without looking up.

"I'm a reporter with *Newshound*," Nik said.

"Don't quote us," the white cop said.

"You haven't said anything," Nik said.

"And we ain't gonna," the cops said in unison and walked away.

Nik looked around for someone else to approach and noticed a couple of the cars in the parking lot had US government license plates, not a guarantee that they belonged to the FBI or another federal security agency, but a pretty good indication.

He was wondering what the feds were doing at the motel when he saw two DC detectives he recognized, a man and a woman, emerge from a second-story room and make their way down the stairs. Nik had come across the pair before on stories he was covering. The man was friendly enough; the woman, not so much.

"Detectives Jenks and Goetz," Nik called out when the pair reached the bottom. "It's Nik Byron."

Yevette Jenks, a hard-nosed senior homicide detective, was an ex-marine and twenty-year veteran of the DC police force.

Her partner, Jason Goetz, was a former middle-school teacher who had fulfilled his boyhood dream when he joined the police academy. How a world-weary Black woman and a gay white suburban dad had partnered up would always remain a cosmic riddle to Nik.

"You swallow the Pillsbury Doughboy?" Jenks said when she saw Nik approach.

"Murder hornet stung me," Nik said. "It's an allergic reaction."

"Hi, Nik. I think the extra weight looks good on you," Goetz said emphatically.

"What are the two of you doing here?" Nik asked, ignoring the jabs directed at his bulging waistline.

"We got transferred to the Seventh District in Anacostia six months ago to help train their homicide investigators," Goetz said. "It's quite an honor," he added.

"Yeah, real fuckin' feather in our caps," Jenks said. "I could ask you the same, Byron. What are you doing in this neck of the woods? Anacostia ain't exactly Georgetown."

Nik had first encountered Jenks when the homicide detectives were investigating a killing in DC that Jenks believed Nik had witnessed but refused to talk about. Their paths had crossed again when Geoff Tate, one of the world's richest men and the CEO of the country's largest artificial intelligence company, was shot and killed by his young wife.

"Slow news day," Nik said evasively.

"Uh-huh. Ain't buying it. Come on, Goetz," Jenks said and started walking away.

"Hold on, Detective Jenks," Nik pleaded. He explained he was working on a story about Xion. "But we don't have much to go on. We heard about the suicide of their chief scientist and decided to check it out. Can you tell me anything at all?"

Jenks stopped. "Not much. Definitely a suicide. Guy was swinging from a length of rope when we arrived. I appreciate he didn't use a gun like most men and spray gray matter all over the walls. Less mess this way."

"He leave a note?" Nik asked.

"Yeah, but the feds got ahold of it first, and they won't let us have a look. It's their investigation now."

Nik said, "Why the feds? When did they start taking an interest in suicides?"

"I don't know. It's hush-hush. Not even sure what federal agency we're dealing with. They ain't big on sharing."

"They were rude," Goetz interjected, "and mean."

"So, you figure Rothschild left his office in Rockville, drove thirty miles to a run-down motel in Anacostia, and killed himself?" Nik said.

"Something like that," Jenks said.

"What's that supposed to mean?"

"He didn't leave his office. He was a patient at St. Elizabeth's down the road. He walked away from campus, came here, rented a room, ran a rope through the false ceiling, and strung himself up."

"St. Elizabeth's, the psychiatric hospital?"

"Yup, cuckoo's nest," Jenks said. "Apparently the guy had some issues."

"Apparently," Nik said.

"Let's go, Goetz," Jenks said and started walking away again. She stopped and turned back around. "And, Byron?"

"Yeah."

"You owe me now, and I will collect."

"Sure thing, Detective," Nik said, brushing off the comment.

"There's one other thing," she said.

"What's that?"

"You might want to try keto. I hear it really works," Jenks said with a cackle. Goetz winced and gave Nik a quick wave goodbye.

The two detectives were gone by the time Zach returned. The intern told Nik the motel clerk, a female student at the local community college who worked a couple days a week behind the desk, rented the room to Rothschild about seven p.m. the previous evening. The clerk told Zach that the man paid for the room in cash, which she said was not unusual for Anchor Inn customers.

"She described Rothschild as friendly but nervous," Zach told Nik. "The clerk said Rothschild was constantly pacing and looking out the window at the parking lot the whole time he was booking the room. She asked him if he was expecting someone, but he didn't answer."

"She say anything else?" Nik asked.

"Yes. Rothschild asked if the room had Wi-Fi access. It does. He also had a visitor."

"How do you know that?"

"Another customer, a woman who frequently rents rooms by the hour, saw Rothschild and a woman on the balcony. She told the clerk they were having an intense conversation," Zach said.

"A hooker? The woman who saw Rothschild and this other woman is a hooker?"

"The clerk didn't say that in so many words, but, yeah, that would be my guess," Zach said.

"What were they arguing about, Rothschild and this other woman, payment?" Nik said.

"She couldn't hear but said the woman was definitely not a regular," Zach said.

"Cops know about this?" Nik asked.

"Don't think so. The customer didn't want to get involved, and the clerk said she only learned about it after the cops had already interviewed her."

"That it?"

"Well, there's this," Zach said and held up a piece of paper.

"What's that?"

"I exchanged phone numbers with the clerk. Name's Missy. She's cute."

"Dog."

CHAPTER 5

Narda resolved to bide her time now that she had located Puck. The attack would come at a place and hour of her choosing. Besides, she figured too many people had seen her enter the campsite the prior evening and then leave Sassafras the next morning with the younger woman. If Puck somehow accidentally died on the trail that day, questions would be raised. It was too risky.

Instead, Narda assumed the role of a fellow voyager and fed Puck made-up stories about her life—she said she was an architect from San Francisco—during the twenty-mile trek from Sassafras to Fontana Dam.

"I was such an idiot," she faux-confessed as they struggled up one particularly steep section of the trail, "to ever believe he was going to marry me after dating for nearly five years."

"What happened?" Puck huffed back over her shoulder and stopped to catch her breath and take a sip of water.

"I woke up one Saturday morning and gave him an ultimatum. By that afternoon, he had packed up his things and moved out of the apartment. Five days later, Bobby was living with a trust-fund coed from Berkeley. That's when the idea came to me to hike the Appalachian Trail. In retrospect, best thing that ever happened to me," Narda said.

After another hundred yards of sharp incline, the trail leveled off and the pair rounded a corner. In the distance, shrouded mountains, like the shoulders of a slumbering giant, loomed.

"Isn't this beautiful?" Puck said, scrambling past boulders to an outcropping that overlooked a deep ravine, the Smoky Mountains framed in the background. "Let's take our picture together," she said, perched on the ledge, staring down at Narda.

Narda watched Puck balancing on the outcrop, momentarily occupied in thought, and said, "Be careful, Puck. You wouldn't want to fall." Puck looked down at the bottomless canyon below, nervously laughed, and stepped away from the edge.

"Tell you what, give me your phone, Puck," Narda said and held out her hand. "I'll take your picture first and then climb up and get a selfie with both of us with the mountains as a backdrop."

Puck offered up her phone, and Narda shed her pack and stepped up on a fallen tree on the other side of the trail from where Puck stood, to get a panoramic view of the scene. She steadied herself and started clicking away, taking both vertical and horizontal pictures. When she finished, she joined Puck. She held the phone in her right hand and stretched out her arm to frame the shot, but just as she clicked the shutter, she dropped her head to obscure her face.

Narda jumped down and was hoisting her pack on her back when Puck said, "Hey, wait a minute, we need to take the picture again. All I can see is the top of your head."

Narda waved her off. "Come on, Puck. We've still got a ways to go, and we'll have plenty more opportunities to take pictures along the trail."

After climbing most of the morning, the trail started to descend to Fontana Dam through a series of switchbacks. The downward journey was easier but monotonous, and Puck suggested they sing songs to pass the time and to ward off any bears or mountain lions that might be lurking in the densely forested areas just off the trail.

There were only a few songs the pair both knew, mainly ABBA, so for the final five miles of the trek, the duo alternated between singing "Dancing Queen" and "Fernando." Puck had a hard time maintaining a rhythm since Narda constantly sang off-key, but they carried on and joked about Narda's tin ear.

The trail was uncrowded, not unusual for that time of year, and when they did come across others, it was usually a solo hiker or the occasional small group, but for the most part, they had the footpath to themselves. The spring and summer months attracted the most hikers. In late autumn and early winter, like now, kids had returned to college, professionals to their desk jobs, and the trail was uncongested. Puck pledged to return again next fall if at all possible.

"So what do you do for a living?" Narda asked.

Puck told her she had been laid off from a research job at a biotech company in the DC area. When Narda pressed her about what kind of research, Puck was intentionally vague, mindful of the government nondisclosure documents she had signed.

To switch subjects, Puck, a plant biology major, started pointing out various wildflowers along the route and singing out their names: "Painted trillium, also known as *Trillium undulatum*," she called over her shoulder and pointed to the low-lying broad-leafed flower. "Yellow trout lily, or *Erythronium americanum*. Red trillium, *Trillium erectum*. Canada mayflower, formal name *Maianthemum canadense*."

And so it went until they reached Fontana Dam in the late afternoon. Puck went directly to the general delivery window at the local post office to see if there was a letter from her mother. There was.

Narda checked in at the Hike Inn and got a room for one night. Puck did likewise but booked a two-night stay. She was unable to convince Narda to remain an extra day, and the next morning, the two parted company, but not before exchanging contact information—Narda's fake, Puck's real—and destinations.

"Newfound Gap is the last stop on the trail for me," Puck said. "That's forty miles from here, mostly uphill all the way. From there, I'll catch a shuttle to Asheville before eventually making my way back to my mother's house. You?"

Narda said she hoped to make it through to the Virginia border, roughly 110 miles northeast, before the weather turned. She gave Puck a quick pat on the shoulder and wished her traveling companion well. She then set out in search of a spot to stage the ambush.

Ten miles east of Fontana Dam at Devils Tater Patch, a one-way, isolated stretch of trail that sits at 4,775 feet elevation near the North Carolina–Tennessee border, Narda discovered an abandoned animal den carved into the side of a steep bank, an ideal location. The forest canopy that covered the trail in the summertime was gone now, and she had an unobstructed view of the footpath for 150 yards.

Narda took up her position, heated some soup, and waited.

A cold, sharp rain mixed with sleet unexpectedly fell overnight, making the trail slick, and Puck briefly considered staying an extra day at Fontana to let the ground dry out, but then thought better of it. The temperature had dropped nearly fifteen degrees from the day before, and she worried the change in weather might signal the first signs of a winter storm. She decided to push ahead.

Puck was sitting in Hike Inn's small dining room, swirling a forkful of pancakes in a pool of maple syrup on her plate with one hand while swiping through photos on her iPhone with the other, when she realized she never did get that picture of her and Narda together.

Wonder if I'll ever see her again? she mused.

"You must be in a big hurry," Puck's waiter, a rangy, dark-eyed transplanted Texan who had paused at Fontana for a couple weeks before resuming his thru-hike to Georgia, said when he stopped to ask Puck if she wanted a coffee refill. The waiter's name was Cody, but he went by Rawhide, the name he adopted on the trail, a common habit among thru-hikers.

Rawhide was the same waiter Puck and Narda had for dinner the night they'd arrived. Narda had flirted aggressively with the server, and Puck suspected the two might have slept together, judging from the sounds she'd heard coming from her travel companion's room later that evening.

"Why's that?" Puck asked.

"Most of the other guests who were supposed to check out this morning rebooked for another night after that downpour last evening. They're waiting to see if that rain turns to snow as predicted. You were in sixteen, right? You're the only one who hasn't."

"No such thing as bad weather," Puck said, recalling the mantra from Outward Bound, "just bad gear."

"Well, the good news is that you'll likely have the trail mostly to yourself."

Puck downed the last of her coffee, paid her tab, relaced her boots, and texted her mother that she was setting off on the last leg of the trail and would call her in a couple days when she reached Newfound Gap, her terminus. She had been wearing shorts for most of the journey, but today she switched to a rain jacket, long cargo pants, and a baby-blue University of North Carolina stocking cap.

The trail started climbing the moment Puck departed Fontana, and the slippery footing slowed her progress. Puck had resupplied at the local store, and her backpack was now ten pounds heavier with additional food, warmer clothing, and extra fuel for her camp stove, making the climb even more difficult. She removed the rubber pads from her hiking pole tips for better traction.

Her goal that day was to reach Thunderhead Mountain, approximately twenty miles from Fontana. But as midmorning turned into early afternoon, she thought that unlikely and instead set her sights on Spence Field Shelter, a few miles shy of Thunderhead.

Puck skipped lunch and only stopped briefly for bio breaks. She'd come across only one other hiker that morning, a retired Wake Forest botany professor heading in the opposite direction toward Fontana. Rawhide was right. The rain and cold weather had convinced most hikers to remain hunkered down for the day.

Puck had been listening to a podcast about the naturalist Edward O. Wilson when her iPhone flashed a warning that her battery was running low. She switched off the device and removed her earbuds.

She marveled at the stillness of the environs and realized the wood thrushes that usually filled the air from dusk to dawn with their flutelike voices had gone silent. The cold snap must have driven them down the mountainside to lower altitudes and warmer temperatures.

Puck continued to pick her way along the trail and almost tripped over an exposed tree root, sidestepping it at the last moment. She was just about to start a short, steep descent on the trail when she heard a thud behind her. She turned and saw a woman dressed in black sprawled on the ground, face-down, having stumbled over the root that Puck had just barely avoided.

"What?" she said, bewildered at the sight of the fallen woman. "Narda, is that—" But before she could finish her thought, the woman was on her feet and lunging at Puck.

Puck didn't think. She reacted and swung her hiking pole like a saber, slashing Narda across the cheek with the metal tip, drawing blood. The blow temporarily stunned Narda and gave Puck just enough time to take another lash, this one back-handed, but Narda saw it coming and dodged.

Puck's momentum spun her partially around, her back now exposed, the heavy pack shifting on her shoulders, throwing her off-balance. Narda sprang and drove her hiking boot into Puck's sciatic nerve.

Puck's knees buckled from the pain and under the weight of the backpack, and Narda locked an arm around Puck's neck in a choke hold and began to squeeze. Just before she passed out, and with Narda on her back, Puck rolled her shoulders forward and the two of them tumbled down the steep embankment until they slammed into a fallen tree, the backpack ripping loose.

They came to rest alongside a mountain stream surging from the recent rain, Puck bloodied, her eyes watery, unfocused, mouth full of dirt and grit. She staggered to her feet, traumatized and unstable, and when she tried to walk, her legs gave out and she fell backward into the creek's chilly waters. Before she knew it, Narda was on her once again, hands at her throat, shoving her head underwater, a crazed look in her eyes, hair full of twigs and dead leaves, nostrils flared, mouth frozen half open.

Puck reached down her right side and unholstered the canister of bear spray on her hip and shot it into her attacker's eyes and open mouth. Narda bawled and flung herself off

Puck and plunged her head into the water. Puck crawled out of the streambed, unclipped the day pack from her rucksack, and splashed down the creek, deeper into the timber, not knowing where she was headed, Narda's pained screams echoing behind her.

CHAPTER 6

Samantha Whyte hurtled along the corridor of the US Capitol Building, the heels of her shoes clacking away like a typewriter on the marble floors, her lavender scarf billowing behind like a wind sock, and veered right down a hallway and out a side exit that opened onto a path just steps from Constitution Avenue. Her boss, Eva Summers, the US senator from Colorado and an influential member of the Senate Select Committee on Intelligence as well as Homeland Security and Governmental Affairs, was wrapping up a hearing on national security threats and would soon return to her office in the Russell Senate Office Building. Sam wanted to be there to greet her when she arrived.

The sky was the color of pewter and a steady rain was falling. Sam made the usual eight-minute walk from the Capitol to the Russell Building in half the time and was sitting outside Summers's office when the senator stormed in, a clutch of aides trailing in her wake.

"I need to see you," Summers said and pointed when she saw Sam on the outer-office couch and motioned her inside. "The rest of you stay here. And, Timothy," she said to her receptionist, "bring me a cup of tea. You want anything?" she asked Sam.

"Some water," Sam said.

Summers, a former US Olympian in double trap shooting, was one of a half dozen Democrats considering a run for the presidency, an election now less than twenty-four months away. She had just received new national polling data that showed her in a virtual tie for second place with a Midwest governor and behind the front-runner, the former vice president. The numbers were encouraging, but it was still early.

"Why is your hair all wet?" Summers said when Sam closed the door behind her.

"I decided to walk. Needed the fresh air."

"Explains why I didn't see you on the train," Summers said, referring to the underground light-rail that connects the Capitol to the Russell Building. "You see the numbers?"

"I did. That's why I'm here," Sam said. "I'm getting calls and text messages from the press asking if you're going to officially declare your candidacy. I can pretty much guarantee prime spots on CNN and MSNBC."

Sam had joined Summers's staff as press secretary after two years working as the lead investigator and chief spokesperson for the Northern Virginia County Sheriff's Department. Before that, she was a political reporter for the *Washington Post* and was plugged into media and political circles in DC.

Summers removed her yellow blazer, hung it on a hook behind the door, kicked off her shoes, and dropped into her desk chair. The senator was handsome, in the way women are who spend most of their lives growing up in the outdoors, with rugged yet feminine features, her skin smooth and nut brown from the sun. She had an easy manner and a disarming laugh that belied a punishing interrogation style that made her feared on Capitol Hill.

The shelves behind the desk were lined with family photos; paintings of Colorado's mountains; and Olympic medals hanging from red, white, and blue ribbons encased in gold frames from her days as a world-class athlete. Colorado and US flags were planted in one corner and a large potted fern in the other.

Summers pulled out a desk shelf and propped up her right leg and started rubbing the knee. She had torn her ACL in a skiing accident, and it ached whenever it rained.

"What about Fox?" Summers asked and put on a pair of reading glasses to scan the printout of the polling numbers. "I'd sure like to get a triple bagger when we do this."

"It's not out of the question," Sam said. "Your Olympic medals in trap shooting and your lifelong support of the Second Amendment weigh heavily in your favor over there."

"Yeah, but they hate my—quote—liberal positions on FISA warrants, Gitmo torture, and assassinations. What's the name of that woman reporter Fox hired from the local television station? Bet we could get her to do a friendly interview," Summers said, snapping her fingers, trying to recall the name. "Breck, Libby Breck? Something like that."

"Elizabeth Blake," Sam said, "but I'm not sure that's such a good idea, Senator. She's very ambitious and would do anything to boost ratings. We'd be taking a big risk to trust her."

Sam didn't mention that Blake had a personal vendetta against Nik and had vowed to sabotage his career if she ever got the opportunity.

"Work on it," Summers said. "See if you can bring her around."

The receptionist knocked on the door and entered, holding a tray with a steaming teapot, flatware, a cup with the senator's slogan—"Summers Year-Round"—etched on the side, lemon wedges, a small glass jar filled with honey, and a bottle of water. He set it on a side table next to the senator's desk.

"Anything else?"

Summers smiled. "No, thank you, Timothy. That will be all."

After he backed out of the office, Summers opened a bottom desk drawer, retrieved a flask of brandy, and poured a thimbleful into the cup. She held up the flask and offered it to Sam. Sam shook her head no.

"The Intelligence Committee is releasing a widely anticipated report in two weeks on the role of foreign money and influence in our country's top research universities and think tanks. I'd like to hold off making any comment about my candidacy until then. Let's issue a statement saying I'm not paying attention to the polls and that I'm focused on shoring up our country's intelligence defenses."

"Sounds good," Sam said. "Oh, that reminds me, you still want to give the *Post* and *Times* reporters background briefings on the report before it comes out?"

"Yes. Set that up for next week."

"Good. I'll let them know."

"Now, before we talk about this Xion Labs matter you've asked me to look into, tell me about that baby of yours," the senator said and poured herself another shot of brandy.

For the first time in several months, Sam and Nik found themselves alone on a weekend evening, Isobel in the care of a night nanny.

"Talk about disruptive technology," Nik said, uncorking one of their favorite bottles of red wine while Sam stood at the stove in bare feet and the same cream-colored blouse and navy skirt she had worn to work and stirred a simmering Bolognese sauce. "Who knew a creature no larger than a loaf of bread and incapable of uttering a single word could bring two adults to the brink of capitulation?"

"You're exaggerating," Sam said. She tasted the sauce. "Yummm. That's delicious. She's a sweetheart."

"You sure we're talking about the same child?" Nik asked. "Tufts of strawberry-blond hair, green eyes, pudgy legs, about this long?" he said and spread his hands apart. He handed Sam a glass of wine, filled nearly to the brim. "I gave you a healthy pour. Figured you could use it. Cheers."

"Oh, stop it," she said. "Cheers." She leaned in and kissed Nik.

Sam lit candles, turned down the lights, and placed warmed plates heaped with tagliatelle pasta on the dining room table while Nik selected a playlist on his phone. Over dinner, they talked mostly about the baby, how their lives had changed, and possible future dates for their wedding that had been canceled by the virus.

"I forgot what it was like to have a quiet meal together," Nik said after they had finished and he was clearing the dishes.

"So, you want to hear what I found out about Xion?" Sam asked casually.

Nik dropped the pile of plates back down on the table with a crash and settled into his chair. "You know I do. I can't believe you waited this long to bring it up."

"I wanted to focus on us, not work."

"Fair enough," Nik said and refilled their glasses, emptying the bottle. "So, tell me."

"Well, it's not much, to be honest, but were you aware Xion is one of the suppliers of vaccines to the US stockpile?" Sam asked.

Nik shook his head. "Nope. Not a clue. Until a couple days ago, I had never heard of them at all."

"You're not alone; neither had Senator Summers, and she sits on the Intelligence Committee."

"How's that possible?" Nik said. "Given what we've just been through with the pandemic, I would have thought that type of information would be of vital national interest."

"You would think so," Sam said and took a sip of wine. "But you'd be wrong."

Nik picked up the empty bottle, looked at it dolefully, and gestured with his chin to a rack of wine on the kitchen counter. "What do you think?"

"Sure, why not," Sam said. "We get to sleep in tomorrow."

Nik eased out of his chair and into the kitchen. "So what happened?" he asked, opening the bottle and topping off their glasses.

"Secret, single-source no-bid contracts, that's what happened. Hundreds of millions of dollars in contracts awarded to biotech companies like Xion, and that just might be the tip of the iceberg."

"Really? Who approved the contracts?"

"The White House, using an emergency authorization that was granted during the early days of the outbreak. Who exactly in the White House is unclear. They intentionally circumvented procedures, to cover their tracks, and, apparently, the senator believes, did so with DARPA's tacit approval."

"DARPA, the Defense Advanced Research Projects Agency?" Nik said. "I'm confused. What's DARPA got to do with any of this?"

Sam explained that the Pentagon's secret research agency had a long but little-known history of studying deadly viruses. Well before the COVID-19 pathogen took root on the world stage, she told Nik, DARPA had already established an antibody program, the Pandemic Prevention Platform, or P3, in anticipation of just such an occurrence.

"In fact, it was DARPA that funded the first two US companies to enter clinical trials with a vaccine for the novel coronavirus, and P3 was at the forefront of a potential COVID-19 antibody treatment," she said.

"Let me make sure I got this straight," Nik said. "You believe someone in the West Wing, in conjunction with the Pentagon, is running a shadow infectious disease program."

"Sure looks that way from where we sit," Sam said, "but you need to be careful. We may be misreading this. Doesn't help that the White House is stonewalling and Xion might just be a bit player."

"I will," Nik said, "but the cloak-and-dagger stuff doesn't make sense. Building up a national vaccine stockpile is reassuring, a positive for the administration. Why would they want to keep that a secret?"

"The senator doesn't know why, either, but she intends to find out. And, Nik, remember our agreement. You need two independent sources to confirm what I've told you before you can use it. Right?"

"Right," Nik replied, and thought, *Where the hell am I going to find those?*

"Now," Sam said, pushing away from the table and moving toward Nik. She loomed over him, hiked up her skirt, and straddled his lap. "If you don't take advantage of this beautiful, slightly tipsy woman before she falls asleep, you're a bigger fool than I thought, Nik Byron."

Nik grinned. "My momma didn't raise no fool," he said and stood, Sam's legs clamped around his hips like a vise, and carried her to the couch.

He pushed up her skirt, thrilled to discover she was naked underneath.

CHAPTER 7

The graveside service for Deidre Steward took place at St. Paul's Church Rock Creek Cemetery on a blustery, unseasonably warm midweek morning that was threatening rain. The Reverend Joshua Barnes officiated, and he stumbled over Steward's first name, calling her Debbie at one point. It was an understandable mistake. While a member of the congregation for a number of years, Steward was not a regular churchgoer, though she often visited the cemetery grounds of the three-hundred-year-old Episcopalian parish to sit, read, and mediate, Rev. Barnes recalled.

When the lightly attended ceremony concluded, Nik and Zach, who had been standing off to one side under a large sycamore tree, split up and mingled with the few mourners who remained behind.

On the way in, Nik had noticed dozens of plain white crosses marking gravesites and asked a caretaker about them. He was told most of those graves were Covid-related deaths that were awaiting permanent headstones.

"Stone carvers got work backed up as far as the eye can see. Never been nothin' like it in my thirty-seven years," the man said.

A woman in a simple black dress, kerchief, and shawl draped around her shoulders drifted away from the gathering, down a stone pathway, and took a seat on a granite bench that was surrounded by a low hedge. Nik, his raincoat billowing in the wind, followed.

"That was a nice service," he said when he drew near.

The woman wore large square sunglasses that covered most of her face, and held an umbrella in her hand. She looked up at Nik, who had the light at his back. "I guess so," she said. "Frankly, I'm tired of people dying, going to funerals and memorial services. It's draining."

The woman opened her purse and took out a pack of cigarettes and a lighter. "Do you mind?" she asked but didn't wait for Nik's approval and struck the lighter. "I haven't smoked in years, but I started again recently. Nerves, I guess."

"Not at all," Nik said. "Anne and Thom, you mean, their services?"

"Yes," the woman said and exhaled a stream of smoke. "And others."

He paused. "Others?"

"Dr. Rothschild," the woman said.

"Of course," Nik said.

The woman removed her sunglasses, her eyes moist, and fixed Nik with a suspicious gaze. "I don't believe I know you." Without the sunglasses she looked older, careworn, the skin around her eyes crisscrossed with dozens of fine lines, like spiderwebs.

"I apologize. I should have introduced myself. My name's Nik Byron," he said and touched his chest. "And you are?"

"What lab do you work in? I haven't seen you around Xion, have I?"

"Ah, that's because I don't work at Xion," Nik said. "I'm sorry. I didn't mean to imply that I did."

"How did you know Deidre?"

"Well, that's an interesting question." Nik attempted to deflect the woman's inquiry.

She cut him off. "You didn't know her, did you?"

He hesitated. "No, not well," he admitted.

"And you didn't know Anne or Thom, either, I'm guessing."

Nik looked down at the ground for a moment and then back at the woman. "True. I didn't know them, either."

The woman stood and dropped her cigarette on the stone path and crushed it with the toe of her shoe. "What are you, some kind of creep who stalks mourners at funerals for kicks?"

"I'm a reporter," Nik said.

"A reporter? For who?"

"*Newshound*. It's an online—"

"I know what *Newshound* is." She cut him off again.

"Recently there's been a number of unexplained deaths of people who once worked at Xion," Nik said rapidly before the woman could walk off. "I'm trying to understand why. I know Xion is in the business of manufacturing vaccines, and I'm wondering if there's a connection there somehow."

The woman looked over her shoulder. There were only three or four people left at the grave site. She turned back to Nik. "You got a lot of nerve, showing up here."

"I've tried to speak directly to company officials," Nik said, "but they won't return my calls. I was hoping I might have better luck with some of Deidre's colleagues."

"You're joking, right?" the woman hissed. "We all have strict nondisclosure agreements."

Nik tried to stall. "Look—"

"No, you look. I'm not going to talk to you. Now please show a little decency and leave me to grieve in peace."

"Okay," Nik said and backed away. He removed a business card from his coat pocket and placed it on the granite bench. "In case you have a change of heart, and, truly, I am sorry about Deidre and your other colleagues."

The woman didn't look at the card. She put her sunglasses back on and turned a shoulder to Nik.

Zach was waiting for Nik at his vehicle when he returned. "Well, that was a clusterfuck," he told the intern and unlocked the doors with the key fob, motioning for him to climb in.

"Why, what happened?" Zach asked, and Nik described his encounter with the woman. He turned the engine over and put it in drive. "Sorry I dragged you out here for nothing."

"Not for nothing," Zach said.

"You found someone willing to talk in spite of the nondisclosure agreements?" Nik said enthusiastically, pumping the brakes.

"They didn't sign an agreement."

"How'd they manage that?"

"They don't work for Xion."

"Hmm," Nik said, less interested, pushing the vehicle forward. "Who was it?"

"Puck Hall's DC roommate. She met Deidre through Puck, and the three of them became good friends."

Nik smiled and turned to face the young man as the vehicle sped along the cemetery's serpentine lanes. "You keep this up, and I'll be working for you someday."

The intern blushed at the compliment and shifted his weight on the seat. "Watch out," Zach said.

Nik turned his attention back to the road and managed to swerve just in time to narrowly avoid a collision with a granite headstone. "That was close," he said with a grin. "What'd she say?"

"Said she talked to Puck's mother yesterday and that she's really worried that she hadn't heard from her daughter. She fears she may be lost or hurt."

"Yeah, you kinda suspected that, but did she say anything about their work at Xion?"

"She didn't know what they were working on at Xion but said that it was top secret. One night when they were all at a bar together and had too much to drink, she said Deidre and Puck were joking. Deidre said if the long hours they were working at the lab didn't kill them first, then the experiments they were conducting probably would, so they might as well go ahead and drink themselves to death."

Nik shook his head. "I don't get it," he said. "What kind of vaccine kills people?"

He wheeled out of St. Paul's Cemetery and turned left on Webster Street. That's when he saw the large billboard for a local undertaker, a smiling man and woman looking down on passing motorists. Beneath their beaming faces, the ad read: "Marion's Mortuary, We Put the Fun Back in Funerals."

CHAPTER 8

US President Ronald Warfield was seated in a small room off the Washington Hilton's main stage, where he had just delivered a fundraising speech to a group of petrochemical executives, when Dr. Lance Craine, the president's chief health preparedness officer, hustled in a petite woman dressed in a drab, ill-fitting outfit.

Craine was one of a handful of the administration's extreme hard-liners who viewed the virus that had emerged from Wuhan and swept the globe killing millions as an intentional act of—if not war, then economic sabotage. To a person, these hard-liners pledged retaliation, and Warfield had tapped Craine to lead the charge.

The sixty-six-year-old Craine was the perfect candidate for the job. A retired Air Force colonel with advanced degrees in medicine and national security and an expert in bioterrorism, Craine was equal parts soldier, physician, and political infighter.

He was also virulently anti-communist and anti-Sino, having been orphaned as a young child when guerrilla fighters loyal to Mao had slaughtered his missionary parents in

Taiwan. As a youngster, Craine had bounced around from relatives who didn't want him to foster parents who had neglected and abused him before he finally found a home at a boys' military academy, where he excelled in science and mathematics.

Craine had President Warfield's ear, and he bent it every chance he got to remind the commander in chief of the human and economic toll the virus had inflicted on the United States and of the president's sworn duty to protect the country's citizens.

"First the Chinese attempted to hack our computer systems to steal our advanced technologies, and now they're trying to cripple us. You let them get away with this, sir," Craine warned darkly, "and it will only embolden them. This time, they were merely testing our defenses, probing for weaknesses. Next time, instead of several hundred thousand US casualties, it will be tens of millions."

The woman, who had been standing motionless, cleared her throat.

"Mr. President," Craine said, turning to her, "I'd like to introduce you to Dr. Wen Qi, the Chinese virologist I told you about. She used to be a researcher at a little-known sister lab to the Wuhan Institute of Virology and worked closely with China's Ministry of State Security before fleeing to our country. She did her doctorate work here in the United States."

"It's an honor, sir," Dr. Wen said, bowing low.

"Let's make this quick," Warfield snapped, squirming in his chair, uncomfortable in the presence of a foreigner in the claustrophobic space. "I don't have all day."

"Of course," Craine said. "Dr. Wen, can you tell the president about your work at the ministry, and, please, be concise."

"My team created the COVID-19 virus," the woman said matter-of-factly, staring up at the president with intense eyes magnified by thick glasses. “It is lab made, not natural, as Chinese authorities would have you believe.”

“Why did they create it?” Warfield asked.

“To study how best to combat the spread of mutated pathogens if our enemies launch germ warfare first. They believe Russia, Iran, and America conduct similar programs.”

“It’s called gain-of-function research,” Craine explained. “Scientists alter a virus to make it either more deadly or more transmissible in order to better predict new pathogens and ways to counter them. It’s not an uncommon practice.”

“That may be true,” Warfield thundered, “but germ warfare is entirely different and not something we condone in the United States. We have laws against bioweapons that we adhere to. Isn’t that so, Lance?”

“Absolutely, sir.”

“My country did not intend to weaponize, initially, but once the virus accidentally escaped the lab and spread among the general population, authorities saw an opportunity to hamper China’s adversaries since it already had measures in place to contain an outbreak within its own borders. That’s why China’s economy bounced back so quickly while the rest of the world suffered. It had the playbook.”

“And this lab, is it still in operation?”

“No. It closed. Government afraid of repercussions. Many of the scientists were placed under house arrest to keep them quiet.”

“How come our scientists insist the virus is naturally occurring, that it came from animals?” Warfield asked.

“Your scientists are mistaken. We designed it to look that way.”

“But they’ve isolated a close cousin to the virus in bats,” Warfield persisted. “I’m told it has nearly an identical genetic makeup.”

Wen was unmoved. "Fake," she dismissed. "Also human-made constructions."

"Dr. Wen has research papers to back up her claims," Craine said and fished a folder out of his briefcase and handed it to the president, who dismissed the documents with a wave of his hand.

"I have one last question, Doctor. Why did you leave China? Why turn your back on your country?"

"Easy." She shrugged. "To save the world."

After Dr. Wen was escorted from the room, Warfield rounded on Craine. "She better be fucking telling the truth, Lance."

"I have every confidence in her credibility, sir," Craine lied. He had told a few of the hard-liners that he didn't know if Dr. Wen was telling the truth or not and, what's more, didn't particularly care. He said she was probably a crackpot, but she had served her purpose.

"Because if she's not, a lot of people could die."

"Mr. President, the Chinese knowingly remained silent and allowed the virus they created in their own labs to ravage our cities and citizens when they could have prevented it. Any harm visited on them now is of their own doing."

"Where are we on Black Bird?" Warfield asked.

"Been ready to go for months, sir. Just waiting for your approval to move to testing, sir."

Warfield reached into the inside breast pocket of his suit coat and removed a small mirror. He studied his reflection and patted the sagging skin under his chin with the back of his hand. The skin had started to take on the look of stretched taffy, and Craine knew his media consultants had recommended plastic surgery before the election. Warfield ran a hand over his lacquered hair and bared his teeth. He probed his gums with the nail of his baby finger, clearing a piece of chicken from lunch. He replaced the mirror then reached into his outer pocket and produced a spray bottle and squirted it into his mouth.

"You see that leggy brunette sitting in the front row during my speech, skirt barely covering her snatch?" the president said, making a popping sound with his lips. "She eye fucked me the whole time."

"I didn't notice, sir," Craine said blandly. He had often complained to the president's handlers about Warfield's increasingly brazen infidelities, but to no avail. "If he doesn't start focusing on what matters, there's not going to be a second term," Craine warned.

"Get her name from the Secret Service and invite her up to the suite to discuss my administration's chemical policies."

"I'll see what I can do," Craine replied.

"And, Lance?"

"Yes, sir?"

"You have my permission to move forward on the next stage of Black Bird."

"Excellent news, sir."

"And you're certain no one's going to raise any questions?"

"Not a peep, Mr. President, you have my word. We intentionally have targeted isolated populations, and I plan to personally oversee the operations, sir."

"Very good. And, Lance?"

"Yes, sir?"

"Now get your ass out there and find that woman before she gets away."

CHAPTER 9

Puck emptied the contents of the day pack she had escaped with onto the ground and sorted through the pile. There were a half dozen Coleman fire starters, a Leatherman tool her father had given her with her name engraved on the side that she was never without, a large coil of rope, a Grabber Space emergency blanket, a small LED headlamp, a whistle, camp soap, a tin cup, toilet paper, hand warmers, antibiotic cream, a handful of energy bars, matches, ibuprofen, an Ace bandage, gauze, tape, iodine pills, toothpaste, and a toothbrush.

She had a folding knife, an empty bear spray holster, a small water bottle, and a carabiner with two eye-hook screws attached to it hanging from her belt. She had left behind her satellite phone, sleeping bag, warm clothes, tent, food, and compass. She assumed her mobile phone had slipped out of her pocket either when she had rolled down the hill or had fallen into the water while wrestling Narda.

The rush of adrenaline Puck had initially experienced after fending off the attack had faded now, and her body ached and she convulsed with chills whenever she stopped moving for too long. She worried about going into shock and was thankful she had dressed in a quick-drying shirt and pants that morning.

She had a gash on her left knee that she was fairly certain went to the bone, and she had begun to limp badly but refused long rests, wanting to put as much distance between herself and her attacker, who, she was certain, would pursue once the bear spray had worn off, if she wasn't already on her trail.

Puck rolled up her pant leg and dressed the wound with the antibiotic cream, gauze, and the Ace bandage. The bleeding had slowed, but the knee was swollen and covered in deep-purple bruises the color of plums. With the leg partially stabilized by the wrap, she cut a sturdy limb from a hickory tree for a walking stick and continued on.

After the attack, Puck had walked the stream for a ways until she came across a low bank and climbed out. She found a game trail that, more or less, paralleled the creek. It made for easier walking for her, but the same would also apply to Narda, who, if she had two good legs, would overtake her in a couple days if not sooner.

Darkness came early in the mountains this time of year, and Puck began searching for shelter for the night. She had no idea where she was, what direction she was walking, or if she was headed closer to or farther from civilization. She told herself, repeatedly, not to panic.

Puck harvested wild leeks from the forest, fished crawdads out of the creek, and cut shelf mushrooms growing from a tree she spotted along the trail. It wasn't the first time she had foraged her meal from the wild, and the ingredients would make a decent stew when she stopped for the night.

The game trail narrowed and branched off in two directions, one deeper into the woods, the other turned back toward the creek. Puck followed the creek trail to the water's edge and could see where the path continued on the far side, but the water was swift here, and she worried about falling if she attempted to cross with her unstable leg.

Puck backtracked to the other route and soon learned why the trail crossed the river where it did. A slab of granite the size of a pyramid had calved off the mountainside above, blocking the way. She had no choice but to turn around and ford the creek.

Once safely on the other side, she discovered a boulder field, most likely the result of a landslide that had been triggered when the face of the mountain had given way. She found a clearing between a pair of boulders as big as Volkswagens and made camp for the night, the rocks sheltering the wind and concealing the flames of her campfire.

Puck heated her dinner in the tin cup, gobbled it down, drank iodine-laced water from the creek, and rewrapped her still-oozing knee. She unfurled the space blanket and wound it tightly around herself and settled into a sitting position, her back against a giant rock, the fire warming her, the blade of the folding knife open and clutched in her right hand.

She fell asleep and dreamed of her father.

Puck bolted awake and looked around, the space blanket rustling noisily like a candy wrapper. She heard a sound off to her right. The fire had died, and it was as dark as the bottom of the ocean. The sky above was clear, and the stars looked like distant sparklers on the Fourth of July. She guessed it was around four a.m.

She heard the noise again, closer now, and flicked on the light of her headlamp just in time to see a family of raccoons heading toward the creek, probably to hunt crawdads. Puck was stiff and stretched, and when she did, the pain in her knee exploded.

She quickly ate two more ibuprofen and came to the grim realization that she couldn't outrun Narda and that she was probably going to die in these mountains, she just couldn't understand why. Was her pursuer a deranged serial killer, stalking hikers, or had Narda mistaken Puck for someone else? None of it made sense.

The dream of her father slowly returned to Puck. She remembered him telling her she could do anything if she just believed in herself.

"First we fail in thought," he quoted one of his favorite sayings to her in the dream, "and only then afterward in action."

A drunk driver had killed Puck's father when she was a sophomore in high school. Her father had been her volleyball coach, biggest fan, and confidant, and the ache that had settled in her heart after he was killed eventually faded but never truly left her.

Puck then recalled her college volleyball teammates and the nickname they had bestowed on her and thought, *Fuck all. If you're going to die here, Puck, at least go down fighting.*

She started devising a plan.

CHAPTER 10

When they arrived at *Newshound*'s offices later that evening, Nik put Zach to work scouring local media archives for recent death notices that mentioned Xion while he searched company-related profiles on LinkedIn looking for the woman he had met at St. Paul's Cemetery. "She said she was tired of attending funerals and implied there were others," Nik said before giving Zach his marching orders.

After two hours of scrolling through countless internet pages, the pair had nothing to show for their efforts.

"I've gone back nearly two years," Zach reported.

"And nothing?" Nik asked.

"Zilch."

Nik pushed his wire-rimmed glasses up on his forehead and rubbed his eyes with the palms of both hands, trying to concentrate. "It doesn't add up. Why would she volunteer that? It's not like I asked. It's not even like I knew to ask."

"Maybe she was referring to personal friends or family who have died recently, not coworkers," Zach offered.

"Maybe," Nik said, "but I don't think so." He stood and grabbed his coat and satchel. "Come on."

"Where we goin'?" Zach asked.

"You'll see. Doria," Nik called out to the copy editor as he headed out the door, "you're in charge."

Doria glanced up from a story she was editing and squinted, a sour look on her face. "'Bout time. Maybe this place has a future after all," she said and put her head back down and continued to edit.

Zach trailed Nik down into the parking garage, where they climbed into Nik's Land Cruiser. In addition to the condominium near DC's swanky Kalorama neighborhood, the $75,000 vehicle was one of the few luxury purchases that Nik had allowed himself to indulge in after he came into a small fortune when *Newshound* had a successful public stock offering.

For years, Nik had driven an old Land Cruiser, a bare-bones but classic-looking vehicle. This new model had all the modern technology and bells and whistles, but it was like driving a couch. He gunned the engine and motored up the garage ramp and darted out into a nearly deserted street.

"You gonna tell me where we're headed, or do I have to guess?" Zach said as Nik shot down Independence Avenue to Fourth Street before jogging east on E Street.

"No need. We're here."

Zach buzzed down the passenger-side window and stuck out his head. He was looking up at a six-story glass-façade building across the street from the US International Trade Commission.

"The city morgue?"

Nik dialed his phone, and it automatically connected to the vehicle's audio system. "Yup. You know why they have bars on the morgue's windows, Zach?" he asked.

Zach shook his head. "No idea."

"People are dying to get in," Nik chortled.

"Byron, your jokes suck," a voice said over the speakers.

"DeShaun," Nik said. "How you doing?"

"I'm a little busy right now, Nik."

"This won't take but a minute."

"Ah, okay. Whaddaya want?"

"Can you let us in?"

"What?"

"We're out front."

"Right now?"

"Yeah. Now."

DeShaun Bailey was the assistant chief medical examiner for the District of Columbia, a Spelman College undergrad with a medical degree from Stanford University. DeShaun and Nik were teammates on the Washington Cannons, an adult baseball team for thirty- to forty-year-olds. Bailey was the Cannons' ace pitcher, Nik its so-so second baseman.

"I really shouldn't, Nik. The last time—"

"That was totally my fault, DeShaun," Nik cut in. "I promise not to touch anything. Please, this won't take long."

"What's this about?" Bailey asked after he let the pair in and Nik made quick introductions.

"It's kind of a shot in the dark," Nik said and explained that they were looking for any recent deaths of people who might have had an association with Xion Labs.

"You mean, besides Bernard Rothschild?"

"Yeah, yeah. Besides Rothschild. We know about him."

Bailey wheeled his chair over to a computer monitor and punched the keyboard. "This is our central database. We have over two hundred identifying fields for victims who end up here. This might take a few minutes."

"We're in no hurry," Nik said.

"Huh," Bailey said after about forty-five seconds.

"That was quick," Nik said. "What did you find?"

"Nothing. No hits. Sorry."

Nik sighed. "Like I said, it was a long shot. Thanks anyway."

"You plan on playing again this year?" Bailey asked and looked at Nik's expanding waistline.

"Baby fat," Nik said. "Not to worry, it'll be gone by the time the season rolls around."

"Gotcha," Bailey said as he walked to the front door, unlocked it, and let Nik and Zach out. "I really thought you were here to ask about Rothschild," he said, holding the door open.

"Unless someone commits suicide in a very public manner, like jumping from the Washington Monument, we politely ignore it," Nik explained. "Besides, the guy had psychiatric problems."

"I'm not talking about the suicide."

"Oh?"

Bailey studied Nik for a moment, unsure if he should continue. "I'm talking about his body."

"What about it?"

"It's gone. The feds grabbed it."

"Guess that was to be expected," Nik said. "They were at the motel where it happened. Pushed the local cops aside."

"It's not so much that they took the body. It's *how* they took it."

"What do you mean?"

"They came in dressed in space suits with their own oxygen supply and hermetically sealed the corpse. The only other time I saw anything like that," Bailey continued, "was when I was doing a rotation in Zambia with Doctors Without Borders and a male patient died shortly after being admitted to the hospital."

"What was that guy's cause of death?"

"Cardiac arrest."

"So, why all the extra precaution then?"

"They thought he had Ebola."

CHAPTER 11

A strong wind was blowing up the isolated canyon outside of Provo, Utah, and the smell hit Lance Craine a quarter mile from the site. Inside two hundred yards, his nostrils burned and he started to gag. His companion, a bald-headed, reedy man with skin the texture of dead leaves, handed Craine a gas mask. "Here, put this on. It'll help with the smell," the man, an official with the US Department of Agriculture, said, and slipped one over his head as well. He helped Craine adjust his mask before walking on.

The pair crested a ridge and peered down at row upon row of corrugated sheds glimmering in the sun as far as the eye could see, the sides propped open, and within the sheds a warren of cages. Dozens of individuals in hazmat suits and face shields swarmed in and out of the buildings, hauling out the cages and dumping their contents into front-end loaders that idled nearby, exhaust pipes burping nosily in the mountain air.

"I wouldn't advise gettin' any closer," Craine's companion said and threw up his arm. "Better to keep a safe distance."

Craine had a hard time hearing the man through the gas mask, but he got the gist of what he was saying and stopped.

Craine shouted a question. "When did you say the first mink got infected?"

"I didn't, and we're not sure. Coulda been a couple days, maybe a bit longer. Hard to know for certain."

"And it spread to the whole colony?"

"Like a whirlwind. Five thousand mink. Had to exterminate the entire population. Couldn't risk it."

"How do you think they got infected?"

"That's the head-scratcher. All the workers who have come in contact with the animals tested negative for the coronavirus."

Craine nodded but otherwise didn't respond. He knew how the mink had gotten infected. He had ordered it.

Trillions of viruses circulate in the atmosphere every day. There are more viruses on the planet than there are grains of sand in all the world's deserts and beaches. In fact, there are more viruses than there are stars in the universe, and there are ten times as many stars as there are grains of sand. Scientists estimate that eight hundred million viruses descend daily on every square meter of the earth, dropping from clouds overhead as they're pushed along by the jet stream. A coronavirus is microscopically small. So small, in fact, that five hundred of them could fit on the head of a pin.

But despite their pervasiveness, the vast majority of viruses pose no threat to humans, and rarely do they spawn pandemics, but the ones that do have a few things in common. First and foremost, they depend on modern transportation to get from one corner of the globe to the other.

One thousand years ago, it was the Vikings, in their sturdy sailing vessels, who, historians believe, exported the smallpox virus to the New World, killing millions. Later it would be steamships plying the world's rivers and seas that silently carried deadly cargo. And today it is air travel.

The other characteristic these deadly diseases share is that, for the most part, they jump from animal to human. The plague was transmitted from rodents to humans by fleas; Middle East respiratory syndrome, or MERS, one of modern history's most lethal viruses, was spread to humans by camels; and SARS-CoV-2, the strain of coronavirus that causes COVID-19, rode in on the wings of bats, if you believed the story the Chinese were peddling.

Lance Craine knew this, of course, but what he didn't know, what baffled him, in fact, was why the Xion virus didn't spread from animals to humans in the wild as it had in the controlled experiments his team had successfully conducted in offshore black sites operated by the US government.

"And you say none of the workers got sick from the animals?" Craine quizzed the man from the Agriculture Department.

"Nope, and, quite honestly, we were surprised, because we have documented cases of the virus jumping from humans to minks back to humans."

"Lucky bastards," Craine said.

"Don't ya know."

CHAPTER 12

Puck decided to make her last stand at a bend in the river where the game trail veered away at a ninety-degree angle and large sugar maple, hickory, and hemlock trees crowded in from all sides, the understory thick with shrubs and vines. The location provided the element of surprise that she would need to execute a sneak attack, but even then, she knew the odds heavily favored Narda.

Puck reasoned a frontal assault on only one good leg was sure to fail and that she needed a diversionary tactic to stand a chance against a stronger, better-equipped opponent who would be anticipating an ambush.

Even though it was only a short distance, it took Puck most of the morning to roll a large speckled boulder up from the river and onto the trail. She stopped multiple times to rest her knee, and once, when she failed to brace herself properly, the rock rolled halfway back down the hillside toward the river and only came to rest after she managed to throw a log in its path. She thought she would cry.

Puck was tired and her skin clammy from sweat when she finally managed to position the rock under a massive hickory branch that overhung the trail. She cut open her day pack and fashioned a sling to cradle the rock that she then bound with the coil of rope. She took the other end of the rope and looped it over the branch and wrapped it partway around the tree's base and then ran the free end through the carabiner that she had screwed to the tree's trunk to create a crude block and tackle.

With a grunt and a groan, Puck began to slowly hoist the rock off the ground and up into the branches. When Narda rounded the turn in the trail, she would find herself almost immediately beneath the suspended boulder, which Puck figured to weigh between twenty-five and thirty pounds and hung about fifteen feet off the ground. At that weight and that height, the falling rock would easily splinter human bone.

Puck tied off the rope with a slipknot, laid its tag end alongside the path, recrossed the trail, and began to carve out a small cave in the tangle of vines near where the trail turned, providing her a clear view of the approach. The hideaway was on the downhill side of the trail, and Narda would be slightly above Puck when she drew even to the entrance.

By late afternoon, Puck had finished her preparations and collapsed in the vine cave, exhausted, and fell asleep, clutching her walking stick.

Narda did not appear that day, nor early the next morning, and Puck began to think perhaps the woman wasn't pursuing her after all. Maybe Narda had concluded, not unreasonably, that Puck would perish soon enough on her own, lost in the wilderness without food or shelter.

Later that afternoon, Puck was rechecking the knot she had tied in the rope when a murder of crows, braying loudly, exploded from its perch in the branches overhead.

Someone's coming, she thought, and dove back across the trail into her hideout, pulling vines down over the opening to conceal her position.

Minutes passed, and Puck began to hyperventilate. She fought to control her breathing, but that only heightened her anxiety, causing her to guzzle more air. She became lightheaded and closed her eyes. As she did, her father's image swam before her. Her galloping heart slowed, and a peacefulness, like a cloud of warm steam, settled over her.

Puck could now hear Narda's footfalls on the trail, moving methodically, cautiously.

"Puck," Narda's voice rang out unexpectedly. "I know you're close by. I found the ashes of the fire you built between the rocks down below and saw fresh blood on the ground. You're hurt, Puck, let me help you."

Puck stiffened and clamped her hands tightly around the walking stick, its end sharpened to a spike.

"Puck, what happened back there was a terrible mistake. I didn't mean to attack you. I thought you were someone else out to hurt me." Narda's words ricocheted around the forest, bouncing off trees and slamming into rocks before slowly dying out. "I can explain everything if you just give me a chance."

Narda was close, maybe thirty yards off. She would be at the spot where the path turned in less than a minute. "There's a major snowstorm headed our way, Puck," Narda continued. "We need to stick together if we're going to make it out of here."

Puck steeled herself, and when she looked up, there was Narda only steps away, her face covered in red splotches, one eye partially swollen closed from the lingering effects of the bear spray.

Narda hesitated, looked over her shoulder, and then peered into the underbrush before tentatively stepping forward, a small revolver in her left hand, the side closest to Puck.

Just before the path veered, Narda froze, vigilant, listening. She shifted the gun to her right hand and crouched, no doubt wary of the trail's sudden ninety-degree turn.

She was so close now that Puck could read the labels on her clothing and backpack and see bruises on the backs of her hands and arms from the fall they had taken down the mountainside.

Narda straightened, head down, eyes sweeping the trail side to side. She stepped around the bend, but before walking beneath the suspended boulder, she stopped, having spied the tied-off rope and followed it with her eyes to where it looped around the tree and up into the branches until she saw the rock swaying overhead.

"What the fuck," she muttered, rooted to the spot, staring skyward, bewildered. It was the moment Puck had hoped for. She burst from the vines, the walking stick held like a spear, and charged, catching Narda momentarily off guard.

Had the gun remained in Narda's left hand, she simply would have had to raise her arm and fire, point-blank, at the onrushing Puck. But instead, it was in her right, away from the attack, and she was forced to twist around before discharging the weapon, the backpack restricting her movements, and when she did, she opened her front side to Puck.

The spear lanced Narda just below the left rib cage and above her hip, drawing blood and fluids, and she let out a gush of air with a painful "oooof." She pitched forward, dropping the gun in front of her on the trail, and grabbed the spear with both hands to prevent Puck from plunging it deeper.

But Puck, instead of thrusting the spear farther in, yanked it back, the bloody rod slipping through Narda's hands, and coiled for a second charge.

Before Puck could strike, Narda lurched and grabbed the revolver. A split second later, Puck spun away, dropping the spear and flinging her body across the path toward the rope that lay nearby. She grabbed the end and tugged just as Narda leveled the gun and fired.

The boulder crashed down on Narda, pile driving her face into the earth.

Puck lay on the ground, rope entwined in her fingers, snow starting to fall, blood pooling in the dirt where she'd been shot, and blacked out.

CHAPTER 13

"It's time to either phone or get out of the booth, Nik," Mia Landry advised her colleague over early morning coffee at the Sugar Shack, Nik's favorite go-to breakfast spot. "You've been sitting on this Xion story long enough. Publishing might kick something loose."

Nik and Mia were seated at a table in the rear of the small shop, customers wrapped in heavy coats spilling out the front door and down the street, waiting to place an order.

The temperature had dropped overnight, and there was frost on the windshield of Nik's vehicle when he had picked Mia up from her apartment that morning. Mia, chilled, as always, was wearing a purple wool beanie, purple mittens, and had a white scarf knotted at her neck, her cheeks rosy.

Nik blew on his coffee and looked longingly at Mia's glazed cinnamon roll, having opted for oatmeal for himself, but said nothing. They were longtime workmates; Nik recruited and mentored Mia right out of Northwestern as a junior reporter for *Newshound*'s Midwest operations.

Mia had excelled in the position, and when Nik had relocated to DC, she and two other staffers had followed him to the nation's capital. Shortly afterward, Mia had launched *Dateline Washington,* a podcast devoted to the singles scene, which became an overnight success and led to her promotion as head of *Newshound*'s podcast operations.

Later, after Nik was pushed out of his job as *Newshound*'s deputy editor by his chief rival, Mia had helped salvage his career by offering him a spot in her small, but growing, podcast empire.

"Yeah," Nik finally conceded. "I've been thinking the same thing, but I'm not quite sure how to approach it," he said, scooping up a spoonful of oatmeal. He made a face and swallowed. "I don't want to focus on the three—quote, unquote—accidental deaths of the Xion employees, but I don't know how to avoid it, and, at this point, that's our strongest angle."

"You worried about the competition?" Mia asked.

"Always. We tip our hand, and the *Post* or some other media outlet will throw a platoon of reporters at the story and steal it right out from under us. It's happened before."

"Don't focus on the deaths, then," Mia offered, removing her mittens and rubbing her hands together to warm them. "I wish they'd close that front door. It's freezing in here."

"What's left?" Nik asked, having already briefed Mia on the background material he and Zach had gathered in their reporting. "Rothschild's suicide is off-limits, and I haven't been able to get anybody to corroborate the tip about Xion being handed government no-bid contracts for vaccines, and I'm not even sure how relevant that is anyway."

"If it were me," Mia said, biting tenderly into her pastry, leaving Nik in suspense while she slowly chewed and then washed it down with coffee, "I'd write about the girl."

"Puck?"

"Yeah, her. Young, accomplished, professional woman, hiking the Appalachian Trail by herself, lives in DC, was a star volleyball player at the University of North Carolina. Lost in the wilderness. That's a helluva story."

Nik nodded his head slowly and sipped at his coffee. "That's not a bad idea. We've been concentrating on the people who died, the credentialed scientists. You might be right."

"Of course I am. Anything else I can help you with?"

He hesitated. "Well, since you asked," he said sheepishly, "you gonna eat the rest of that cinnamon roll?"

Mia gave Nik a sad look, shook her head, and then slid her plate and an extra fork in front of him. "Knock yourself out, big fella."

Nik and Zach cobbled together a story about Puck Hall that traced the missing woman's 165-mile solo hike along a southern stretch of the Appalachian Trail from Georgia, where she started her journey, to Fontana Dam in North Carolina, her last-known stopover, where she had rested up for two nights before resupplying and setting out for Newfound Gap, her final destination.

They located other hikers who had encountered Puck and even interviewed a waiter, Cody Fisher, from the Hike Inn, who had served her breakfast the morning she departed from Fontana Dam.

"Frankly, I was surprised she decided to continue on her route after that storm blew through the night before," said Fisher, a Texas native who had taken a temporary job at the inn before continuing his thru-hike. "The rain and sleet made parts of the trail extremely hazardous, and a number of veteran hikers who were staying at the inn decided to lay over a couple extra days to let conditions improve before tackling it again. That was the smart thing to do."

Olivia Hall, the young woman's mother, pleaded for help in locating her missing daughter.

"She was supposed to check in with me four days ago when she reached Newfound Gap. It's not like Puck. One or two days, maybe, but four days, something's not right. I'm worried sick," she told the reporters. "I'm asking anyone with information to please contact local authorities."

Those who knew Hall best—college roommates, friends, volleyball teammates, professors at the University of North Carolina at Chapel Hill—all attested to her resourcefulness and competence.

"Hands down, she's the toughest, most resilient individual I know," Ginny Sloan, Hall's UNC volleyball coach, told the reporters. "If anyone can survive in those mountains, it's Puck."

Government officials and experienced Appalachian Trail hikers speculated that Hall had wandered off the trail in the dark and gotten lost, but they were cautiously optimistic she was still alive and would be found if they could reach her before a forecasted winter storm hit the mountains. The temperature was already dropping below freezing most nights and would soon be in the single digits.

Lauren Kline, a spokesperson for the National Park Service, said a coordinated search had been launched for the missing twenty-four-year-old. Twenty volunteers, including park rangers mounted on horseback, and tracking dogs, were scouring the area between Fontana Dam and Newfound Gap. So far, no traces of the young woman had been found, and attempts to geo-locate the satellite phone she was known to be carrying had been unsuccessful.

"We remain hopeful, but we are keeping an eye on the weather conditions and may have to call off the search if the storm that's forecasted materializes," Kline told *Newshound.*

"But as of this moment," she added, "nobody here is at the give-up stage."

The story noted that Hall graduated with a dual major in plant biology and bioinformatics, an interdisciplinary field of study that combines biology, computer science, mathematics, information engineering, and statistics. She attended the university on a four-year mathematical scholarship, and, until recently, had been employed by Xion Labs, a biotech company in the Washington, DC, area.

Near the bottom of the story, they buried mention of the three former Xion employees who had recently died in what they termed "alleged accidents," hinting that the official findings might be in question.

The last paragraph noted that, before graduating from college and joining Xion, Hall had earned a coveted internship with the Federal Laboratories Consortium Mid-Atlantic Region, where she worked as an analyst at one of the labs. One of her jobs during that semester was to help track what was then an unknown pneumonia sickening people in China. That virus, they reported, was later dubbed COVID-19.

CHAPTER 14

God spoke to Reid Brimlove on January 1, 2015, when he had woken up in bed naked next to his yoga instructor, her young Puerto Rican lover, and a snake after a particularly debauched New Year's Eve. The voice the twice-divorced real estate agent and lapsed Southern Baptist heard that morning ordered him to leave Destin, Florida, and move to Porthill, Idaho, on the Canadian border, where he was to establish a church and call it the Shepherd's Staff.

The forty-two-year-old Brimlove had never set foot in Idaho before in his life, nor had he communed with God, but the experience humbled and transformed him. He heeded the Lord's word and, by Easter of that year, sold everything he owned and purchased two hundred acres of forested property near Stein Mountain and set about clearing the land and building a church and compound for his future congregants, who God had assured him would flock to the sanctuary.

Brimlove, a naturally charismatic salesman with chiseled features, black hair as thick as tar, and a restless masculinity, chronicled his ongoing church-building efforts and religious visions (God appeared to him in various transfigurations, but most often as a Seminole chief) in his blog, *The Staff*, which had a small but devoted following.

It took him nearly three years and every penny he had to complete the project, but by the time he opened the Shepherd Staff's doors, seventy-five believers had moved to the tiny, remote location, and several hundred more potential worshipers had sent Brimlove donations and pledged to uproot their lives and make the move in the near future.

Brimlove described the Porthill area as a second Garden of Eden, set among the majestic Selkirk, Cabinet, and Purcell mountain ranges and blessed with some of the state's most fertile soil and abundant natural resources.

Brimlove didn't have the funds to reach a national television audience, so he turned to small cable outlets and social media to amplify his profile and broadcast his message. He promised religious seekers "spiritual enlightenment and heavenly riches" the moment they entered the Shepherd's Staff community.

One year after christening the church, the Reverend Brimlove's flock had grown to 125 Shepherds, as they were known, and their families, and each day brought more promises of relocation and financial commitments. God, he said, had instructed him to purchase additional land, this time in Oklahoma, and he made plans to build a second church and start a school in Porthill for the children of the parish.

Then the pandemic hit, donations dried up overnight, and what little employment there was to be had around Porthill vanished. Not long after, Shepherds started fleeing, and those who stayed turned to begging to support themselves. It didn't take long for the residents of Boundary County, Idaho, already suspicious of the religious order, to lose patience with Brimlove and his followers and vote to ban panhandling on public property.

Five years after Brimlove had established the Shepherd's Staff, the sect's congregation had dwindled to twenty-seven die-hard believers and became isolated from the surrounding communities, growing some of their own food, homeschooling their children, administering folk remedies to the infirm.

Every week, they made the rounds to local food banks, shelters, and churches to gather up what supplies and staples they could, and recently a Good Samaritan had taken to anonymously leaving canned goods at the entrance to the compound for the members.

Cut off from the outside world, Reverend Brimlove's pronouncements took a turn from sunny optimism to dark foreboding, and he told his followers to prepare for the End of Days.

The first sign that the reverend's prophecy was at hand was when a Shepherd awoke early one morning covered in oozing blisters, with a searing pain in his lungs and a crippling headache. By ten a.m., he was coughing up tablespoons of blood and what looked like specks of lung tissue. By noon, he was dead.

In less than seventy-two hours, more than half the Shepherd's Staff congregation was dead, and those that remained, clinging to life, died in the fire that swept through the structure later that day, too weak to save themselves. The fire incinerated everything in its path, including a pantry full of adulterated canned foods. Turns out, the anonymous donor who was leaving food for the congregants wasn't a Good Samaritan after all.

CHAPTER 15

It was a little past six p.m. when Dr. Stanley Lowenstein emerged from the front entrance of St. Elizabeth's Hospital. He headed down Sycamore Drive SE toward the Congress Heights Metro station.

Lowenstein tugged his coat collar up around his neck and quickly set out for the station, quietly humming a tune from the musical *Hamilton*. He appeared not to be paying attention to the people around him and was startled when Nik stepped in front of him, blocking his path.

"Dr. Lowenstein?"

Lowenstein blinked slowly at the stranger, like a tortoise, seemingly trying to recall if he knew the man. Clearly, he concluded he didn't, and tried to brush past. Nik again stepped in his path.

"Yes?" an exasperated Lowenstein asked.

"Dr. Lowenstein, my name's Nik Byron. I'm a reporter for *Newshound*."

Lowenstein looked around and then back at Nik, as if unsure if Nik was actually addressing him, or if he had him confused with someone else.

"I wonder if I could have a minute of your time?" Nik said.

"What's this about? Why would a reporter for—who is it that you say you work for again?"

"*Newshound.* It's an online newspaper," Nik said.

"Never heard of it. Now, if you'll excuse me, I'm late as it is," Lowenstein said.

"This won't take long, Doctor," Nik said.

"Really, I don't have time for this," Lowenstein said, irritated, and puffed out his cheeks before turning around and walking away.

"It's about Bernard Rothschild," Nik said at the man's retreating back. "Your former college classmate."

Lowenstein stopped and slowly swiveled his head, a hard squint in his eyes. "What about him?"

After *Newshound* published the story about the missing female hiker, Nik and Zach started to dig into the backgrounds of the deceased Xion employees. Nik researched Bernard Rothschild and Thom Berg while Zach concentrated on Anne Paxton and Deidre Steward.

Rothschild had an impressive academic and professional record before joining Xion as its chief scientific officer. He had degrees in medicine and epidemiology from some of the nation's most prestigious universities and had published extensively on deadly pathogens and pandemics.

Nik's research had turned up a photo of Rothschild, an undergraduate of the Massachusetts Institute of Technology, at a reunion with a classmate, drinks in hand, beaming smiles, wearing bright-red blazers with the MIT insignia on the breast pocket, arms draped over shoulders. The fellow graduate was Dr. Stanley Lowenstein.

"I thought it was strange that it was reported that Rothschild wandered away from St. Elizabeth's. I mean, the hospital is a high-security institution," he said. "It's where the guy who shot Reagan was confined. People just don't pick up and walk away."

Nik stopped, expecting Lowenstein to respond. When he didn't, Nik continued, "So I thought maybe you could explain to me how a patient walks off the campus without setting off all kinds of alarms."

Lowenstein finally broke his silence. "He wasn't a patient."

"Not a patient? Really? What was he, then?" Nik asked.

"Officially, he was a temporary in-resident doctor. It's a professional courtesy we extend to medical personnel who need time away from the pressures of life," Lowenstein said.

"And unofficially?" Nik asked.

"Bernard Rothschild was a dear friend and colleague and a brilliant scientist. He asked for my help and a place to stay, and I gladly gave it to him," Lowenstein said and looked around, apparently uncomfortable with the conversation in such a public setting. "Follow me," he said to Nik and turned on his heel.

"Where to?" Nik asked.

"My office," Lowenstein replied, "where we can talk in private."

"You'll miss your train," Nik pointed out.

"It's the Metro, Mr. Byron," Lowenstein said and started briskly walking back toward the hospital. "There's one every eight minutes."

Nik was propped up in bed, pillows tucked under his arms, Isobel balanced on his stomach, Sam by his side, Gyp asleep at their feet. It was a drizzly Saturday morning, and Nik was elated when Sam told him they didn't have any plans for the whole day.

The first couple weeks working the night shift at *Newshound* had invigorated Nik but left him exhausted. He was pulling double duty, trying to report on the Xion story during the day and overseeing the newsroom in the evening. While Zach, nearly half Nik's age, found the overtime work exhilarating, Nik increasingly found it unsustainable, though he was reluctant to admit it to anyone.

Sam traced slow air circles around the baby's face with her index finger, reciting a children's rhyme, before zeroing in and tweaking Isobel on the tip of her nose, setting off peals of giggles. "This Dr. Lowenstein," Sam said, "says he was stunned when he heard Rothschild committed suicide?"

"Yup. Said something was definitely troubling Rothschild but that he wasn't mentally unstable."

"And you think he's right?" Sam said.

Nik shrugged. "If anybody would know, it would be Lowenstein. Guy's a shrink and Rothschild's friend. He talked openly about their long personal and professional relationship. I was surprised he spoke so candidly, but he said he was speaking as Rothschild's friend, not his therapist. Said he never treated Rothschild professionally."

Sam started pulling on the baby's toes, singsonging "This Little Piggy," which caused Isobel to squeal even louder and kick her feet in the air. The dog lifted its head to investigate the commotion, determined it was harmless, and went back to sleep. "So what does he think happened?"

"He doesn't know but believes whatever it was, it had to do with Rothschild's work at Xion. Said the scientist told him he had made a terrible mistake and that he needed to fix it," Nik said.

Sam slid out of bed and pulled on a robe. "I need more coffee. Want a refill?"

"Sure. No cream," Nik said. "I'm on a diet, remember."

"Riiight," she replied. "Lowenstein have any guesses what the terrible mistake was?" Sam asked, tousling Isobel's hair before collecting Nik's empty coffee cup.

"Nope. Not really," Nik said and started bouncing the baby up and down. "He thought maybe it had to do with Rothschild's decision to join Xion in the first place. He speculated the scientist might have felt guilty about leaving academia to chase a big payday in the corporate world."

"Hmm," Sam mused, sounding unconvinced, and left to retrieve the coffee.

"There was one other thing," Nik called after her.

Sam reappeared a few minutes later, a copy of the *Washington Post* tucked under one arm, with small bowls of fruit stacked atop the coffee cups, which she gingerly placed on the bedside table. "What was that?"

"Lowenstein said he found a notebook that Rothschild left behind at the hospital."

"Full of incriminating evidence, I hope," Sam said.

"Not exactly," Nik said and eyed the fruit bowl suspiciously. "It was filled mainly with sketches and a few notes."

"Sketches? What, of nudes?" Sam said with a smirk.

Nik shook his head and laughed. "Nope, unfortunately. Birds. Drawings of birds, all in great detail."

"That it? Just birds?"

"The words 'Project Black Bird' were printed in block letters on the inside cover, and Lowenstein said there were scribblings in the margins on some of the pages."

"What do you think it means?"

"Dunno," Nik said, "but my guess, it has something to do with what those dead scientists were working on."

"You need to get a look at that notebook," Sam said.

"Small minds think alike," Nik said and stabbed a piece of melon with his fork and popped it into his mouth.

CHAPTER 16

Lance Craine, the former Air Force colonel and the president's chief health preparedness officer, landed the government jet at Boundary County Airport, two miles northeast of Bonners Ferry, Idaho, and made the thirty-minute drive up State Highway 1 to Porthill in a rented SUV. As an expert in bioterrorism, Craine personally wanted to oversee the evacuation of the corpses from the Shepherd's Staff's charred compound and make certain the bodies were properly handled before they were removed to a secure government facility for disposal.

He also needed to head off rumors circulating in the area about the cause of the deaths before they spread uncontrollably and to reassure residents that a mass murderer wasn't on the loose. Despite his promise to President Warfield that the deaths of the Shepherd's Staff congregation would go unnoticed, news of the die-off was already circulating online.

Craine called an afternoon press conference at the Boundary County Sheriff's Office that eventually had to be moved from the courthouse to the local SaveUmart parking lot to accommodate the nervous local population, half of whom were wearing sidearms.

Squat, with pasty skin and cheeks like small saddlebags, Craine was not a particularly imposing figure. A band of white hair ringed his bald pate, and when he spoke, he tended to talk out of one side of his mouth. In an effort to command attention, for the occasion he dressed in his official service whites, with the shimmering brass buttons, gold piping around the collar, epaulets on the shoulders, adorned with ribbons, medals, and multicolored pins.

Folks in Boundary County were not used to interacting with federal officials, and the uniform had the desired effect of giving Craine an air of authority, at least initially.

After quick remarks thanking the sheriff and local politicians, Craine told the gathering that the president had personally dispatched him to the scene to investigate the deaths at the Shepherd's Staff compound.

Craine cleared his throat and had started to read a vacuous prepared statement full of medical mumbo jumbo when a hefty woman at the back of the crowd dressed in Carhartts and a camo hat called out, "We heard they all had their throats slit from ear to ear and the women were sodomized."

Craine had lifted his head and was nudging his glasses back up on the bridge of his nose to see where the question came from when a man shouted, "Is it true they had six-six-six carved into their foreheads?"

Others in the crowd started to stir, and the sheriff and local politicians who had been standing at Craine's side eased away. Craine had misjudged the mood of the residents. They were distrustful of Washington bureaucrats, and he needed to calm their fears before they turned on him.

"Ladies and gentlemen, please, please, if you just give me a minute," he beseeched, his pleas all but drowned out by the rowdy spectators.

A tall, dark-haired man in an olive-green military fatigue jacket who was filming the press conference with his smartphone turned to the crowd and raised both arms over his head, palms damping down the air. "Let's hear what he has to say," he shouted above the din. "It's the least we can do since he's come all this way."

That seemed to settle the throng. "Bert's right," another woman said, referring to the speaker, Bert Sanderson, the editor of the local newspaper. The man, Craine was relieved to see, appeared to be respected and well liked.

"Thank you," Craine acknowledged Sanderson. Craine crumpled up his prepared remarks and improvised.

"The fact of the matter is those poor folks at the Shepherd's Staff died as a result of asphyxiation. They ran out of funds to purchase a supply of fuel oil for the winter, and, to compensate, they used propane tanks to heat a great room in the compound where they all slept. The fumes rendered them unconscious, and after they had passed out, the unattended heaters caught some bedding on fire and burned down the building around them."

Craine paused to judge the impact his lies had on the crowd. He could see a number of the residents turn toward their neighbors, heads bobbing, to discuss what they had just learned. The explanation had the ring of truth to many of them who had used portable propane tanks themselves in the past and knew of the dangers they posed if they were not properly vented.

Seeing he had gotten the upper hand, Craine seized the moment and quickly added, "I'd ask we all bow our heads and say a short prayer for their souls."

Heads lowered to chests, as if one, and a low rumble rose from the gathering as everyone offered up blessings.

CHAPTER 17

Glenn Bauer, the forty-six-year-old CEO of Xion Labs, was trapped in a darkened, airless room in a nondescript building near Baltimore/Washington International Airport in late 2019 with a dozen other pharmaceutical execs listening to a presentation about a new class of opioid drugs when his cell phone exploded with text messages about the rumored outbreak of a novel coronavirus ravaging Wuhan, China.

One of the incoming messages was from Tony Gilroy, Xion's head of sales. "This just might be the Hail Mary we've been praying for, boss. Get our crack marketing team to rebrand Xion meds antiviral so my guys have something new to peddle."

Bauer was in no mood for marketing gimmicks. Xion was already under state and federal investigations for selling a drug that caused transverse myelitis, the inflammation of the spinal canal. The condition could be treated if discovered early enough, but, undetected, it could lead to long-term disabilities.

Xion's own director of regulatory affairs had warned Bauer about releasing the vaccine prematurely. "To imply we have efficacy data that supports a wide distribution to the general population at this point is a stretch," she wrote to Xion's management team in an email that was later leaked to plaintiffs' attorneys.

Desperate to boost quarterly revenues, Bauer had refused to heed the advice, and the company ended up facing a raft of multimillion-dollar lawsuits charging it with "willful misconduct," the trigger phrase that allows consumers to sue vaccine companies if they are able to prove management ignored or intentionally covered up defects in its products.

Bauer immediately texted Gilroy back: "Do your fucking job, Tony, and sell the shitty drugs we already have in the pipeline and stop chasing your tail. Unless people develop this corona illness from drinking beer, don't bother me again with this horseshit. Nobody gives a rat's ass about Wuhan, China, wherever the fuck that is."

Bauer silenced his phone and turned his attention back to the speaker.

Six months later, with his company under legal siege and revenues in a free fall, the Xion CEO had a change of heart.

Bauer was in his office, watching CNBC in alarm as his company's stock cratered after news of a class-action lawsuit against the firm for willful misconduct in the production and distribution of its vaccines, when the call came in from the White House.

Lance Craine was phoning to inform Bauer that Xion was in the running for a massive government contract to begin work on a vaccine program to restock the federal government's dwindling stockpile. Xion had produced limited supplies of vaccines in the past for the government, but this new contract was potentially fifty times the magnitude of prior orders.

What Craine needed to know was if Xion was interested and if the company was capable of quickly scaling up production to produce several hundred million doses of the vaccine. The answer to both questions, Bauer assured Craine, was yes.

"Shouldn't be a problem," Bauer said, and then added the caveat "Naturally, we'd have to find room in our schedule. There's been a huge surge in demand for our products lately."

Craine was also watching CNBC and knew that to be a lie and that Xion was in financial distress. That was the main reason he had chosen it. "Well, perhaps the timing's not right, then."

"No, no, that's not what I meant," Bauer quickly backpedaled, his bluff having been called. "Of course, we'll make it happen. I was just thinking out loud."

"Are you absolutely certain? This is a top priority for President Warfield. If there's any doubt in your mind about Xion's ability to give its full attention to this program, we should end this conversation now."

"One hundred percent certain," Bauer said.

"Good to hear," Craine said. "There are some strings attached—details, really—that you would need to agree to up front before proceeding."

"Anything for our country," Bauer said helpfully.

"First, this is a no-bid, sole-source contract estimated at three and a half billion dollars to supply vaccines to the US stockpile," Craine said.

Bauer let out a low whistle. "Fan-fucking-tastic. That's right in our wheelhouse."

"That part is, but wrapped inside that contract is a separate covenant that would require Xion to commit to participating in a top-secret experimental bioweapons research program," Craine said, pausing to let that sink in. "Now pay close attention, because this is the important part. Xion would need to manufacture a coronavirus, the vaccine to counter it, and an antibody treatment to be available for patients who might acquire the virus pre-vaccine."

"Uh-huh," Bauer said, distracted by the downward march of Xion's share price across the television screen.

"You will receive separate instructions on the transfer and dispositions of the funds. It's the administration's intention to use Xion as a central clearinghouse for our national vaccine strategy. Your company will receive excess monies that it will then transfer to other companies involved in the program designated by us."

"Don't see a problem," Bauer said.

"Excellent. I think we can do business together, then," Craine said and laid out the details of the plan.

In his late fifties with thinning hair, a distracting tic in his right eye, and a noticeable stoop from years of bending over microscopes, Bernard Rothschild was beloved by his staff but distrusted by senior management. He dreaded meetings with Xion's CEO. But the chief scientist had been summoned to the boss's office, so off he went.

He thought Bauer, a six-foot-four ex-jock with a set of teeth as sparkly as a strand of Christmas lights, was a bully who, despite being the head of a biotech company, was hostile to the scientists, belittled their work, and resented the money the company spent on research and development. Rothschild also hated the fact that Bauer insisted on calling him Bernie, a name he had despised since childhood.

After some perfunctory chitchat about the past weekend's Baltimore sporting events, Bauer got down to business and told the scientist that he was ordering Xion to halt all nonessential research projects in order to focus its energies on a new government program related to COVID-19.

"Are we in the hunt for future vaccines?" an excited Rothschild asked, straightening and throwing back his hunched shoulders. "The staff will be thrilled to hear the news."

"Well, Bernie," Bauer replied dryly, "sorta but not exactly."

"What's that supposed to mean?" Rothschild asked.

Bauer explained that Xion, as well as a handful of other biotech companies, had been tapped to resupply the government's depleted vaccine stockpile.

"In addition, Xion has been singled out to do gain-of-function research to create the next generation of coronavirus and the vaccine to prevent it. This administration is convinced that China deliberately targeted the United States with the COVID-19 pathogen and believes the only way to protect our country in the future against such attacks is to build up our defenses and get out in front of these wicked diseases before the next one is unleashed. Thus the need to manufacture a virus."

"Oh," Rothschild responded skeptically. "I see."

"It's a highly sensitive mission, Doctor, and it's classified top secret. If word of it were to leak, it would damage our national security and Xion's reputation. Understood?" Bauer said and tugged down his reading glasses to the tip of his nose as he stared menacingly at Rothschild over the rims.

"Of course," Rothschild said, offended at the implication that he or his staff would in any way compromise their integrity or security clearances.

Rothschild didn't like Bauer in general, but he *really* didn't like him telling him how to do his job, and, for once, he refused to be intimidated by him. "And do I have your assurance that this experimental coronavirus is to be contained in the lab and only used to manufacture an antidote and vaccine?" Rothschild pushed back.

"Absolutely. Why else would we do it? We're not the Chinese, Doctor."

"I just wanted to hear it for myself."

"The research needs to be tightly controlled and compartmentalized. One department cannot know what the other one is working on," Bauer emphasized.

"That might be a little difficult," Rothschild replied.

"If you're not up to the task, Bernie . . . ," Bauer started in.

"I didn't say that," Rothschild shot back, the tic in his right eye firing like a ship-to-shore signal lamp.

"Good," Bauer said. "I want Anne Paxton's lab to oversee the mutation of the virus. You decide which labs to use to manufacture the vaccine."

"Anne's our top virologist and nationally acclaimed. She would have been my recommendation as well," Rothschild said, annoyed that Bauer was stating the obvious.

"Oh, by the way, the project is code-named Black Bird," Bauer added.

"Black Bird?" Rothschild said. "Why Black Bird?"

"No fucking idea, but what I do know is that I'm personally gratified that my country has seen fit to ask Xion to carry out this critical patriotic mission, Bernie," Bauer said and exhaled a long stream of blue cigar smoke that settled over Rothschild's head like a mushroom cloud. "Don't fuck it up."

CHAPTER 18

Doria Miller was editing one of Zach's stories, the intern stationed rigidly at her shoulder like a mannequin, expressionless, when Nik staggered into the newsroom ninety minutes late, having slept through the alarm he had set. It was starting to become a habit.

Miller lifted her boxy head, wrinkled her nose, and gave Nik a scornful look as he walked past her desk. He ignored her and tossed Zach a quick nod before taking his seat and signing into his *Newshound* account, scrolling through endless emails, company memos, and various news alerts and announcements.

He opened his satchel and took out a thermos of coffee and poured a cup that he inhaled. He refilled the cup and called over to Wil Dutton, the assistant night editor, "Willy, miss anything?"

"Naw, not much," Dutton, a lumbering, raw-boned thirty-five-year-old with a crew cut and large ears, said. "I'm putting the finishing touches on the story rundown now. I'll shoot it over to you in a few minutes. You might want to take a look at the story on the Senate Intelligence Committee report on the gusher of foreign money pouring into US universities and think tanks."

"Okay, I'll do that," Nik said and pulled the story up on his computer.

Sam had told him Senator Summers's committee planned to release the report, and he already knew the highlights—foreign governments, but primarily China, had quietly funneled millions of dollars into domestic institutions, endowing chairs and underwriting research, all with the aim of buying influence.

Nik was reading a section about how professors and researchers had appeared to compromise their independence by secretly accepting money from Chinese government sources when he looked up to see Zach, arms crossed, waiting patiently by his desk.

"Give me a second, Zach. I'm almost finished with this piece," Nik said and went back to reading. After a few more minutes, he closed the file and called out to Dutton, "Story looks good, Willy. Send it to Doria for a copyedit and then publish."

Nik turned back to Zach. "Hey, what's up?"

"They called off the search," Zach said.

Nik gave him a puzzled look.

"For Puck Hall, the missing hiker. A snowstorm hit the mountains. I got a call from my source at the National Park Service."

"Right, sorry. I'm a little tired," Nik said. "How bad's the storm?"

"Whiteout conditions."

"They say when they'll resume the search?" Nik asked.

"Storm could last a few days. On the record, they're officially postponing the search. Off the record, they have no plans to resume it until the spring thaw, and at that point, it won't be a rescue mission any longer but a body recovery effort."

Nik interlaced his fingers and shelved his hands on top of his head. He closed his eyes and thought about Puck Hall's mother. *It must be torture for her.* He sighed, and realized those thoughts would probably not have occurred to him before becoming a parent.

"Write a story that they temporarily halted the search due to weather conditions," Nik instructed Zach. "Skip the part about recovering the body in the spring for now. Let's give it a couple days and see how it plays out. Maybe she'll turn up."

"Okay," Zach said and started to walk away. "Oh, I almost forgot." He stopped and turned back to face Nik. "My source at the Park Service said a television reporter has been calling nearly every day for status updates on the search for Hall. Looks like we got competition."

"I wouldn't worry about it," Nik said with a shake of the head. "It's probably just a reporter from the Halls' hometown television station. Send me your story when you finish it."

Nik and Wil were discussing whether to send a reporter to cover a large pro-democracy protest outside the Saudi ambassador's residence when Zach reappeared, his cell phone pasted to his ear. "Hang on," he said into the phone before addressing Nik. "Turn your television to Fox News."

Nik, perturbed, picked up the TV remote and punched in the station. The sound on the small desktop TV was muted, but there on the screen in front of him was Elizabeth Blake, a political correspondent for Fox News, who had, until recently, worked as a reporter for a local Washington, DC, television station.

A chyron crawled across the bottom of the screen that read: "Mountain rescue called off due to winter storm, missing girl presumed dead."

"Aw, shit, Lizzy," Nik said, addressing the TV. "Did you really have to report the part about the girl being presumed dead?"

Blake and Nik had a complicated history, and he knew she'd do anything for a scoop, but he was puzzled why a national reporter—and a political reporter, at that—would care about a missing hiker. *Something isn't quite right with this picture,* Nik was thinking to himself when Zach blurted out, "That's her," gesturing toward the television set.

"That's who? What the hell are you talking about, Zach?"

"That's the woman the motel customer saw on the balcony arguing with Bernard Rothschild before he killed himself. She's the one he was talking to," Zach stammered.

"Lizzy Blake?" Nik said, confused. "Are you sure?"

"I'm on the phone with Missy, the motel clerk. Remember, we exchanged phone numbers. She's standing in the lobby right now with the customer and they're watching the news. The customer says she is one hundred percent positive it's the same woman," Zach said.

"Aw, shit," Nik uttered and unmuted the television.

CHAPTER 19

Puck woke, the sun's blinding light shining in her eyes, covered in a mound of newly fallen snow, her body cold and sore from head to toe, her injured knee barking when she shifted her weight.

She turned her head away from the sun's glare, but the light followed her movements and grew closer, brighter. That's when she realized it wasn't the sun at all but a powerful flashlight, and she squirmed to a sitting position.

"Be still," a raspy voice ordered.

It was dark and Puck couldn't see who was talking. She raised her right arm to shield her eyes from the light and, when she did, howled in pain, the bullet Narda had fired having passed through the fleshy part of her shoulder. She moaned and sank back down on the ground.

"I'm hurt, mister," Puck finally managed to say. "I think I've been shot."

"Uh-huh, I can see that," the man said. A large raspberry-colored stain coated the ground where Puck had been lying.

"I'm in a bad way," she moaned again.

"Nowhere near as bad as that woman over yonder," the voice replied. "Head cracked open like a walnut."

"She tried to kill me," Puck defended herself.

"Mm-hmm. That's your side of the story. She can't tell hers," the man said, drawing farther away from Puck but keeping the light trained on her face. "Who helped you lift that rock up in the tree?"

"What?" Puck said. "Oh, the boulder? I rolled it up from the creek and hoisted it myself."

"You don't say."

"It's true," Puck said and started to shiver, her teeth clacking like castanets. "Mister, I'm freezing. You got anything I can use to cover up?"

The man doused the light and they were plunged into darkness; black dots, the size of pieces of coal, danced in front of Puck's eyes. She could hear the man moving about but couldn't see him.

She reached up with her left hand and switched on her headlamp. He was standing not two feet away, hovering like smoke, ghostly, in the snow. He was a clean-shaven Black man of indeterminate age with a large head, wide-set eyes, face rutted with lines, and he was dressed in an old-fashioned plaid wool coat that had patches sewn on the sleeves. He wore a watch cap pulled down over his ears and leather gloves cinched on his hands, snow piling up on his shoulders and head. He unbuttoned the coat, shook off the snow, and draped it over Puck.

"Need to get movin'. This is a bad storm. You able to walk on your own?" he asked.

"Yeah, I think so," Puck said. "Where we headed?"

The man didn't answer right off, but looked around, assessing the situation, wind howling, temperatures plunging, snow falling harder by the minute, a gun-shot woman, maybe a murderer to boot, he was probably thinking. "My cabin. It's a few miles from here. I'll return for the body later. Hopefully it'll be okay for a bit before the animals find it and start eatin' on it."

Puck stiffened at the comment but didn't respond. The man's wool coat revived her, but her shoulder started to throb now that her nerve endings were no longer numbed by the cold. "I have some ibuprofen stashed over there in the vines. Think you could get it for me?" she said and motioned toward the spot.

The man walked across the path and swept the vines away from the opening with his hand. "This your hidey-hole?" he asked, shining his flashlight inside and reaching in for the small vial lying atop a rock.

"Yeah," Puck said. "I guess you could call it that."

He stepped back over to Puck and handed her the ibuprofen. "Lemme have a look at that shoulder of yours," he said and knelt in the snow next to her. She slipped the coat off and pulled down the sleeve of her shirt, wincing in pain.

She was lucky, the bullet having passed clean through without striking an artery or bone, but it was an ugly wound and would need to be attended to before an infection set in.

"I've seen worse. Good news is the bleeding's stopped for now," he said and then made his way over to Narda's body. The boulder that had landed on the now-dead woman had rolled off and come to rest in a small depression in the earth a few feet away.

The man removed Narda's backpack and pried the revolver from her fingers, stiff from cold and the onset of rigor mortis. He tucked the gun in his waistband and lifted the pack over his shoulder.

He was adjusting it when he stepped on something under the snow. He kicked at it with the toe of his boot and uncovered

Puck's walking stick. He examined the sharpened rod, its one end encrusted in dried blood.

"Sticks and stones," he said. "This yours?"

Puck nodded. He handed her the stick, and she used it to steady herself. She leaned into it and did a series of knee bends, shallow at first, then deeper, to get her circulation flowing and loosen up her limbs.

She hobbled over to the cave and collected the folding knife, the Leatherman tool her father had given her, and her toothbrush. She left everything else behind and pulled the vines back over the entrance after she had stepped out.

A steady snow was falling, and the game trail had all but disappeared. Darkness slowly receded, only to be replaced by a flat gray light. Puck could make out the shapes of hemlock branches, weighed down by the heavy snow, poised over the trail like vultures ready to swoop down on stragglers.

"Let's go," the man said and set off with powerful strides. Puck followed but, after a couple minutes, called out, "Wait, stop."

The man looked back over his shoulder. "What now? We got no time to be stopping every few minutes if we're gonna stay ahead of this storm."

"It's not that," Puck said. "I need to look in her backpack."

The man pursed his lips but didn't say anything and slid the pack from his shoulders. "Make it quick."

Puck rifled through Narda's belongings but didn't find what she was looking for. "Stay here," she said. "I'll be back in no time." She set off down the trail.

The man placed the pack on the ground, sat down on it, and called after her, "You got ten minutes. Not a second more," as he looked at his watch.

Puck hurried back down the trail, trying not to slip and fall on the snow. When she reached the site, she dropped to the ground and patted down Narda's pockets. She felt a jackknife in the right pocket and a set of keys in the other.

She wedged her arms under the body, first the left, and then, gingerly, the wounded right, and rolled the corpse over. Narda's face stared up at her, eyes blank, lips peeled back, a snarl frozen on her half-open mouth as if in midscream.

Puck gagged and turned away.

She took a moment to compose herself before unzipping Narda's coat and checking her inside pockets.

In the left breast pocket, she found what she was searching for and retrieved Narda's mobile phone. She pushed the home button, and the screen lock popped up, asking for a six-digit pass code.

Puck stared at the phone in disbelief and began rubbing her hands together furiously to create friction and heat. After several seconds, she picked up Narda's hand, removed her glove, and placed Narda's right thumb between her warm palms for twenty seconds and then pressed it to the home button.

The screen bloomed open. Puck thought about severing Narda's thumb to take it with her, but then she poked around in the phone's settings file and discovered she could delete Narda's six-digit code and replace it with one of her own to activate the device. Having done that, she then placed the phone in sleep mode.

Puck double-timed it back up the trail, her old tracks already covered by the fast-falling snow, but when she got to the spot where she had left the man, he was gone. Her shoulders slumped.

"Over here," a voice said from the trees. "Needed to relieve myself. You find what you were looking for?"

"I did," Puck said and held up the cell phone.

"Ain't gonna do you much good out here," he said. "No reception."

"Yeah, I know," Puck said, "but maybe there's some information stored on it that could explain why she attacked me."

The man grunted. "Name's Cliff, by the way."

"I'm Puck."

"Puck, huh? Figures," Cliff said.

"Why's that?" she said.

"Rhymes with 'luck,' which you surely must have, young lady. I weren't planning to check my trap lines down this way for another week, and ain't another soul but me in these parts this time of year. You'd've froze to death in six hours in these conditions, as sure as I'm standing here, had I not come along."

"I'm grateful," Puck said. "I'm only here—wherever here is—because I was trying to escape from that woman. I met her on the trail. I thought she was a friend."

"Save it. You can tell me your story when we're safe and warm in the cabin," Cliff said. "We stand around jawing much longer, and we'll both die of exposure. We'll be lucky to make it back in time as it is."

Cliff turned and started walking. Puck fell in behind, struggling to match his stride, the wind and snow whipping her face.

CHAPTER 20

Lance Craine switched off the TV as a feeling of relief washed over him. Or maybe it was the Scotch. Either way, things were working out better than he could have imagined.

The Shepherd's Staff bodies had been disposed of quietly, and what little interest there had been in the tragedy had died off, so to speak, as Craine had predicted it would. Even that local-yokel newspaper editor in Idaho had stopped pestering him with questions about official autopsy reports and death certificates. Enthusiasm for the story waned the more time passed.

And now, a deadly blizzard was lashing the North Carolina mountains. With any luck, the young research assistant would die in those mountains, one way or the other, and, with her, one of the few remaining links to the Black Bird virus.

Craine recalled that Xion's CEO, Glenn Bauer, hadn't fully comprehended his meaning when he told him that Anne Paxton's department, along with Rothschild, would have to be eliminated after their work on the virus was completed. If it wasn't clear to him then, it was now.

When Craine was still at the Pentagon, his colleagues had war-gamed various military conflicts with China over the years, all of which ended in millions of casualties and large parts of each country laid to waste. The most promising strategy he heard of called for sinking China's entire naval fleet in seventy-two hours, but even that had a one-in-a-thousand chance of succeeding.

No, Craine had surmised that the best way to defeat China was not with bombs but with bugs, both the viral and software-related kind.

To be successful, the bugs would have to be planted in such a way that they couldn't be traced back to the source, and in the case of the pathogen, the trick would be how to inoculate Americans in case the virus rebounded on the US.

Craine belched loudly, scratched his left ass cheek, and poured himself another tumbler of Scotch. He picked up the pathologist's report on the Shepherd's Staff deaths from the coffee table and reread it. It was gruesome, to be certain, but on the plus side, the virus was extremely effective.

The Black Bird virus didn't dismantle the body's immune system as much as it decapitated it. They would need to use extreme caution in handling the pathogen.

All Black Bird needed to do to cripple China, Craine had argued, was instill enough fear in the citizenry to destabilize the country, and the best way to accomplish that goal, he reasoned, was to seed the virus in China's impoverished provinces. The rest would take care of itself.

Craine had arrived at that conclusion by studying how Chinese authorities had first responded to the spread of COVID-19.

After denying there was an emerging epidemic and then attempting to cover up the disease, China's leaders had sprung into action and moved forcefully to contain the spread. Whole regions of the country were locked down and quarantined, but that was mostly true in prosperous cities where the middle classes resided. Government officials made the decision to spare no expense to protect those citizens.

That wasn't the case in remote villages, which were home to broad populations of poor and illiterate peasants. Beijing largely ignored those folks, and they were left to fend for themselves. What few medical supplies they did receive were inferior.

China's leaders came to realize that their strategy of protecting the well-off at the expense of the less fortunate had backfired, and they were then confronting two lethal challenges: the virus and a potential uprising by peasants. Based on China's long history, Communist authorities knew one could be as deadly as the other.

China eventually subdued the disease in remote areas, but only after thousands of people had needlessly suffered and died. Long after medical personnel departed, there remained a deep bitterness and suspicion toward Beijing in the countryside, where inhabitants felt isolated, betrayed, and sacrificed.

It was clear to Craine that China's poor were a powder keg just waiting to explode. All someone needed to do was light the fuse. Craine found a match in, of all places, Pittsburgh.

The National Aviary in Pittsburgh is home to one of the largest live bird collections in North America. It harbors some six hundred birds and more than two hundred species, and it was there, on a dull, wintery afternoon, that Lance Craine first got the inspiration for Project Black Bird.

Craine was in Pittsburgh for a presentation on infectious diseases at Carnegie Mellon University, and it was only by a fluke that he even visited the aviary that February day. The presentation was unexpectedly rescheduled until the next morning, and Craine found himself with an extra four hours on his hands.

Searching for something to do, he asked the hotel's concierge, an avid birder, for suggestions and was directed to the National Aviary. Craine was astonished by the variety of birds he encountered as he toured the forty-thousand-square-foot facility. He admired African penguins, the smallest of the penguin family; Eurasian kestrels, which can literally hover in midair like a hummingbird; and Vietnamese pheasants, which, with their brilliant midnight-blue plumage, look more like peacocks than they do a game bird.

Eventually he found himself standing in front of the exhibit for *Corvus brachyrhynchos*—the common American crow.

Reading the accompanying brochure, Craine was surprised to discover that crows are capable of recognizing individual humans by their facial features. The birds have been known to dive-bomb people who have harassed them in the past and reward shiny objects to those who have been kind to them.

But that's not what caught his eye that day. No, what intrigued him was the pivotal role the black bird played in the transmission of the deadly West Nile virus. The genetic composition of a crow, he learned, makes the bird ideally suited to host and spread the lethal disease.

As Craine made his way back to the hotel from the aviary later that evening, shivering in the winter air, an idea took root.

CHAPTER 21

"You best not be yanking my chain, Byron," Detective Yevette Jenks warned as she emerged from the passenger's side of a late-model four-door sedan, gravel crunching like broken glass underneath the heels of her shoes. "'Cause I ain't in no mood to be playin' no games."

Jenks's young partner, Detective Jason Goetz, popped out from the driver's side like a jack-in-the-box and waved. "Hiya, Nik."

It was a late Tuesday afternoon and the sun in the sky above Rock Creek Park was dying like lights slowly dimming in a movie theater.

"Detectives Jenks, Goetz." Nik greeted the officers with a nod.

It was Nik's day off, and he had debated whether to seek a meeting with the detectives but, in the end, felt he had little choice after seeing Elizabeth Blake's newscast and learning of her presence at the Anchor Inn shortly before Bernard Rothschild had died.

Blake had somehow managed to outmaneuver Nik on the story, and he was desperate to regain an edge. "Thanks for making the time. 'Preciate it."

"What's this about, Byron?" Jenks demanded, jerking her head toward her partner. "Goetz here says you were evasive on the phone. Said something about information concerning Rothschild. Up to me, I wouldn't've come."

"He's right. It does concern Rothschild, but before I divulge what I know, we first need to establish some ground rules," Nik said.

"Who died and made you queen for the day?" Jenks said.

"Maybe we should listen to what Nik has to say, Detective Jenks," Goetz said deferentially.

"I dunno," Jenks said dismissively. "Byron's not exactly been forthcoming in the past."

"Fine, if that's the way you want it, Detective, then this will be a really short meeting," Nik said, "but I think you'll find what I have to say interesting."

Jenks's service revolver was holstered at the small of her back, and she shifted it to her right hip, folded her arms across her chest, and leaned on the hood of the sedan. "Go on," she said, a bored look on her face, "but make it quick."

"For the record, it's not my habit—" Nik began.

"Spare us the fuckin' sermon, Reverend," Jenks sawed Nik off midsentence. "You're the one who asked to meet with us."

"Fair enough. What I'm about to tell you consists of some hard facts, some secondhand information, and some informed conjecture on my part, most of it having to do with Rothschild."

"Sounds like you got a whole lotta nothin'," Jenks said.

Nik ignored the detective and continued. "What I need from you, in return, are assurances that you will not breathe a word to anyone about where this information came from," he said, "and that you will share with me any leads you get based on what I'm about to tell you."

Jenks stared coldly at Nik but didn't speak.

"Do we have a deal?" Nik finally asked.

Jenks looked at Goetz, then back at Nik, and slowly nodded her head. "But if you're bullshittin' me . . ."

"Hear me out, then decide for yourself," Nik said, and when Jenks didn't interrupt, Nik continued, "When I saw you at the Anchor Inn that day, what I didn't tell you is that three former Xion employees, like Rothschild, recently died violent deaths. All three were ruled accidental, and had their death notices not arrived in our offices around the same time, there's a good chance we would not have made the connection to Xion. We believe the three—Anne Paxton, Deidre Steward, and Thom Berg—were working on a sensitive government project at Xion and that Rothschild oversaw their work." Nik paused. "Follow me so far?"

"How'd they die, these three former employees?" Jenks asked.

"Allegedly, skiing accident in Washington, boating accident in North Carolina, and drowning in Florida. We've requested the official death certificates but haven't received them yet."

"Go on," Jenks said, uncrossing her arms and boosting herself up to sit on the car's hood. Goetz was leaning against the grille, scribbling notes on a digital tablet.

Nik started again. "There's a fourth person who also worked in the same lab."

Jenks said, "This other person dead, too?"

"Maybe. We don't know, but she is missing. We wrote about her. You may have seen our story. Her name's Puck Hall," Nik said.

"You got anybody alive we can talk to?"

"Not really, but that does bring me to Rothschild. A source who was a close friend and associate of Rothschild's is convinced he didn't commit suicide. Said, mentally, Rothschild was stable as the Rock of Gibraltar."

"That right? This source, how they so sure?" Jenks asked.

"Just a gut feeling. Said Rothschild admitted he had made a—quote—terrible mistake, but my source was pretty certain Rothschild was referring to his decision to leave teaching and go to work for Xion."

"Huh. Anything else, or is that it?" Jenks asked and slid down from the hood of the car.

"That's pretty much it," he said. Nik intentionally left out the part about Elizabeth Blake's meeting with Rothschild.

"Good. 'Cause now I got some hard facts for you to chew on," Jenks said. "We finally got a look at Rothschild's suicide note."

"Really?" Nik said apprehensively. "What did it say?"

"Yeah, really. It seems the good doctor had become obsessed with a certain young female research assistant at Xion, a cute little thing. Pursued her every chance he got. Stalked her online. Even threatened her career if she didn't reciprocate his advances. He got pretty graphic. Need me to paint you a picture?"

"No, Detective," Nik said. "I think I get it. What happened?"

"She rebuffed him, that's what happened. Turned the tables on Rothschild, secretly recorded him, said she was going to go to management, the police, the media. He couldn't handle the rejection and public humiliation, so he killed himself. Wrote in his note that he made a—quote—'terrible mistake,'" Jenks said. "Sound familiar?"

"This young research assistant . . ."

"Goetz, why don't you tell 'im?"

Detective Goetz gave Nik a pained smile. "It was Puck Hall."

"I don't believe it," Nik said, looking at Goetz, stunned.

"It's true, Nik," Goetz said. "We saw Rothschild's suicide note. He named her."

Jenks opened the car door and dropped into the passenger's seat while Goetz climbed behind the wheel. Jenks closed the door and lowered her window. "Next time someone tells you they got a gut feelin', Byron, you might want to take it with a grain of salt," she said.

"I'll keep that in mind, Detective," Nik said.

The sedan started pulling away and then stopped. Jenks stuck her head out the window.

"People," Jenks said, shaking her head, "just when you think you got 'em figured out."

"I . . . ," Nik began to respond but didn't finish.

The car rolled on and left Nik standing there, staring down at the tops of his shoes, disoriented, feeling a fool. He was still standing there some time later when a park ranger pulled up and informed him the park was closing shortly and he needed to leave.

CHAPTER 22

Nik met Mo Morgan and Mia Landry that evening at the Third Edition in Georgetown, their one-time after-work watering hole. When the trio had first arrived in Washington, they had gathered weekly at the bare-bones bar for what they dubbed "boozehounders," nights of hard drinking, gossip swapping, and scheming to undermine Li'l Dick Whetstone, *Newshound*'s former chief editor, who had it in for the transplanted midwesterners.

But with Nik's impending parenthood and Mo's vow of sobriety, the frequency with which they gathered for boozehounders had slowed markedly over time, and when the pandemic hit, they had ceased altogether.

Covid had upended their lives in big and small ways. Mia had been recruited to be *Newshound*'s technology czar, in charge of making sure all staffers were equipped with the tools and resources they needed to work remotely, while Mo became a logistics expert, sourcing face masks and personal protective equipment (PPEs) for *Newshound* employees from vendors.

Before he had gone on paternity leave, Nik had been put in charge of overseeing coverage of the protests that had erupted in the city following the death of George Floyd and helped reporters and photographers safely navigate the sometimes hostile and even violent demonstrations.

The biggest blow had been the loss of Frank Rath, their longtime colleague and mentor, who died from complications from the virus in a Washington hospital, no family or friends in attendance. They conducted a well-attended Zoom memorial for Frank that went on for hours while participants exchanged stories about the notorious journalist.

All three were now happy to revive the boozehounder custom, even if just for one night, because of what the occasion signaled—that their lives were slowly returning to normal.

The trio huddled in their regular booth in the back of the bar away from the crowds and pool tables but not so far that they were out of eye contact with Pete, their favorite bartender. Nik was drinking Budweiser, Mia white Russians, and Mo nonalcoholic beer. After their second round, Pete sent over a large basket of cheesy nachos on the house.

Mia and Mo were both on the short list to replace Whetstone as chief editor, and a raw, palpable tension, like an overfilled balloon set to burst, had developed between the pair. Nik had noticed it, as had everyone in the newsroom, and he worried it might erupt at the bar. He needn't have. Mo lanced the tension with a toast to Mia as soon as the first round of drinks hit the table:

Here's to good Irish friends
Never above you
Never below you
Always beside you
Cheers!

Nik then gave his two workmates a quick summary of his meeting with the detectives and how what he had assumed about Xion, Rothschild, the dead researchers, and Puck Hall had been wrong. And not just marginally wrong, but 180 degrees wrong.

"I had it ass-backward," he confessed. "Couldn't have been more off base. I was so sure of . . . ," he started to say before letting his thought trail off.

"Well, that explains what Lizzy Blake was doing at the Anchor Inn," Mo said. "Hall must have followed through on her threat to sic the media on Rothschild and got in touch with Blake. The MeToo movement takes another scalp."

Mia stirred her drink contemplatively. "How's the nonalcoholic beer?" she asked Mo.

"Tastes like ditch water," he said and took a swig. "Wanna sip?"

Mia squinched up her nose. "No, thanks. I'm not certain the two of you are looking at this the right way."

"Why's that?" Nik asked.

"Well, I don't know how those three scientists died or why, but you can't convince me that young woman turned the media loose on Rothschild," Mia said.

"The cops saw the suicide note," Nik countered. "He named her."

"I've been hosting the *Dateline Washington* podcast for singles for over a year now, Nik, and I'm telling you that's not how a twenty-four-year-old female in her first job out of college handles that situation."

Nik polished off his beer and flagged Pete. "You want another?" he asked his tablemates. Mo shook his head.

"I'm good for now," Mia said, "but let's get some real food."

Mo ordered a burger with fries, Mia a pastrami sandwich, and Nik a house salad. "Diet," he explained. "So what does she do instead?"

"She tells a friend, confides in a mentor. Maybe she talks to a lawyer, but doubtful. What she doesn't do is threaten to destroy a prominent scientist's reputation by going to the media," Mia said and took a bite of her sandwich. "God, I missed these," she said, a rivulet of Russian dressing running down her chin.

"Hold on," Mo protested. "You have to admit that it explains Hall's spur-of-the-moment decision to hike the Appalachian Trail. Her mother even said the idea came out of the blue. It's obvious she regretted outing Rothschild and wanted to go somewhere no one could find her, put distance between herself and what was going to be a media shitstorm."

"You made more sense when you were drinking," Mia said.

"No argument there." Mo frowned.

Mia continued, "Why run? The woman Rothschild allegedly described in that note was seeking attention. No reason for her to flee once she got what she was after. I'm not buying it," she said.

The three fell quiet, concentrating on their food. Nik finally broke the silence. "I'd give anything to know what Lizzy's working on."

"Looks like you're going to get your wish," Mo said.

"Whaddaya mean?" Nik asked.

Mo nodded to the television set suspended in the corner of the bar. Nik and Mia swiveled their heads around to see what Mo was looking at. There on the screen was a picture of Lizzy Blake. A bold headline across her chest read: "Fox Exclusive—Former Xion scientists implicated in superbug scandal."

Nik moaned. "My day just keeps getting better 'n' fuckin' better," he said and called Pete over to ask him to turn up the sound on the TV.

CHAPTER 23

Elizabeth Blake wanted nothing more in life than to be a correspondent for a national news operation. It's what she had dreamed of as she worked her way up the food chain, moving from one backwater television market to the next, in search of bigger stories and more exposure, willing to put up with terrible hours, low pay, and sexual come-ons from fossilized station managers if it meant getting ahead.

Her managers consistently rated her as one of the best reporters on staff in annual reviews, and, to a person, they characterized her as a fierce competitor with ambition as her number-one trait. Several went so far as to call it "blind ambition."

When she finally landed in Washington, DC, as an investigative reporter for an affiliate of a major broadcast organization, she was one small step away from fulfilling her fantasy.

Then fate intervened and she collided with Nik Byron. Her career had imploded quicker than the time it takes to change a channel.

To be sure, Blake's undoing was largely self-inflicted. She convinced a *Newshound* employee to remove secret files Nik had obtained on Yukon Inc., the nation's largest artificial intelligence company, and turn them over to her. What Blake didn't foresee was that Nik would get wind of the scheme and alter the documents, betting the erroneous information would find its way into Blake's on-air reporting. It did, and the story had blown up in her face.

Incensed and embarrassed by the foul-up, Blake's bosses kicked her to the curb, and it had taken her nearly a year of volunteering for every assignment, no matter how demeaning, to rehabilitate her career. Eventually her hard work had been noticed and led to a job offer at Fox News, but Blake had vowed to settle the score with Byron if she ever got the opportunity.

As fortune would have it, that opportunity dropped in her lap one day via an unsolicited tip. She was on a deadline and almost hadn't taken the call when it came into the newsroom. It was from an anonymous caller, the receptionist said, and they had an important tip.

"Fuck," Lizzy said under her breath. To the receptionist, she said, "Put 'em through."

"Lizzy Blake," she said brusquely when she picked up the phone. The caller seemed to be in no hurry and asked Lizzy how her day was going. "Fine. I'm really busy just now. How can I help you?"

"How familiar are you with Xion Labs?" the caller asked.

"Exxon?" Blake replied, only half paying attention to the caller. "Who the fuck doesn't know about Exxon?" she barked, irritated at herself now for answering the call from someone who was obviously a crank.

"Not Exxon. Xion. X-I-O-N." The caller spelled out the name and chuckled, which pissed off Blake even more.

"I don't have time for this bullshit," she snapped. "Either tell me what this is about or I'm going to hang up."

Dead air.

"Hey?" she said after what seemed like a half minute. "You still there?"

"You're right. Maybe the *Post* would be a better fit," the voice finally said. "Or *Newshound.* Their reporters are already sniffing around the story."

Lizzy bristled at the mention of *Newshound.* "I'm still here, aren't I? Sorry if I was abrupt just then. I'm under deadline pressure. What about Xion Labs? What did they do?"

"It's not what the company has done," the caller said calmly, "it's what a small group of malcontent scientists was attempting to do."

"And what was that?"

"Something very disturbing, I'm afraid. Steal vaccines intended for US citizens as well as secret vaccine patent formulas."

"To do what with?" Lizzy asked.

"Offer it up on the black market to rogue drug companies. Those formulas are worth billions," the voice said. "The company only discovered the plan after the scientists had been fired from their jobs."

"Where are these scientists now?" she asked.

"Dead, for the most part. Word is they crossed the wrong people."

"Well, that's interesting, but if everybody's dead . . . ," she started to say.

"There are two people who are still around. One is a junior staffer, the other is the former chief scientific officer at Xion. His name's Bernard Rothschild, and right now, he's at the Anchor Inn motel over in Anacostia."

"What's he doing there?" Blake said.

"Hiding out is my guess. Trying to avoid getting arrested."

"What about this junior staffer, where is he?"

"She. And she disappeared into the wilderness. Rumor is she was Rothschild's lover."

"How is it that you know so much about this?" Blake quizzed.

"Me, I'm just a concerned citizen. Tell you what. Check out these people," the caller said and rattled off Paxton's, Steward's, and Berg's names. "See for yourself if what I said is accurate. If not, drop it. If it is, go talk to Rothschild. He's in room eleven. But I wouldn't wait. He might not be there long."

"How can I reach you?" Lizzy said.

"You can't. Give me your cell phone number, and I'll be in touch."

Lizzy recited her number and was starting to ask another question when the line went dead.

CHAPTER 24

Samantha Whyte surveyed the ballroom of the Grand Hyatt hotel and couldn't have been more satisfied with the turnout. All the major networks had assigned reporters to Senator Eva Summers's press conference, as had the top cable channels. Sam spotted a knot of reporters in the back of the room from the *New York Times*, the *Washington Post*, Bloomberg, and the Associated Press. In the far corner, a female reporter from *Axios* was talking to her counterpart from *Vice*. Sam was disappointed not to see anyone from *Newshound*.

Sam had arranged for Summers to make the rounds of the Sunday talk shows and do friendly sit-downs with CNN and MSNBC. She was still negotiating with Fox over who would interview the senator, but it looked like Elizabeth Blake, to Sam's unease.

Sam's boss was running behind, exactly as planned. The press conference was scheduled to start at four p.m. Summers would walk on stage at precisely 4:18, not so late as to be rude, but just late enough to allow the reporters to get their socializing out of the way and add some drama to the event.

The stage was festooned with American flags and a large overhead screen projecting scenes of the Washington Monument, the Lincoln Memorial, Martin Luther King's march on Washington, and other iconic symbols from the country's past.

It was no secret that Summers intended to declare her candidacy for the office of the president of the United States. What was less known was exactly why she was running and how she intended to attack the incumbent.

At 4:18, Summers swept onto the stage dressed in patriotic colors—a navy-blue pantsuit and a white blouse, with a red scarf looped around her neck—surrounded by staffers, a Bruce Springsteen song pumping up the crowd. After a preamble that touched on her western roots, family, the Olympics, and her political career, she announced her intention to seek the land's highest office.

She then launched a broadside against the current administration, condemning President Warfield for a reckless foreign policy, abandoning allies, undermining the US intelligence community, and putting his own interests above that of the country.

Summers accused Warfield of using the pandemic to roll back civil liberties, punish opponents, and pay off political favors.

"This administration has secretly funneled billions of taxpayer dollars to shadowy companies under the guise of fighting the virus, and it has stonewalled all attempts by my committee to get information on the program. It's a dark chapter in our country's history and a national disgrace," Summers said.

"The American public deserves better, and I pledge to restore trust in our government if elected," she said, and added, "I'll take questions now." The room erupted in shouting.

"Sanctimonious bitch," President Ronald Warfield sneered at the television screen before switching off the set in the Oval Office.

"The dyke doesn't stand a chance against you, sir," Courtney Sachs, the White House's director of communications, assured her boss as she busily scrolled through her phone. Sachs was seated on a beige love seat off to one side of the room, legs tucked under her, skirt bunched up around her thighs, unnaturally blond hair hanging loosely down around her face and over dark eyebrows as black and straight as pieces of electrical tape.

"You really think that?" Warfield said and cocked an eyebrow at Sachs.

"Absolutely. She's not in your league, Mr. President. Hell, she'll be lucky to make it out of Iowa, if she even gets that far."

"No, no, not that," Warfield said. "The dyke part."

"Oh, for sure. She went to an all-girls school, played college sports, was on the women's Olympic shooting team. Definitely."

"Didn't know," Warfield said, shaking his head. He thought Summers was hot, wouldn't mind getting his hands into those pantsuits of hers.

"Golf, softball, basketball. Full of 'em. Lacrosse," Sachs added.

"Hmm." Warfield scratched his chin, thinking that his wife, Susie, had attended an all-girls school and played college sports, as did his daughters. "But she has a husband, a family."

"As if that matters," Sachs cackled.

Warfield had hired and retained Sachs because of her undying loyalty, not for her political acumen or personal assessments. That, and he found her physically attractive, in a slutty kind of way. He knew this about Summers: she would be no pushover as an opponent. He had followed the senator's career and thought her politically gifted, tough, quick on her feet. He admired her for being able to connect with people in what appeared to be a genuine manner, even if, as he suspected, it was fake.

What's more, as a member of the Senate Homeland Security Committee, she was in a position to cause Warfield serious political headaches by investigating the vaccine program.

Warfield harbored no doubts that the Chinese had lied to the world about the origins of the coronavirus, and, like most, he was horrified by the toll the disease had taken and appalled by the cavalier posture Chinese authorities had adopted. Furthermore, he was incensed when Chinese politicians attempted to pin the spread of the virus on US military personnel in Asia.

But as time passed, Warfield came to view the virus in an entirely different light. He no longer saw it through the narrow prism of a global health crisis; rather, he recognized it for what it truly was—a twenty-four-karat, gold-plated political opportunity—and he was determined not to squander it.

So when Lance Craine had approached him with a scheme to funnel hundreds of millions of dollars into a secret bioweapons program, Warfield had wholeheartedly embraced it.

"I'm getting tweets from the press asking for a comment on Senator Summers's announcement," Sachs called over to Warfield, absentmindedly twirling locks of her hair around her left index finger. Warfield found the gesture distracting and a turn-on. "Anything you care to say, sir?"

President Warfield furrowed his brow and steepled his fingertips, as if deep in thought. "Yes, as a Christian, I remain open-minded about my opponent's motivations no matter how radically different her political and lifestyle choices may be from my own and those of millions of freedom-loving and God-fearing Americans," he said, Sachs tapping away at the keyboard on her smartphone.

"That's beautiful, sir," Sachs said breathlessly. "I'll post that to your Twitter account immediately. It says absolutely nothing but everything all at the same time."

"Thank you, Courtney," Warfield said. "It's a gift."

"It certainly is, sir. It most certainly is."

CHAPTER 25

Leza Burdock was standing in line at the Twisp Bakery on a cold ash-gray day, a steady snow falling outside, waiting to place her lunch order for a hot-brewed chai tea and a roasted chicken wrap before driving out to a nearby ranch to help with the foaling of a mare, when her mother's text arrived. Leza never knew what to expect from her mother, who had only recently gotten a smartphone and was still new to texting. She often just sent a random link—it could be for her daughter's daily horoscope, a coupon for tampons, or Hollywood gossip. And as often as not, she never attached a note explaining the reason for the link.

The text this day was a bare link to a news story about Xion. What little media Leza consumed consisted primarily of cooking shows and PBS miniseries. She found news programming depressing, ever more so since the death of her partner, Anne Paxton.

Leza assumed the link would take her to an updated story about Puck Hall, the missing hiker. Her mother had previously sent her a link to a story from a site she had never heard of before—called *Newshound*—about Hall that had mentioned

Anne and her deceased colleagues. Leza was curious why the reporters had referred to their deaths as "alleged accidents." Anne's death was clearly an accident, an extremely tragic one at that.

Leza had cried when she read the *Newshound* story, thinking about her own loss, what Anne's life was like in DC before they met, the deaths of the other scientists, and Puck Hall, now lost somewhere in the Smoky Mountains. It was almost too much to bear.

On the few occasions that Anne had talked about work, she had spoken glowingly about the bright, gifted young researcher. Anne had predicted Hall would rise fast and have a successful career, and she was proud of the small role she had played in mentoring the young woman.

After reading the story, Leza had called the newsroom to ask to talk to the reporters and find out why they had written "alleged accident," but as she waited on hold to be transferred, she hung up, seized by a panic attack.

Leza found it hard to remain in her cabin after she returned from Anne's funeral in Chicago. While they had only been together a short time, Anne was messy, and her personal belongings—books, shoes, earrings, keys—were scattered everywhere. Leza couldn't walk into a room without feeling Anne's presence. Her one escape was her veterinary practice.

She finally found the willpower to box up Anne's things, and that's when she had come across Anne's journals, tucked under a pile of sweaters in a pine wardrobe that Anne had bought at a local flea market shortly after the two moved in together.

Leza thumbed through the pages of the journals, impressed by Anne's neat, compact handwriting. *Never would have guessed,* she thought, but couldn't bring herself to read the entries and packed up the notebooks with the rest of Anne's belongings and stowed it all away in the small attic above the garage. She would write to Anne's parents in a few weeks and see if they would like her to ship Anne's things to them in Illinois.

Leza's lunch order arrived, and she paid in cash and left a 25 percent tip, far more than she normally would have, but Anne, who had waitressed throughout college, had convinced her to be more generous toward food service workers.

Leza walked out to her truck, the driver's side door stenciled with her name and occupation: "Leza Burdock, Large Animal Veterinarian." She slid behind the wheel, Otto, her Dalmatian, sitting in the passenger seat, wagging his tail. She set her tea in the cupholder, placed the wrap on the console, and pressed the ignition button.

"Don't even think about it," she admonished the dog when he caught scent of the food and lifted his nose to sniff the air in the cabin. "You're already too fat."

The truck's windows were fogged from Otto's breath, and Leza switched on the defrost to clear the windshield. She sipped her tea and clicked on the link her mother had texted her. As she waited for the site to load, her phone vibrated with an incoming call.

"This is Leza," she answered.

"The mare's water just broke, Doc." It was the rancher's foreman calling.

"She's early," Leza said. "Keep her calm. This is her third foal. She's an old hand at this by now and should be fine. I'll be there in less than fifteen minutes." She tossed her cell phone on the dashboard and raced out of the parking lot.

Leza arrived home well after midnight, exhausted from the grueling birth, the sky clear, a full moon sparkling off the snow like a laser-light show. What normally would have been a thirty-minute foaling procedure had taken nine-plus hours to perform. The foal had become twisted in the mare's birth canal in what is known as an abnormal presentation, its back facing out, instead of its front hooves.

Complicating matters, it was a large foal, and Leza struggled to get the animal properly oriented for delivery. Each time she managed to get it aligned the right way, the foal would kick and flip back over, distressing the mare even further. For a while, Leza feared she might lose both mother and offspring.

Finally, at 10:29 p.m., the mare successfully foaled, but Leza remained for several more hours monitoring the vital signs and health of the pair. When she was satisfied the animals were stable, she headed home.

Leza hung up her coat, slipped off her boots, fed Otto, pulled out a chair at the small kitchen table, and sat down to eat a light snack before going to bed. She opened the calendar on her phone to check her schedule for the next morning and was relieved to see it was a relatively quiet day, just a few inoculations here and there throughout the county.

She quickly looked at her email. Nothing urgent. She noticed she had several missed calls from her mother and remembered the text she had received earlier that morning. She opened the text message again and clicked on the link and launched a site that, in turn, launched a video player.

The sound on her phone was muted, and she missed the introduction. She turned on the volume just in time to hear a reporter, a woman, announce:

"Officials believe they have uncovered an attempt by now-deceased Xion Lab scientists to steal highly valuable patented US vaccine formulas and sell them to third parties on the black market. Company officials only discovered the plot after the scientists were fired from their positions earlier this year, and reported it to federal authorities. The lab was headed up by the late Anne Paxton, a virologist, who died in a skiing accident out west . . ."

"Awww, hell no," Leza shouted angrily. There was no way that the Anne Paxton she knew would steal so much as a dime, let alone some secret vaccine formula.

Leza sat in stunned silence for a moment and then bolted from her chair, upending the kitchen table and startling Otto, who began barking wildly. She sprinted from the house, through snowdrifts to the garage, and climbed up into the cramped attic, her wet moccasins slipping on the rungs of the pull-down ladder. She dug through Anne's belongings until she found the box that contained the journals, ripped it open, retrieved the notebooks, sat down on a battered suitcase, and started to read.

CHAPTER 26

A musician was playing jazz standards on the piano when Maggie entered the bar of the Jefferson Hotel. The interior was dimly lit, and she did a double take when she spotted Nik. She couldn't recall the last time she had seen her ex-husband and hardly recognized him now. Nik had let his hair grow out. It was shaggy and fell over his shirt collar, stopping just short of his shoulders. He wore it swept back off his forehead and tucked behind his ears. His normally three-day-old stubble had blossomed into a full-on beard.

But the real shock was his weight. She'd had never seen Nik so heavy in all the years they had been together. He looked lumpy, like he was sheathed in a sleeping bag, and the bar's parquet floors let out a noticeable squeal when he walked toward her.

"Maggs, you're a sight for sore eyes," Nik said and leaned in and kissed her on the cheek. He sniffed the air. "Is that Shalimar?" he said.

"You know it is, since it's the only perfume I've ever worn, and you're quite the sight yourself," Maggie responded, recoiling slightly. "What's happened to you?"

"You mean the beard and hair," Nik said, and ran his hand over his head. "Sam likes it long."

"The hair, yes, but . . ." Maggie spread her arms apart, palms upturned, and gestured at his girth.

"Oh, the extra weight, it's just temporary," Nik said with a dismissive wave of the hand and laid his satchel on the bar and took the seat next to Maggie, the barstool moaning under his heft. "A combination of Covid and the baby. I've already knocked off a few pounds. I'll be back in the gym and in fighting shape in no time."

"If you say so," Maggie said, eyes wide, and scooted her stool over to give him more room at the bar. Nik opened his phone and quickly shared a dozen pictures of Isobel with Maggie. The pair then spent the next ten minutes catching up on each other's lives.

Maggie had taken the day off work to do some early Christmas shopping, and she was dressed casually in camelhair slacks, a cranberry cashmere top, and ankle-high leather boots. Her dark hair was cut in a bob, her face relaxed, worry free. She had never looked so good.

Maggie and Nik had had a volatile marriage and, at times, contentious divorce, but they had reconciled and were, if not actually friends, friendly and fond of one another.

Maggie was a successful partner in one of DC's largest law firms and also a former assistant US attorney. She had been an invaluable—if somewhat reluctant—source for Nik over the years.

Nik told Maggie that while researching court documents related to the class-action lawsuit against Xion, he had discovered that her law firm, Woodward, Stallworth and Moran, was acting as a consultant in the case to the lead plaintiffs' attorneys.

Nik ordered a lite beer and turned the conversation toward business, launching into a detailed account of the reporting he and Zach had been doing on Xion over the past several weeks.

When he finished, Maggie shook her head and said, "I don't know, Nik. I'm not sure I feel comfortable talking to you about this."

"You want another drink?" he asked, ignoring Maggie's hesitancy.

Maggie examined her glass. "Okay, but just one more. I have somewhere I need to be."

"Chardonnay?"

Maggie nodded yes.

"I'm curious," Nik said and caught the bartender's eye to order another round, "why isn't Woodward, Stallworth handling the Xion case itself, given your experience and what's at stake?"

When Maggie was at the AG's office, she had successfully prosecuted a number of pharmaceutical companies for price-fixing, fraud, and kickbacks and had earned a reputation, well deserved, for taking on the CEOs of health care giants.

"They haven't lost faith in me, if that's what you're hinting at," Maggie said defensively.

"Thought never crossed my mind," Nik said, "but it's not like law firms to pass on a potential big payday."

"If you really must know, it's because vaccine manufacturers have been granted virtual immunity by Congress against lawsuits. In order to prevail in court, plaintiffs have to prove what is known as willful misconduct—that management knew their product was dangerous to the public but proceeded to manufacture, market, and distribute it anyway. That's a high bar to clear, even when the facts are on your side. Acting as a consultant, Woodward, Stallworth and Moran gets paid regardless of the outcome of the case."

"You're bloodless," Nik said, rocking his head back and forth.

"Gee, I'll take that as a compliment," Maggie said and took a sip of her white wine, a thin smile on her lips.

"So why the reluctance to talk to me about Xion if you're acting as a consultant on the case? I don't get it," Nik said.

"Even as consultants, we're still bound by attorney-client privilege. Everything connected to the class-action lawsuit is off-limits," she explained.

"Perfect," Nik responded enthusiastically, "because I ain't the least bit interested in the lawsuit or transverse myelitis, whatever the hell that is. I just need someone who has visibility into Xion. Every time I call the company for a comment, officials claim national security and hang up."

"Tell me, why aren't you asking Sam about this?" Maggie said. "I'd think she'd have the inside track since her boss is running for president."

"Yeah, well, I tried that route, but now that Senator Summers has declared her candidacy, Sam says she can't be seen playing favorites. She's about as helpful as the Xion officials."

"Smart girl. By the way, when are the two of you going to get married and make it official? That baby of yours will be in college before you know it if you don't get moving, and, besides, I bought your wedding gift ages ago and it's taking up space in my closet."

"Hope it was expensive," Nik said.

"It was. Top-of-the-line Cuisinart, and if you don't tie the knot soon, I'm going to keep it for myself, and I don't even like cooking that much."

"I'll get right on it," he said.

"What exactly is it that you're after, Nik?" Maggie asked, checking her watch.

"Well, that's the problem. I don't know for sure. It's all a little murky," he confessed.

Maggie looked at him skeptically. "Seriously, you're asking for my help, and you don't even know what you're looking for? How's that supposed to work?"

Nik contemplated his beer in silence for a moment. "Anything would help. Xion has received huge no-bid contracts from the government for vaccines. Why would Warfield's administration hand out money to a company that was up to its ears in lawsuits and possibly on the verge of failing?"

"Nik, do I need to remind you that you're in Washington, DC? It's called politics."

"I do have one lead," Nik offered.

"Oh, and what's that?"

"Something called Project Black Bird."

Maggie gave Nik a blank look. "You plan on telling me what Project Black Bird is, or am I supposed to guess?"

"I think it's related to the research Rothschild and the other scientists at Xion were working on before they died."

"And you think that because . . . ?" Maggie quizzed.

Nik's elbows were propped up on the bar, and he ducked his head between his arms and whispered, "Because of a notebook Rothschild kept."

"Well, that's a start," Maggie said encouragingly. "What's in this notebook?"

"Some writings but mainly drawings," Nik said.

"Of . . ."

"Birds," he mouthed.

"What?" Maggie said. "You're kidding, right?"

Nik shook his head.

"Jesus, Nik."

"I know—" He started to defend himself when Maggie cut him off.

"Nik, don't take this the wrong way, but you're losing it. Have you looked at yourself lately? You're a mess. You're out of shape, unkempt, and now you're talking conspiratorially about birds of all things, for fuck's sake."

"I believe I said it was murky," Nik replied heatedly.

"Not happening, Nik. I've helped you out in the past, often against my better judgment, but I'm not getting anywhere near this hair ball because some guy who liked to sketch birds cracked up and killed himself," Maggie said and stood and looped the strap of her purse across her chest defiantly.

"There are four dead scientists, Maggie, that ought to tell you something," Nik said.

"It tells me life can be unpredictable and cruel, Nik, and I would have thought you would have learned that lesson by now."

"Wait," Nik said as Maggie started to walk away. He reached into his satchel and withdrew Rothschild's notebook and flipped it open on the bar. "All I'm asking is that you just take a look at this for yourself and decide if these are the drawings and notes of some mad scientist or if there's maybe something more there."

Maggie hesitated. She looked at the notebook opened on the bar, back at Nik, and then back at the notebook.

"Where did you get this?" Maggie said and slowly reached over to the notebook and turned a page and studied the contents.

"A source," Nik said. "And I've confirmed that it belonged to Rothschild."

When Maggie finished examining the sketchbook and reading the notes in the margins, she closed it and handed it back to him. "I dunno, Nik," she said. "Not sure what to make of it. Guy sounds paranoid to me. I'll keep my eyes open, but no promises."

"That's all I'm asking."

CHAPTER 27

Cliff staggered over the threshold of his cabin and collapsed to his knees, spilling Puck out of his arms and onto the floor. He was half frozen, eyebrows caked with ice, the tip of his nose discolored from the onset of frostbite.

On the way back to the cabin, Puck's damaged knee began to seize up and blood started to pour again from the gunshot wound in her shoulder. Cliff had carried the woman for much of the way in blizzard conditions as the storm intensified, and by the time they finally reached their destination, Puck was swimming in and out of consciousness, Cliff near exhaustion.

The main room of the cabin was bare, an iron bed pushed in one corner, four wobbly spindle-backed chairs around a Formica-topped table, a faded braided rug over a wood-planked floor, a potbelly stove centered in the middle of the room, animal hides tacked to the walls. Snow drifted in under the door, and wind blew in from cracks around the frame.

Hands numb and fingers stiff from the bitter cold, Cliff struggled to light a fire in the stove that he used to both heat the cabin and cook his meals. On the third attempt, the fire took, and he slowly coaxed it to life, stoking it with a stick as he layered on dried kindling one piece at a time.

Cliff added split pine logs to the stove, closed the door, and watched as the flames lapped at the wood. Once circulation returned to his legs and arms, he walked over to Puck, scooped her up from the floor, and laid her on top of a worn patchwork quilt that covered the bed. She barely stirred. He placed his hand on her forehead. She was burning up with fever. He checked her injuries. She had lost a lot of blood, but the bleeding from the bullet hole had finally stopped, and he bound up the wound as best he could. The knee was disfigured, swollen to twice its normal size, the flesh around it mealy, drained of color. Later he'd cut some ice from the small pond out back and pack it around the knee, but he worried about infection setting into the bone.

Cliff entered a side room and returned with a black bear pelt and covered Puck with it. He went back outside and hand cranked a portable generator. A single light flickered on in the cabin, and a small refrigerator hummed to life.

He reentered the cabin and opened the refrigerator and removed a pot of venison stew and warmed it on the stove. He poured some of its contents into a tin cup, took a chair from the table, and sat it next to the bed.

He shook Puck awake. "Here, you need to eat," he said and propped up her head and offered her small scoops. Puck ate a couple spoonfuls and then held up her hand. "Thanks, that's all," she croaked and slipped back under the pelt and fell asleep.

Puck woke in the middle of the night, unsure where she was or how she had gotten there. The only light was an orange glow, like a miniature setting sun, in the middle of the room. She had been dreaming about her father. He was standing on the opposite side of a deep but narrow crevasse, encouraging her to leap toward him. She backed up to get a running start, and flung herself at her father's outstretched arms. Halfway across the divide, suspended in midair, she awoke. She laid there, in the cold and darkness of the cabin, heavy-headed, someone snoring nearby, before drifting back to sleep.

The next morning, when she opened her eyes, Cliff was hunched over the open door of the stove, poking the fire, a black cast-iron Dutch oven sitting atop the stove like a crown. Through a window above a sink, Puck could see the storm still raging outside.

"Good morning," Puck said feebly at Cliff's back. He raised his hand to acknowledge her but didn't reply and didn't turn around. "Where's your bathroom?" she asked.

Cliff pointed to a door, and Puck swung her legs over the bed and onto the ice-cold floor. She was weak from the loss of blood, and the movement caused her to feel faint. She placed her hands on the bed to steady herself. She found her boots under the bed and stepped into them and made her way, haltingly, toward the bathroom.

When she emerged, she sat back on the bed with a sigh.

Cliff turned away from the stove and faced her. "How you feelin'?"

"Weak, feverish," Puck said, her face looking washed out and weathered as faded newsprint, eyes sunken, red-rimmed.

"You lost a good deal of blood. Knee looks bad, shoulder, too. You gonna need doctoring," Cliff said. "I can set a bone, but I ain't equipped to deal with no infection."

"Thank you for your help. I would have died out there. Think anyone's looking for me?"

Cliff shook his head. "Not in this storm, they're not," he said. "You hungry?"

"I could eat something."

Cliff removed the lid from the Dutch oven and picked out two large golden biscuits, steam rising off them like smoke signals, and set them on a plate that he placed on the table next to a knife, coffee cups, honey jar, butter dish, and coffeepot.

Puck gathered all her energy, pushed off the bed, and shuffled over to the table. She sat down and poured herself a cup of coffee, spilt the biscuits in half, and covered them in butter and honey. She took a bite, chewed quietly, and washed it down with the coffee. "Real good," she said after she swallowed.

"It's my momma's recipe," Cliff said.

"All those animal pelts, you trap those?" Puck asked, nodding to the doorway that led to the bathroom. The bathroom connected to a back room that was stacked, floor to ceiling, with red fox, beaver, muskrat, and bear hides.

"I did. My ancestors have been trapping in these mountains since the beginning of time. That's how I make my livelihood. I'm a trapper. They're legal, if that's what you're wondering," Cliff said and eyed Puck cautiously. "Leastways, most of 'em. Why, you planning on turning me in?"

"Oh, no. That's not what I meant," Puck said. "Why haven't you sold them?"

"Waitin' for prices to tick up. Domestic market's dried up for fur with all those PETA protestors, and overseas markets are flooded with pen-raised pelts."

"I see," Puck said and finished the last biscuit. She started pecking at the crumbs left on the plate.

"We need to talk about what happened out there," Cliff said as he stood, picked up Puck's plate, and carried it over to the sink. "People gonna want answers why that woman's dead when this storm stops. Boulders just don't fall from the sky and crush people's skulls all by themselves."

"I told you, she was trying to kill me."

"That's what you keep saying," Cliff said and stared out the window at the snowstorm, "but why you?"

"I don't know why," Puck said and then remembered Narda's phone.

She was still wearing Cliff's coat and reached into an inside pocket and retrieved the device. "This might tell us," she said and tapped in a numeric code. The screen lit up.

Puck swiped through screens, studying the apps. She clicked on the photo icon and gasped. She was staring at multiple pictures of herself taken surreptitiously in and around Washington, DC.

"Find somethin'?" Cliff asked.

"Yeah, photos," Puck said, bewildered. "Of me."

"Lemme see," Cliff said, and she turned the phone toward him. There were pictures of Puck standing by the Lincoln Memorial, on the steps of the US Supreme Court, outside a sub shop in Georgetown, running along a trail in Rock Creek Park.

"It's like she was obsessed with me. Stalking me. I don't understand."

Puck glanced back down at the phone in her hand and clicked on a folder labeled "Communications." Nestled in the folder was an icon for Signal, the encrypted messaging app. The last message in the queue read: "Found Girl. Now just a matter of time," and she repeated the message to Cliff.

"None of this makes any sense," Puck said and pushed away from the table.

"Where you headed?" Cliff asked.

"I can't stay here," she said and stood.

"You ain't goin' anywhere in this storm, and besides, she's dead. She's no threat to anybody now," Cliff said.

The sudden move made Puck's head spin, and she slumped back into the chair and exhaled loudly. She started scrolling frantically through the Signal app for more messages to read, and when she was done with that, popped open other apps and folders. She was skimming a financial document detailing large cash deposits into an offshore account, and that's when the phone's battery died.

CHAPTER 28

Leza was still reading Anne's journals when the sun rose the next morning. She had moved back inside her house and was sitting in an overstuffed chair in front of the fireplace wrapped in a red-striped woolen blanket. Anne had started keeping the journals nearly three years earlier, and she had been fairly religious about jotting down her thoughts, impressions, and occasional observations of the day's events each night before she went to bed. None of the notations were particularly long, and there were some gaps in the books, a week here, several days there, but never anything as long as a month.

Many of Anne's observations were mundane—"Beautiful sunset. Dinner with Jon and Louise was splendid! Need to send a thank-you note & ask for enchilada recipe"—but there were also ones on the more personal side—"Received biopsy results. Lump in breast is a harmless cyst. Hooray!"

It wasn't until Leza picked up the last journal that Anne's writing took a turn. At first, Leza didn't even notice it. It was just the odd, random thought sprinkled in among the more routine notations. "Summer office party tomorrow. Should be fun . . . as long as Thom Berg holds his liquor and doesn't start in again with his wild tales. Fireworks! Well, it is a 4th of July party."

Not long after the holiday party jottings, Anne wrote, "Called Thom on the carpet. Told him his conspiracy theories needed to stop. He needs to concentrate on science, not science fiction. Made myself clear. Think he heard me."

After the confrontation with Berg, there was a long period where things seemed to return to normal at work: "Everyone happy with initial test results. Should enter trials with mice soon. Team working really hard."

Then, suddenly, Anne's writings became darker, more cryptic. "Is plan to weaponize our research? God help us. Rothschild would never stand for it."

The entries continued in that vein: "Can't sleep. These people terrify me. Want to wake up and find it was all just a bad dream. Was Thom right all along??? Why didn't I listen to him?"

Then there was this: "Saw something I wasn't meant to see. They can't possibly be serious about human experiments. Told Rothschild. Vows confrontation."

Two days later, she wrote, "Bauer & Craine accuse me of gossiping and deny there ever was a plan to infect human subjects. Attacked us for being disloyal & unpatriotic. Threatened us with prison if we disclosed Black Bird research."

The next entry read: "It's over. Lab shut down, dismantled. We were informed government defunded project. Claims never the intention to go to full-scale trials. Going to get as far away from this place as possible as soon as I can. Never want to hear the words Black Bird again."

The last entry in the journal simply read: "Spring, Methow Valley."

Leza held the journal in her hands, studying Anne's handwriting and weighing the words. She pictured Anne, in her old apartment, cataloguing her thoughts, feelings, and fears. She felt sadness but also a deeper, more soulful connection to her late partner.

She turned the notebook over and looked at the back cover. It was blank, except for two small doodles, one of a cat and the other of a dog, facing each other. Leza didn't know what, if anything, to make of it. She then grabbed the notebook by the front and back covers, turned it upside down, and shook it, the pages flapping open.

A single paper clip fell out. She gave the notebook one more hearty shake, and a newspaper clipping fluttered to the floor, a picture of Lance Craine, President Warfield's chief health preparedness officer, staring up at her.

Leza bent down and picked up the clipping from the floor. She unfolded the paper, and underneath the picture, there was an Associated Press story out of New Mexico.

She read the story slowly at first, and when she was finished, she reread it. Leza set the journal and clipping down on a side table and picked up her iPhone. She scrolled through her contact list until she came across Stephanie Barrett, dean of Washington State University's School for Global Animal Health and a veterinary virologist. Barrett had been Leza's faculty advisor when she was enrolled at Wazzu's College of Veterinary Medicine.

"Leza Burdock, what a pleasant surprise," Barrett said when she answered her phone. "Just yesterday, someone mentioned your name to me in passing."

"I need to see you," Leza blurted out.

"What, no hello?" Barrett said with a chuckle. "Still in a rush, I see."

"Sorry," Leza said. "How are you?"

"I'm well, thank you for asking. From the sound of it, I'm guessing this isn't a social call."

"I've got a problem, and I think you can help."

"Well, why don't you tell me about it?" Barrett replied.

"It's not the sort of conversation we can have over the phone."

"Oh, I see. Are we talking about an animal husbandry problem here, or something else?"

"Both."

"And you can't discuss it over the phone?"

"That's right."

"This is all very mysterious, Leza, if you don't mind me saying so."

"I know, and it can't be helped. I'll explain it all when I see you. I should be there around lunchtime."

"What? You're coming today?"

"Yup. Leaving right now. Figure it will take me four, four and a half hours," Leza said, snatching the final journal and newspaper clipping from the table and her coat from a hook near the front door.

"Well—" Barrett started to say, but Leza was already halfway out the door, Otto at her heels, when she clicked off the call.

CHAPTER 29

Nik was jarred awake by the theme song from *Rocky* blaring from his cell phone. He had selected that particular ringtone to inspire him to get out of bed and work out before leaving for the office. It had not been entirely successful. Good intentions and that sort of thing.

Working the midnight shift had reset Nik's body clock. He got home most nights around four a.m., didn't get to sleep until generally six a.m., slept past noon, tried to squeeze in some exercise, ate breakfast at two p.m., spent a few hours with the baby, and passed Sam on the way out the door while she was arriving home. He hated the routine.

He turned over in bed and retrieved his phone and looked at the clock. It was ten a.m.

"Hello," he said groggily.

"Mr. Byron?" the female caller asked.

"Yeah," Nik said and dropped his face back into the pillow, the phone to his ear, and closed his eyes.

"If you recall, we met at St. Paul's Cemetery. Deidre Steward's burial."

Nik didn't answer and started breathing heavily.

"Mr. Byron, did you hear me?" the caller said loudly into the phone.

"Yes," Nik said, snapping up his head. "Sorry. I was asleep when you called. I work the graveyard shift."

"Graveyard shift? Is that supposed to be some kind of sick joke?"

"What? No. I work nights and sleep days."

"I see. As I was saying, you accosted me at Deidre Steward's service."

"I remember you, but I don't believe I accosted you."

"Whatever. Do you still wish to talk?"

Nik sat up in bed, shaking the sleep from his head. "Yes, of course. Hang on. Let me get a notebook and something to write with."

"No, not now."

"When, then?"

"This afternoon. Is this your cell phone I'm calling?"

"Yes."

"Good. I will text you instructions."

"Okay," Nik said, "but why the change of heart?"

The woman hesitated. "That's my business. Expect my text," the caller said, and the line went dead.

He crawled out of bed and made his way to the kitchen, poured a cup of coffee, and said good morning to Karsen, the nanny, who was cradling Isobel in her arms at the kitchen table. "She's ready to go down for a nap, Mr. Byron," Karsen informed him.

Nik padded over and smiled down at the drowsy baby. He thought she looked more like Sam every day.

He picked up a note Sam had left on the counter, informing him she had to attend a political fundraiser for Senator Summers that evening and would be home later than usual. She had made arrangements with Karsen to remain with Isobel until she arrived, and she reminded Nik that the next evening they were invited to the official opening of the senator's national campaign headquarters in the District of Columbia and a press reception following.

Senator Summers's event had slipped Nik's mind, and he reminded himself to ask Mo to assign someone to cover the night shift for him at work. He generally found an excuse to avoid Sam's social obligations, but he intended to make this one. He had a few things on his mind that he wanted to ask the senator about.

Nik took his coffee and headed back to the bedroom. He would change and get a quick workout in before meeting with the woman from Xion. He walked into the bathroom and glanced at himself in the mirror. Next, he stepped on the scale. He was staring in disbelief at his weight—204 pounds. That woke him up.

Maggie was right. He looked like he'd been living on the street for the past six weeks. He picked up his razor and started shaving his beard. The hair would be next.

They met in the National Gallery under the plaster cast of the relief depicting Robert Gould Shaw leading the 54th Massachusetts Regiment, the all-Black brigade, through Boston on its way to a battle in South Carolina. Nik was admiring the workmanship when the woman approached him from behind and cleared her throat. "Ahem."

Nik spun around to find her dressed identically to the day he had seen her in the cemetery—oversized sunglasses, black dress, shawl around her shoulders, and a kerchief over her head and knotted at her throat. The only variation was that she now had a long coat, also black, folded over her arm.

She removed her sunglasses. Her face was pale, chalk white, and drawn, and she looked like she'd aged years in the short time since he had first seen her. "I don't have much time," she informed Nik.

"Hold on," Nik said. "What's your name?"

The woman crossed her arms, her face impassive, and remained quiet for a moment before replying, "Greta."

Nik said, "Nice to meet you, Greta. Greta what?"

"That's not important. Just Greta."

"It is to me," Nik said.

"I don't feel comfortable standing out here in the open talking, Mr. Byron," the woman said, scanning the gallery. "Can we move somewhere more secluded?"

"Follow me," Nik said and headed for an exit and outside to the Sculpture Garden. They cut across the courtyard, past a looming bronze *Spider*, the *Thinker on a Rock* sculpture, and the *Typewriter Eraser*, until they intersected a gravel path that they followed to the far end of the garden, where Nik motioned to a stone bench tucked behind the *Four-Sided Pyramid.*

"How's this?" Nik asked.

"Fine," she said, slipping on her overcoat before taking a seat. It was cold outside, but not bitterly, and there were other people scattered about the Sculpture Garden, some wandering aimlessly, others rooted to spots in front of the artwork, intently studying the forms, while still others copied figures in sketchbooks they held in their arms or sat perched at easels. None paid the least bit of attention to Nik and Greta.

Recalling their brief encounter at St. Paul's Cemetery, Nik advised the woman, "You're not allowed to smoke here," when he saw her open the small clutch bag she carried with her.

"I know and I've quit," she said and withdrew a small tin of mints, popped it open, and placed one in her mouth. She dropped the tin back in her bag and snapped it shut, not bothering to offer one to Nik.

"You've cleaned yourself up since the last time I saw you," Greta said.

Nik rubbed his bare chin where the beard used to be. "Yeah, thought I was looking a little woolly," he said with a grin.

"Mmm," she responded.

"Okay, Greta, whatever your last name is, thanks for reaching out to me. I very much appreciate it. I have to ask, what about the nondisclosure agreement you mentioned last time?"

"We'll get to that," she said, "and I'm not doing it for you."

"Well, whatever your motivation, I still appreciate it."

"Will you reveal my identity?" she asked.

"Not without your permission. There is, however, one reporter whom I'd like to share your name with. He's working with me on the story. You may have seen him at the cemetery. He can be trusted."

"If you say so."

"Good. First things first, I'm interested in what lab you worked in and if you did any research on the Black Bird program?" Nik said, dropping the name and hoping that it would indicate he knew more about what was going on inside the company than he actually did.

"I'm not a scientist," the woman said stiffly.

"W-what?" Nik stammered.

"I'm not a scientist. I never said I was. What gave you that impression?"

"You said Anne, Thom, and Deidre were your colleagues," he said.

"And they were."

"But you're not a scientist."

"I just told you that. Are you not paying attention to what I'm saying?"

"What are you, then?" Nik demanded.

"I'm a bookkeeper."

Nik's shoulders drooped. "A bookkeeper?"

"That's right."

"So you're not involved in the Black Bird research at all, then?"

"Why would bookkeeping be involved in research? You're not making any sense, Mr. Byron."

Nik ran his hands through his hair and sighed loudly. He was losing his patience. "Well," he began, struggling to come up with an appropriate response, when Greta said, "I process all the incoming government funds to Xion and, in turn, all the outgoing payments."

"Oh," Nik said, curious.

"Follow the money, Mr. Byron, isn't that what reporters are instructed to do?"

"Yes, indeed," Nik said. "That's exactly what we're told to do."

"Very well, then," Greta said and fished the tin of mints back out of her bag and this time offered one to Nik.

CHAPTER 30

Her full name was Greta Louisa Lopes, and she had been a bookkeeper at Xion Labs going on seven years. She worked largely in obscurity, recording revenues as they came in from sales of the company's various products and processing outgoing payments. It wasn't a sexy job, but it was important work, and steady, and she was good at it. At one time, she had contemplated going back to college to get an accounting degree and sit for the certified public accountant exam, but something always seemed to get in the way, and, besides, she had observed the company's auditors up close and wasn't particularly impressed with their work.

She had never been married, though she was engaged once, and lived alone in a four-story walk-up in Adams Morgan. On Tuesdays and Thursdays, she played bridge with a group of women at a local Y, where she swam each morning. She had been a season ticket holder to the symphony for fifteen years but gave up her seats when the female companion whom she attended concerts with moved back to Arizona to take care of her elderly parents.

Other than that, Greta Lopes's main activity was work. While she never cared much for Xion's CEO, Glenn Bauer, she, nonetheless, had always considered herself a loyal employee, and she had wrestled with her decision to call the reporter who had left her his business card that day at the cemetery. But two events caused her to change her mind.

The first was the story by the TV reporter accusing Anne Paxton and her colleagues of trying to steal Xion's proprietary vaccine research. Greta recalled when Anne had voluntarily returned a $150,000 overpayment the federal government had mistakenly made to her lab that had gone undetected by internal controls. She could have easily spent or pocketed the money without a trace. Anne Paxton was not a thief.

The other reason was more personal. When Greta told Nik that she didn't have much time, she wasn't referring to their meeting that day. She was referring to her life. She had been diagnosed with an inoperable brain tumor and given only months to live.

She related all of this to Nik without the least bit of self-pity after he pressed her on her obvious about-face to talk to him. Nik listened intently and sympathetically and made a point not to interrupt or to take notes. He waited patiently until she was done with her story before asking a question, and when he did, it wasn't about her work but about her.

"Do you have any relatives nearby?" he asked.

"A few, but none that I would call close. I have a brother in Florida, and we stay in touch," she said. "But enough about that. You can take your notebook out now. It's time we talked about why I called you in the first place."

Nik waved Zach over to his desk when he saw the intern saunter into the newsroom. With his *Newshound* internship drawing to a close, Zach had been temporarily reassigned to Mia's podcast team, and he and Nik were on different schedules. At Nik's request, Zach had been transferred back to the newsroom for the time he had remaining at the company.

Nik smiled as Zach made his way across the office, recalling the first time he laid eyes on the young intern. Physically, Zach's appearance hadn't changed one bit—he was still a shabbily dressed, undernourished college kid with a flouncy head of brown hair—but he now carried himself with more confidence and had a slight swagger.

Nik thrust out his hand when Zach reached his desk. "Good to have you back," he said and pushed a chair toward the intern.

"Good to be back," Zach said, grasping Nik's outstretched hand. "Love Mia and the podcast team, but I missed actual reporting and writing. What have you been working on?" he said and dropped into the chair alongside Nik's desk.

Doria Miller, the copy editor, was sitting two pods over and raised her head slowly, like a bear that has been roused from a slumber, and peered over the top of the low partition that separated the workstations. "That's what we'd all like to know. He hasn't produced a damn thing since you left," she deadpanned. "Hi, Zach."

"Hi, Doria," Zach said. "Hey, thanks for the letter."

"Don't mention it," she replied. Doria had written to *Newshound*'s HR department recommending Zach for a full-time reporting job after he graduated from college in the springtime. "You earned it."

Doria's comment irked Nik, and he shot her a perturbed look, stood, grabbed his coat off the back of his chair, and picked up his satchel. "Let's head across the street to the all-night diner where we can have a private conversation," he said and cut across the newsroom.

"See ya, Doria," Zach said as he followed Nik out the door. Doria nodded and floated her head back down and resumed editing the story she had been working on when Zach arrived.

Nik related his tale to Zach back to front—starting with his recent meeting with Greta Lopes at the National Gallery, and working his way back to the conversation he had with Maggie, his ex-wife, at the Jefferson Hotel.

Nik told Zach that the bookkeeper said Xion had received a $3.5 billion contract from the federal government to produce vaccines for the US stockpile. At first, the government funding for the program had trickled in, and then, without warning, it turned into a torrent.

"She said there was so much money being wired in—sometimes as much as a hundred million dollars in a week—that they had a hard time managing it. She'd never seen anything like it in her life. They were struggling to keep up with the inflow of funds when one day, out of the blue, they received instructions to start sending the proceeds back out the door."

"Back to the government?"

"No. To the bank accounts of other entities. They were told the accounts belonged to biotech companies that were also enrolled in the vaccine program and that Xion was being used as a pass-through to facilitate the transactions and speed up development."

"Is that legal?"

"Unorthodox but not illegal. According to the bookkeeper, a lot of rules and normal procedures were thrown out the window during the country's race to develop vaccines to counter the pandemic. What was unusual was that funds were wired to unidentified numbered accounts. They had no way of tracing who, exactly, got the money."

A pimply-faced waiter with a pallid complexion stopped by their table to take their order, and Nik used the opportunity to flip through the pages of his notebook. "Oh, this may be important," he said, looking up from his notebook at Zach once the waiter had left. "The bookkeeper said a number of the wire transfers also had the same four identifying letters—*C-R-E-W*—attached to the numbered accounts."

"Crew, as in rowing?" Zach asked with a shrug.

"I dunno what it means, but if we can figure it out, it might point to where the money went," Nik said.

The waiter returned with their order. Coffee for both and scrambled eggs, bacon, whole-wheat toast, and orange juice for Zach, who inhaled the food. Nik was impressed by Zach's appetite and wondered when the last time was the intern had something to eat.

"Anything else?" Zach asked, shoveling a forkful of eggs into his mouth while he mopped up the last of the bacon crumbs with the toast.

"There's this," Nik said as he rifled through his satchel. When he found what he was looking for, he held it up for Zach to see. "She gave me her key card to Xion. She gave notice and doesn't intend to go back into the office. Said it won't be deactivated for another week."

"Whoa," Zach exhaled. "Whaddaya plan on doing with it?"

Nik shook his head. "Not a thing, but I'd be lying if I didn't say it's tempting to go there and poke around."

"That'd be breaking and entering, right?"

"Probably criminal trespass, but still," Nik said and then related the conversation he had with Maggie. When he finished, he said, "I'm not sure anything will come of it, but at least we now have someone close to the company who's keeping an eye out for info related to Project Black Bird."

"And what about the dead scientists? Any new information there?" Zach asked.

"Nope. You know about Lizzy Blake's story."

"Yeah. Doesn't seem plausible," Zach said. "And, Puck Hall, any developments?"

"No news, and that ain't good news. Last check, it was still snowing, making it virtually impossible to restart a search now until spring."

"So, you don't think she could have survived?"

"I don't see how, not in those conditions."

"I keep thinking she's going to turn up one day safe and sound and have the answers to all these riddles," Zach said.

Nik drained his coffee, stood, and pulled on his coat. "Yeah, well, I wouldn't count on it. Now let's go. We've got a lot of work to do."

CHAPTER 31

Cliff stared out the window of his small cabin onto a singularly boundless plane of whiteness. It was as if a sea of snow had flooded the earth, covering every tree, bush, outcropping, and rock. The skies were beginning to show signs of clearing, and he could make out faint rays of light on the horizon as the clouds lifted. He had not left the cabin for days other than to gather wood for the stove or tend to the generator, which he only used sparingly to conserve fuel.

He turned back from the window and looked at where Puck lay on the bed in a state of semiconsciousness, moaning, the infection in her knee having spread, the flesh of the leg reddish, rust colored, the gunshot wound in the shoulder stubbornly refusing to heal.

He walked over and covered her with more blankets and pelts. Puck's condition had continued to deteriorate, and he knew she needed medical attention soon if there was any hope of keeping the leg, and even then, there were no guarantees. A couple more days without medication and proper care, and it'd be her life, not her leg, they'd be fighting to save. Cliff didn't know much about this girl, but what he did know was that she was tough.

He checked the barometer that hung from a peg next to the front door. It was rising, the storm starting to move out of the mountains. If he were going to attempt to evacuate the girl, this would be his chance, and he made his way to the back room where he stored his pelts, unstacked them to expose a hatch in the floor.

He lifted the hatch and dropped down into a crawl space under the cabin, praying the ham radio he had stowed away years ago still worked and had not been gnawed through by rats.

Down below, near the base of the mountain, two men, both ex-military, one in his thirties, squat, thick necked, the other older, sinewy, with a patch over his left eye, waited out the storm. They had been monitoring the signal from a transmitter Narda carried and were growing concerned because her location had not changed in days. Their assumption was she was dead, injured, or holed up until the weather improved.

If dead, they would need to recover her belongings and destroy any evidence before someone else discovered the body. If alive, they were to determine the fate of the girl she had been sent to eliminate, and if the girl was dead, their orders were then to kill Narda.

"How close can the chopper set us down to the beacon signal?" the younger one asked.

"Couple clicks. Then we'll have to hoof it the rest of the way on snowshoes," the older one responded and unfolded a topographical map on the table where they were sitting. "Here," he said and pointed a stubby finger to a spot on the map where the space between the topo lines widened, indicating a flat expanse.

The younger man studied the map. "Our approach is from above. What about skis instead of snowshoes? Be a helluva lot quicker and less work."

"My last two tours of duty were in the Middle East, Iraq. I ain't skied in years. Nope, it's snowshoes. Gear up. We lift off at the first break in the weather."

It was late afternoon, and Cliff was seated at the table in his cabin rewiring the ham radio when he heard the womp-womp-womp of helicopter blades overhead. He grabbed a pair of binoculars hanging from the back of a chair and dashed outside, hopeful it was a rescue squad searching for Puck.

The aircraft was dropping fast, and Cliff only got a quick look at it before it disappeared below the treetops, but it was long enough for him to know that it didn't belong to the National Park Service Search and Rescue Team. From its location, he guessed the helicopter was setting down in a clearing about a mile from his cabin.

He went back inside and continued working on the radio. Maybe he could get it repaired in time to send a message to the pilot. Whoever was in that helicopter had to have seen his cabin. They practically flew right over the top of it.

Maybe it's a private search effort come to look for the girl, he thought to himself. *But what would draw them to* my *location, of all places, in such a vast wilderness?* What were the odds?

Cliff sat there thinking about that, about the injured Puck, and about the dead woman, and got up from the table and retrieved the backpack he had taken off Narda. He had made only a cursory examination of the pack's contents earlier. He had decided if there was a murder investigation down the road, he did not want to be accused of tampering with evidence.

He now poured its contents on the table and started combing through the belongings—flashlights, batteries, dried-food pouches, waterproof matches, maps, a poncho, a single-burner stove, freeze-dried coffee, bandages—all things someone camping in the wilderness would carry and nothing out of the ordinary.

He was shoving the contents back in the pack when he saw it. He had missed it the first time. A small transmitter, the size of a Zippo lighter, and it was activated and broadcasting its beacon.

Whoever was in that helicopter wasn't coming to rescue the girl. They were coming to kill her.

CHAPTER 32

If there was one thing in the world Elizabeth Blake hated more than Nik Byron, it was being snubbed by her peers, and she quietly stewed that none of the other media in Washington had picked up her story about the Xion scientists. The company had confirmed it was looking into "reports" of the possible theft of its proprietary vaccine, she had a copy of Rothschild's suicide note, and the scientists were all mysteriously dead and weren't in a position to dispute her reporting or defend themselves. It was a slam dunk in her mind.

In the tradition of journalists everywhere, Blake had counted on the competition to chase the story and keep it alive to create a feeding frenzy that would, in turn, spawn more stories and validate her reporting. She even called other news outlets, posing as an "interested observer" to goad them into covering the story. It was how the game was played, and it usually worked, but not this time.

Other than a post on an obscure conspiracy website, she couldn't find a single mention of her story anywhere. The silence was vexing, and now her bosses were pressuring her to do a follow-up piece. Blake had assured them she had a major scoop, and they wanted her to milk it for all it was worth.

What's more, the anonymous source who had originally tipped her off to the story had gone dark. She was inexplicably at a dead end, and she was starting to hear whispers in the newsroom questioning her accuracy and reporting methods. She knew if this turned out like the Yukon story, her career was doomed.

Blake hunkered down at her desk and started speed-dialing anyone she could think of who was even remotely connected to the story, praying for a news break no matter how small. After two hours of calling, she had nothing to show for her efforts.

It was four o'clock when she looked up from her desk. She was hungry and agitated and thought about heading down to the company's cafeteria on the first floor for some early dinner but decided against it. She didn't want to risk bumping into her bosses and chose to wait until after four thirty, when she knew they would be in their afternoon planning meeting for that night's broadcast. She reached in a drawer, removed a packet of stale saltines, and ripped it open.

She used the time to reach out to Senator Eva Summers's office. As a member of the powerful Homeland Security Committee with oversight of the government's response to the pandemic and now a presidential candidate, Summers had a duty, Blake felt, to comment about Xion, but the senator had been avoiding her calls.

Blake's call was routed to Samantha Whyte's voice mail, and she left a message with the press secretary demanding an interview with the senator.

At 4:35, she walked down to the cafeteria and was standing in the checkout line, balancing a large bowl of chicken noodle soup on a tray with one hand while pressing the thumb of the other to her mouth as she gnawed obsessively on her lower lip.

Blake was absorbed in her own contemplation and didn't see Christopher Donaldson, the network's chief White House correspondent, slip in behind her. "Hello, Lizzy," Donaldson said. "Penny for your thoughts."

"That bitch—" Blake began to say before catching herself and stopping. She flashed Donaldson a big smile. "Surprised to see you here, Chris." Blake coveted the veteran newsman's job and wanted to stay on his good side since it was rumored he planned to retire after the presidential election.

Donaldson, with his thatch of silvery hair, honeyed voice, and ramrod bearing, was the epitome of a White House reporter. The difference between Donaldson and most television personalities, though, was that he was also a genuinely nice guy and a widely respected journalist. He managed to survive the cutthroat culture of network television by staying away from the newsroom as much as possible.

"Yeah, just dropped in to pick up a new laptop before I head out on the road with POTUS later today. Bitch? To whom were you referring?"

"Oh, that? It was nothing." She shrugged and laughed. "Lucky you," Lizzy said. "Where you headed to this time?"

"President Warfield's taking a tour of the biotech companies that contributed to the vaccine program to personally thank them for helping out during the pandemic. At least, that's the story Courtney Sachs, his communications director, is peddling to the press, but it's hard not to notice he's traveling to all the states that are key to his reelection efforts."

"The life of a White House correspondent," Lizzy said. "I'm jealous."

"Don't be. It's not as glamorous as you think. Hey, that reminds me, any chance you'd be interested in covering Senator Summers's official opening of her national campaign headquarters tonight followed by a press gathering afterward? Obviously I won't be able to make it, and it's invitation only."

"I'm kind of tied up right now with a big assignment, Chris," Blake lied, "but for you, anything." And she reached over and squeezed his arm suggestively.

"Good," Donaldson said and plucked her hand from his sleeve. "I'll inter-office the invitation over when I get to my desk."

"Do you think Nik Byron will be there?" she asked offhandedly.

"Wouldn't surprise me. He is the fiancé of the senator's press secretary. Why?" Donaldson asked.

"Oh, you know."

"Yeah, I know. I know there's bad blood between the two of you. I don't know why, and I don't want to know, but a little free advice, Lizzy: drop it before you wind up doing something you'll regret."

Lizzy gave Donaldson a patronizing smile but didn't reply.

"This is a routine assignment, Lizzy. Don't try to make it bigger than it is," Donaldson said. "Okay?"

"Who, me?"

CHAPTER 33

The woman on Nik's voice mail said she was calling from out west, claimed to know Anne Paxton, and had information that she believed might be related to her death. She didn't say how she knew Paxton or what information she possessed. Nor did she leave a name or phone number, only a message that she would call Nik again the next day at the same time.

He was skeptical. He had received a half dozen anonymous tips from callers about Xion, all promising blockbuster information. None of it had turned out to be useful.

Nik, of course, was aware Paxton had died while skiing out west, so there was the off chance this woman did have a connection to the late scientist, if, in fact, she was actually calling from out there.

Nik had made a mental note to be at his desk the following day when the woman said she'd call back, and then swung by Zach's desk to check in on the intern. He wasn't there.

Neither Zach nor Nik had any success linking the numbered bank accounts provided by Greta Lopes, the bookkeeper, to either an individual or company. When they searched the four identifying letters—*C-R-E-W*—the only plausible result was Citizens for Responsibility and Ethics in Washington, a do-good organization dedicated to rooting out corruption in government.

"This is a joke, right?" the person answering the phone at Citizens said and burst out laughing and hung up on Zach when he asked if the group had ever received any wire transfers directly or indirectly from the Warfield administration.

"I took that as a no," Zach reported back to Nik later.

Nik attempted to get in touch with the bookkeeper again to see if there were any other leads she might be able to provide, but she had gone dark on him. She wasn't returning his calls, and when he drove over to the Adams Morgan address she had given him, he was told by the landlord that she had moved out days earlier.

Nik hung around Zach's desk for a few minutes longer, and when Zach still didn't show, he left him a note saying he'd call in the morning, then rushed off to attend the grand opening of Senator Summers's national campaign headquarters and reception.

CHAPTER 34

Sam stiffened and abruptly broke off a conversation she was having with Nik and Senator Summers's campaign manager when she saw Lizzy Blake enter the building followed by a camerawoman.

"Excuse me. I need to speak to someone," she said and dashed over to Blake with Nik trailing behind. Sam stepped between Blake and the camerawoman. "Who invited you?" she hissed.

Lizzy waved the invitation in front of Sam's face.

"Let me see that," Sam said and snatched the envelope from Blake's grasp. "It's addressed to Chris Donaldson."

"He's traveling with the president and can't make it. Asked me to fill in."

"We said no cameras. We're providing a pool feed for broadcast."

"Oops, guess I missed that. Where's the senator?" Lizzy said, surveying the crowd.

"She'll be here shortly. What are you up to, Lizzy?"

"Me? I'm just here to cover the opening of the senator's national campaign headquarters. Big night."

"That better be all." Sam bristled, eyes snapping.

Feeling the tension mounting, Nik bent his head and gave Sam a peck on the cheek and whispered, "Calm down. People are starting to stare."

Lizzy sneered. "Reporters aren't supposed to sleep with their sources, Byron, or didn't they teach you that in journalism school?"

Nik had not seen Lizzy since the Yukon story and knew she still harbored a grudge and held him responsible for derailing her career.

"It's okay, Lizzy. We're engaged, but I am glad to hear you're beginning to take ethics seriously. Never too late to start."

Lizzy was clearly thinking of a response when Senator Summers mounted the small stage at the front of the hall.

"I've got to go," Sam said, and leaned in toward Nik and whispered in his ear, "Keep an eye on her. I don't trust her for a minute."

"Don't worry about me. I can handle Lizzy," he said before Sam turned and hurried off.

Summers thanked the large crowd of mostly admirers for showing up to support her campaign and started to deliver a few prepared remarks but was cut off by a question shouted from the back of the room. It was Lizzy Blake.

"Senator, the American people want to know why your Homeland Security Committee hasn't opened an investigation into the theft of valuable US vaccine secrets by rogue scientists. They feel they deserve to hear from a presidential candidate, unless, of course, you have something to hide."

Those gathered started booing, but Summers raised her hands and quieted the crowd.

Summers flashed Blake a poisoned smile. "I'm glad you asked that, because I appreciate the opportunity to set the record straight. My committee, unlike your network, doesn't launch investigations based solely on rumor and innuendo, nor do I believe in using hearsay to smear the reputations of good people and dedicated scientists. And if I'm fortunate enough to receive the nomination of my party and win the general election, my administration will follow the science, and not run from it like the Warfield administration."

Lizzy attempted to ask another question but was drowned out by supporters clapping and cheering loudly. "I'll see y'all at the reception." The senator beamed, waved to the crowd, and exited the stage.

"Gee, guess that didn't go like you planned," Nik said.

"Go fuck yourself, Byron," Lizzy said.

Nik had been promised a private interview with the senator at her reception, and he had intended to ask if she was aware of the Xion wire transfers, but Summers only made a brief appearance before announcing she had to return to the Senate for a late-night hearing.

"This is nuts," Nik complained to Sam after Summers's hasty departure. "I have a child with—and am engaged to be married to—the senator's press secretary, and I can't get five minutes alone with her to ask a few basic questions."

Sam frowned apologetically and threw up her hands as if to suggest she was powerless to help. She then made a beeline for a cluster of television personalities to confirm the interviews she had lined up for the senator on the Sunday talk-show circuit.

Nik stormed over to the open bar, where he found Lizzy Blake, eschewed his normal order of Budweiser, asked for a Scotch on the rocks, and began a long night of sulking and drinking.

CHAPTER 35

The men in the helicopter had no way of knowing if Narda was dead or alive, but what they did know, what, in fact, they were certain of, was that her transponder was inside that cabin and broadcasting its signal. They also knew there was a man inside the cabin because they had seen him rush out when their aircraft was beginning its descent.

The presence of others complicated matters. They had to assume whoever was in the cabin was unfriendly and holding Narda against her will—if she was still alive.

Any chance of an element of surprise was gone now. They could blow up the cabin easily enough, or burn it to the ground. No one would be the wiser, not out here in the middle of nowhere. But then, that would leave the girl unaccounted for, which would defeat the whole purpose of the mission.

Their objective was clear: they had to storm the cabin, kill or capture the occupants, and ascertain the whereabouts of the girl. How they were going to achieve that was less clear.

Cliff had precious few options, none of them good.

He could barricade himself and Puck inside the cabin and try to stave off the attack he was sure was coming. The cabin was well built, and he was confident it could withstand a direct assault, but for how long depended on their firepower. Eventually, they would breach the structure.

He might even get lucky and shoot one of them. He figured there were at least two, possibly four.

He could make a run for it. Rig up a sled he could pull and put the girl on it and ski out. It would be slow going, but if he left now, he'd have a good head start and there was a decent chance of escape if they tried to pursue him on skis. But, of course, they wouldn't. They had a helicopter, and they'd hunt him down in no time and shoot both of them from the air. It would be all too easy.

He could leave the girl behind and go for help. He stood a much better chance of escaping that way, but that meant almost certain death for her. He could make a call on the ham radio if he could get the damn thing to work, but even then, whoever was in that helicopter was probably monitoring all channels and would intercept his SOS.

Think, goddamn it, Cliff, he berated himself. *Think.*

They stopped in the tree line high above the cabin and waited. They could see smoke rising from the chimney, but that was the only sign of life down below.

They glassed the terrain, searching for the best approach. The cabin sat in a deep swale, hemmed in on either side by large evergreens. That was to their advantage. They could get near the cabin without ever having to expose themselves. Better still, the snow underneath the trees wasn't as deep as out in the open, the enormous branches acting like giant umbrellas to shelter the ground below. They wouldn't need the balky snowshoes after all, and could come within yards of the cabin.

"Why wait for nightfall?" the young one said. "I say we sneak down there right now when there's still a little light and saw that motherfuckin' hut in half with our ARs. Couple hundred rounds, and they'll come crawlin' out cryin' like babies."

"We could," his partner said, "but we ain't gonna. We got everything to gain and nothing to lose by waiting. We go traipsing down there now, he might be sitting inside his cabin with an old deer rifle and put a slug in one of us. The longer we wait, the more anxious he gets. No, we sit tight."

"I don't like it."

"No one's asking you to. Tell you what, I'll start making preparations and you try to get some shut-eye. It'll be dark soon enough."

When Puck woke, Cliff told her about the helicopter. She looked at him unblinking, nodding her head occasionally as he explained his plan, but he wasn't sure how much of it she actually understood, if any of it, before she passed out again. At least he'd tried.

Cliff determined the attack would come at night and that they would stay hidden in the trees until they were almost on top of the cabin. It was the safest route and the path of least resistance. It was what he'd do if he were in their position.

Earlier, he had spotted movement through his binoculars upslope from the cabin and thought he made out two figures in the trees. He hoped it was only two.

Cliff turned his attention back to the radio. He had pulled it apart to get it in working order and now was piecing it back together.

Just before sundown, he got up from the table, opened the front door, and hollered: "I know you're out there. I saw the copter. What do you want with me?"

His voice, muffled by the snow, echoed up the mountainside before fading into the trees. No response came. He called out again and waited. Still no reply. He was about to yell for a third and final time when a voice rolled down the slope to the cabin.

"We don't want you. We came for the woman and the girl. Send 'em out and we'll leave."

"I don't know what you're talking about. There's nobody here but me."

"The woman had a transponder, and her signal is coming from your cabin. We know she's in there."

"I found an abandoned backpack a couple days ago in the mountains before the storm hit when I was runnin' my trap line. I got it here in my cabin. You're welcome to it."

"Tell you what, you come out with your hands where we can see them, and one of us will come down and have a look for ourselves."

"I'll tell *you* what. I'll throw the backpack out in front of my cabin, and one of you can walk down and get it. That's the best I can offer."

"He's lyin' through his fuckin' teeth. Get him to poke his head out, and I'll take it off," the younger man said, sighting his rifle on the front door.

The older man studied the inside of the cabin through the open door with his spotting scope. He could make out what appeared to be dark blankets hanging on the back wall, a small kitchen table with equipment spread out on top of it, and a doorway near the rear. "Sorry, but no can do," he called down. "Too risky."

"Suit yourself," Cliff said. "Just so you know, I radioed to the ranger station down below when I saw your aircraft. They're on their way up now."

"Nice try, old man. We've been monitoring all the short-band channels. You haven't radioed shit. The cavalry ain't coming to rescue your ass."

"Well, good talkin' to you," Cliff said and closed his door and sat back down at the table and began fiddling with the ham radio again.

They started down the slope toward the cabin two hours after sunset. It was pitch-dark, a moonless night with heavy cloud cover. The only sound was the squeaking of their boots on the dry snow as they crept along the tree line.

They debated the plan before agreeing that they would advance to within twenty yards of the cabin, one on either side. There they would lay down a withering cross fire on the building. After several minutes of this barrage, the younger man would break from cover and sprint to the side of the cabin with the window and lob in a tear-gas canister.

As they approached, the older man thought about what he had seen through his spotting scope when the man had opened the front door of the cabin, and he tried to imagine how those inside would defend themselves, if, indeed, there were others.

He figured the rear doorway that he had noticed led to another room or rooms. Maybe that was where the man had stashed Narda and the girl. Whoever was in the cabin would likely retreat to that area and attempt to seal themselves off from the attack when the gunfire erupted. *Good luck with that.* It might momentarily slow down the assault, but that was about it.

Other than the front door and window, he hadn't detected any other escape routes when the helicopter passed over the cabin earlier that day.

At first, he worried the electronic devices he had seen scattered about the table were part of a bomb-making kit, but then realized they were actually components of a disassembled radio the man was trying to restore. Clearly it wasn't operational.

All in all, it was a pretty straightforward assault and would probably be over in less than fifteen minutes. He assumed the man had weapons in the cabin, but they'd be no match for the unholy wrath they were about to unleash.

He was only a few steps from the attack site when he recalled the dark blankets he had seen hanging on the back wall of the man's cabin. He hadn't paid them much attention until now.

They looked more like rugs than blankets, he thought. *No, not rugs exactly. What? Hides. That's it. Wild animal hides of some sort.*

Then, in midstride, it hit him: *Bearskins. Those were bearskins hanging on the wall.* And in that instant, his instinct was to fall back, but it came a fraction of a second too late.

The bear traps' powerful jaws nearly scissored the men's legs in two, puncturing flesh, biting into muscle, and snapping bones like frozen twigs. Blinding pain convulsed their bodies and short-circuited their brains. Their boots filled with blood. They collapsed, withering in the snow, helpless, mad with agony.

Cliff stood by the cabin's open window and heard the steel teeth clamp down like prison doors slamming shut and the men's anguished cries reverberating around the mountains and through shuddering treetops.

CHAPTER 36

"Mr. Byron. Mr. Byron. Wake up." Nik rolled over and let out a puff of stale air. "Two policemen here to see you," Karsen said and shook his arm.

Nik squinted at the nanny through one eye. His head felt like it was marinating in concrete, and he struggled to bring Karsen's features into focus. It was as if she was standing in a faraway mist. "Wwwwwhat?" he croaked.

Karsen cradled Isobel in her arms, and spoke in hushed but hurried tones.

"Said they're detectives."

Nik propped himself up on his elbows. "What're you talking about?" he said and looked around.

"Not here. I made them wait in the living room. I told them you were sleeping. I brought you some coffee," she said and nodded to the bedside table where a cup sat steaming. "Missus Whyte said you were very tipsy when you got home this morning."

"Oh," Nik said and combed his fingers through his hair and reached for the coffee. He took a drink. He couldn't recall the last time he had felt so hungover or disoriented. "Thank you. The two detectives, one a woman, the other a man?"

"Yes. The woman, she scary."

"Jenks and Goetz," Nik mumbled.

"What?"

"Nothing. They say what they want?"

"No. I asked, but they wouldn't tell me."

"That's okay. Would you please tell them I'll be out in a few minutes?"

Karsen started to back out of the room and stopped. "Missus Whyte, she wanted me to tell you they found your vehicle."

"What do you mean, found my vehicle? It wasn't lost."

"I don't know. I only know what she told me. Said police found it, abandoned, engine running, near Dupont Circle late last night."

Hmmm. So that's what this is about, stolen vehicle, Nik thought as he crawled out of bed.

Detective Jenks was sitting rigidly in a straight-backed chair typing a message on her phone while Goetz was browsing Nik's extensive collection of vintage vinyl jazz albums when Nik emerged from the back of the apartment. He had combed his hair, washed his face, put on a freshly starched button-down shirt and a pair of pressed khaki trousers. He looked presentable, but it was all for show. He felt rotten.

"Sober up?" Jenks asked when she saw him.

"Excuse me?"

"Hi, Nik," Goetz said. "This is an impressive collection you got here. My dad's a real jazz nut. He'd love to see it."

"You smell like you just got sprung from a drunk tank, Byron," Jenks said in her characteristic no-bullshit style. "I'd wager your blood would register ninety proof."

Nik brushed his tongue over his teeth. The inside of his mouth tasted like kerosene. "Happy to show your father my collection anytime, Detective," he said to Goetz. To Jenks, he said, "It's rubbing alcohol. I hurt my shoulder throwing batting practice for my teammates."

"If you say so."

"I do. Now how can I help you, Detective?" Nik said and picked up a coffeepot Karsen must have served the two detectives with and refilled his cup.

"You know Greta Lopes?" Jenks asked and returned to casually studying something on her phone.

"Nik, is this an original Coltrane?" Goetz interjected and pulled an album cover from the collection and removed the sleeve.

"It is, and please be careful with it," Nik said, a hint of panic in his voice. "It's very rare. And, yes, I know Ms. Lopes. So this isn't about my vehicle?"

"What about your vehicle?"

"Apparently they found it last night near Dupont Circle with the engine running."

"And you don't remember leaving it there?"

"I don't remember leaving it there because I didn't leave it there. I'm assuming someone stole it."

"There's been a rash of car thefts lately in this neighborhood," Goetz volunteered.

"Or maybe you had too much to drink last night and blacked out," Jenks said. "But, no, we're not here about your vehicle. When was the last time you were in touch with the woman?"

Goetz had moved over to the couch and sat down and taken out an electronic notebook and a stylus. He looked up at Nik expectantly.

"It's been a while," Nik said and closed his eyes and put his hand to his head to think. He was having a hard time concentrating. "A week ago this Tuesday, I think. No, wait, maybe it wasn't that long ago. I'm a little fuzzy headed."

Goetz started scribbling notes. “Is that when you last saw her or is that when you last spoke with her?” he asked.

“Saw her. I haven’t spoken to her or seen her since then. Maybe if you told me what this is about, I could—”

“She’s dead,” Jenks interrupted. “Strangled to death. Couple homeless folks fished her body out of the Georgetown canal.”

Jenks held up her phone and showed Nik a picture of the deceased woman, eyes bulging, a black kerchief cinched expertly around her neck. He recognized the scarf. It was the same one she had been wearing on the two occasions they had met.

“Jesus,” Nik said and averted his gaze. He felt his stomach heave and thought he might be sick. “When did it happen?”

“Body was discovered early this morning. Looks like she was killed in the last twelve to twenty-four hours. Funny thing is, when we checked her phone records, she had a whole bunch of recent calls from you. Care to explain that?”

“She was helping me out on a story about Xion. She worked there. I presume you already know that.”

“Uh-huh, we do. Landlord at the apartment where she used to live said you were snooping around there a few days ago.”

“When I couldn’t reach her on the phone, I drove by the address she gave me. What are you trying to imply, Detective?”

“Me? Nothing,” Jenks said, shaking her head and turning her phone toward Nik again for him to look at another image on the screen, “but I am curious. That is you trying to enter Xion’s building last night with Ms. Lopes’s key card, isn’t it?”

CHAPTER 37

Glenn Bauer pawed through his desk drawer looking for the slip of paper with the phone number scrawled on it. The Xion CEO was in a panic. The two DC detectives who had just left his office assured him their inquiry was routine, but he wasn't buying it for a minute.

"Did you know anybody who would want to kill Lopes?" they had asked. "What did Lopes do at the company, exactly, and do you have any idea why she was talking to a reporter from *Newshound*? What was Lopes's relation to the dead scientists? Why did she give her notice recently?" And on and on and on.

The security video of the reporter attempting to gain entry to Xion's facilities was alarming.

Thank God the drunken fool was confused and mistakenly tried to access the vivarium where Xion's lab animals are housed instead of the main offices. The bookkeeper's key card isn't authorized to gain entry to the secured area. What in God's name did Lopes tell him anyway? he wondered.

And on top of everything else, Bauer was fighting to fend off the vultures trying to rip Xion apart with their class-action lawsuit.

What a fuckin' shitstorm.

Bauer continued to rifle through his desk drawers until he found the phone number. He was careful not to store the number on his own mobile phone. It was a gamble, calling again, he knew. One too many times, and they might be able to identify him, but he didn't see any way around it. He needed to divert attention. It had worked the first time.

He pushed up from his desk and walked over and closed his office door. He returned and pulled a burner phone out of his briefcase and dialed the number. The phone rang three times before it was picked up.

"Thought you might like to know Nik Byron is a suspect in the murder of a bookkeeper," he said when Lizzy Blake answered her phone.

Detective Jenks hammered Nik with questions for more than an hour while Goetz diligently recorded the session, only occasionally interrupting his partner to ask a follow-up question or get Nik to clarify an answer. It was slow going, mostly because Nik had significant gaps in his memory.

He couldn't recall going to Xion's campus the night before, but clearly he had. That was unquestionably him in the photo. Yes, he had been drinking the previous evening, but not what he would consider excessively.

He vaguely remembered leaving the reception. He thought it could have been between eleven o'clock and midnight and he drove to a bar near Dupont Circle. He didn't recall the name of the bar. A check of his phone revealed that he had ordered an Uber around one a.m. that had taken him to Xion's campus in Rockville. He had asked the driver to wait for him.

No, he had not stolen Greta Lopes's key card. She had voluntarily given it to him when they met at the National Gallery. They could call *Newshound*'s intern and ask him. Nik had shown him the badge and told him how he had gotten it. Goetz stepped out and did just that, and when he returned, he nodded to Jenks to confirm Nik's story.

Nik was sorry, but he wouldn't reveal what information Lopes had supplied him, other than that it had to do with the government's national vaccine stockpile.

Nik had Ubered back from Xion's Rockville offices and returned to his apartment at two thirty a.m., his phone showed. They located the Uber driver, and he told them Nik had talked nonstop the whole trip, but he had his earbuds in and wasn't listening to what he said. The driver also said Nik left him a $250 tip.

"What do you think?" Goetz asked Jenks after they had finished the interview and were walking back to their car. "He telling the truth about Lopes?"

Jenks stopped and weighed the question. "You askin' if I think Byron killed the bookkeeper?"

"Yeah, I guess so."

"Nah," Jenks said and started walking again, "but we ain't gonna tell him that just yet. Byron can be a colossal prick. Let him twist in the wind for a while."

"Who, then?"

"Lopes was killed by a professional," Jenks said without hesitation. "Question we should be askin' ourselves is why."

CHAPTER 38

"What in God's name were you thinking?" Sam bellowed, pacing back and forth, fists clenched, arms flailing, cheeks crimson and puffed out, but before Nik could respond, she rounded on him again. "Do you not understand the implications of this? Of the impossible position you've put me in? My boss is running for president of the United *fucking* States of America, for Christ's sake, Nik."

They were standing in the living room of Nik's pre–World War II condominium with its nine-foot-tall ceilings and thick, soundproof plaster walls in what Washingtonians refer to as Kalorama Triangle, that wedge of land between Columbia Road, Connecticut Avenue, and Calvert Street, just north of Dupont Circle and west of Embassy Row. For the most part, it was a serene neighborhood. Except today.

As Sam peered out their window, she could see two television trucks with their telescopic towers parked out front on Columbia. Farther down the street on the corner, a cargo van belonging to a local radio station sat idling while a couple reporters milled about on the sidewalk. It looked like a small convention.

They were there because Lizzy Blake had aired a story that DC police had questioned Nik in the death of Xion bookkeeper Greta Lopes, whose body had been discovered in Georgetown.

Blake had stationed herself in front of the police precinct and ambushed Detective Jenks when she had emerged from the building with her partner. Jenks had replied "no comment" to the reporter's repeated questions about Nik's alleged role in the homicide, but, to Lizzy, that was just as good as an admission of his guilt.

She had also managed to get her hands on a grainy security video that appeared to show Nik exiting a car and walking across Xion's campus that she posted to the cable broadcaster's website.

Nik had slowly started to recover his memory and recall events of the prior evening. "It's still a bit of a blur, to be honest, but I'm guessing Lizzy spiked my drink when I went to the men's room," he explained.

"How could you be so stupid, Nik?" Sam said, cradling her head in her hands, disbelieving. "You know she's had it in for you ever since the Yukon story. I told you to keep an eye on her."

Sam and Nik had quarreled before, of course, but nothing like this. He had never seen her so angry. She was shaking and gnashing her teeth when she wasn't screaming at him at the top of her lungs.

"Come on, Sam, there's nothing to it," he said, attempting to calm her down. "I didn't steal that woman's employee badge. She gave it to me, and I didn't have anything to do with her death."

"What makes you so certain? You yourself said you're having a hard time remembering what you did last night."

"I said it was a blur. I didn't say I had amnesia. And as far as the video of me on Xion's property is concerned, I made a feeble attempt to break into an animal shelter. It's not a big deal."

"Not a big deal? It's called criminal trespass, Nik," Sam spat.

"It'll blow over," Nik said.

"Really? Try telling that to the pack of reporters prowling on the sidewalk out front. See how far that gets you."

He walked over to the window and looked down at the street. "Good idea, I think I will."

"Nik, don't. I wasn't serious," Sam pleaded as he headed for the door. "Come back. You'll only make matters worse."

Nik huddled around the television screens at the Third Edition with Mia and Mo to watch the evening news programs following the impromptu press conference he had given on the front stoop of his apartment building. Sam had watched from above, anxious and agitated, while his neighbors gave him dirty looks as they shouldered their way past the gang of reporters.

Nik spent fifteen minutes answering every question the reporters threw at him. He scrupulously avoided uttering "no comment," and only called a halt to the proceeding after the questions became repetitive.

Yes, I knew the deceased and spoke with her twice. No, I didn't steal her key card. Yes, that was me in the security video footage on the Xion campus. No, I do not have any idea who might have killed the bookkeeper. Yes, the police have questioned me. No, I will not reveal what Ms. Lopes and I discussed.

The news outlets teased the story throughout the day and told listeners to tune in for an "exclusive report" later that evening. As Nik sat at the bar with his colleagues, nursing a club soda, having lost his taste for alcohol, he feared the worst, and for good reason.

Journalists relish nothing more than the opportunity to publicly disembowel one of their own. They believe it makes them look evenhanded when, in reality, what it makes them is petty and vindictive. Sam knew this, and Nik was about to find out.

At the top of the hour, all three local television stations led off with the murder of Greta Lopes and named Nik as a person of interest in the homicide investigation.

The reports were accompanied by similarly edited video clips of Nik's press conference that seemed to suggest he might have been stalking Lopes ever since his first encounter with her at St. Paul's Cemetery and which left the impression Nik had somehow deceived the dead woman into giving him her Xion employee badge that he then used to try to break into the company's offices.

Even Mia and Mo had to admit the news reports seemed incriminating. Nik came off looking, if not guilty, exactly, then certainly suspicious.

"As they love to say in this town, Nik, the optics ain't good," Mia said.

Mo laid a sympathetic arm across Nik's shoulder. "You know me, buddy, normally I'd say fuck 'em if they can't take a joke. Not sure that would be good advice this time. The woman is dead."

Pete, the bartender at the Third Edition, changed the channel to the final seconds of a Georgetown basketball game, and cheers quickly replaced the somber atmosphere in the bar when a Hoya player sank a buzzer-beater shot to win the game.

A couple days passed before Detective Jenks, at her partner's prodding, reluctantly issued a statement to the local media. The press release read, in part, "The DC police department is aware of news reports linking journalist Nik Byron to the death of Greta Lopes. Byron is not now, and never has been, a suspect in Ms. Lopes's homicide. Any speculation to the contrary is untrue."

But the damage had been done. Sam had packed her bags and moved out, back to her Foxhall Craftsman, taking the baby and the nanny with her. She had also taken Gyp, Nik's dog, to keep guard. As a precautionary measure, *Newshound* management placed Nik on temporary leave pending further investigation.

CHAPTER 39

Cliff waited the better part of two hours, long after the wailing had stopped, before venturing out of the cabin. He approached cautiously, poking a rod in the snow as he moved along. He had laid out a line of bear traps and didn't want to step on one accidentally in the dark.

Both men were motionless when he came upon them. The older man was dead, having bled to death, the younger still breathing, barely. Cliff tucked the revolver he was holding into the waistband of his trousers, shone a light on the younger man, bent over, and levered the rifle from the man's grip and tossed the gun into a snowdrift.

The man opened his eyes and gazed at Cliff, trancelike, his face nearly as white as the snow. The man moved his mouth but emitted no sound. He waited, marshaled his energy, and tried again. "Partner," he eked out.

"Dead," Cliff said.

The man rolled his head over and looked across the open field to the other side where his partner had fallen and lay frozen in the snow.

Cliff removed a flask of moonshine from his hip pocket, lifted the man's head, and put it to his lips. The man swallowed, choked on it, spit it up, and started to cough.

When the coughing spasm passed, the man asked, "The woman?"

"The one with the transponder, the one you were sent for?" Cliff said.

The man nodded weakly.

"She's dead, too."

"The girl?"

"Alive. She's with me."

The man motioned for another drink from the flask, and Cliff tipped it into his mouth. He swallowed the moonshine and, this time, managed to keep the liquor down. The man closed his eyes, and his breathing became labored. Cliff thought he might die, but after a few moments, he opened his eyes again. "Thanks," he murmured.

"Who sent you?" Cliff asked.

The man didn't respond.

"You're gonna die soon, son. You've lost too much blood, and there's nothing I can do for you," Cliff said.

The man slowly twisted his head around and looked back up the mountain.

"Helicopter lifted off couple hours ago, if that's what you're wondering," Cliff said. "Doubt we'll see it again. What was it someone said to me? 'The cavalry ain't comin'.'"

The man dropped his chin to his chest. "War," he uttered.

"Yeah, I figured you and your partner for military," Cliff said. "Me, too. Afghanistan."

The man shook his head and waved Cliff closer. He bent his ear down close to the mouth of the dying man, who whispered, "Fields."

Cliff tilted his head back and gave the man a puzzled look. "You fought in fields, that what you mean? Most of my fighting was in the mountains."

The man locked eyes with Cliff, parted his lips, took a shallow breath, but before he could speak again, he died.

Cliff recovered the men's packs, rummaged through their belongings, discovered penicillin and vials of morphine, released their legs from the bear traps, and trudged back to his cabin, probing the snow out in front of him with his rod for unsprung traps. Maybe he could buy Puck some time after all.

CHAPTER 40

Nik's mystery caller would only give her first name to Nik when she finally reached him, by coincidence, on his last day in *Newshound*'s office.

Nik was in the building that morning packing up his desk after being suspended from the job. He was walking out the door when the receptionist stopped him and told him he had an incoming call.

"Sounds like the same woman who's been calling you every day," the receptionist said. "I've asked to take messages, but she's refused. She wouldn't leave a name or number, either."

Nik paused, wondering if he should ignore the call and have it sent to the city desk. He was in no mood to deal with some random and, more likely than not, irate caller.

In quick succession, he had lost his job, his wife, his child, and his dog. His life wasn't coming apart; it had vaporized right in front of his eyes. Last thing he needed was to listen to a stranger's rant.

"Nik, what do you want me to tell her?" the receptionist persisted.

He set his box down by the front door and told the receptionist to transfer the call to *Newshound*'s small conference room off the lobby. He walked in, shut the door, and picked up the phone.

"Byron," he answered, barely audible.

"Is this Nik Byron?" the caller asked.

"Yeah. Who's this?"

"My name's Leza."

"What can I do for you, Lisa?"

"No, not Lisa. Lee-za, with an *e* and a *z*, not an *i* and an *s*."

"Okay, Lee-za. How can I help?"

"I've been calling you for a solid week. Aren't you ever in the office?"

"I work nights, or, at least, I did."

"Doesn't matter. I finally got ahold of you."

"Yes, you did. What is this about and, please, make it quick, I don't have a lot of time," Nik said, and then thought, *All I have is time.*

"Are you familiar with Project Black Bird?"

Nik was momentarily speechless.

"Did you hear me?" the caller said when he didn't respond.

"I'm sorry, could you repeat that?" Nik said.

"Black Bird. Project Black Bird, are you familiar with it?" she replied.

"Maybe. What do you know about Black Bird?" he asked haltingly.

"So you are familiar with it?"

"Wait a second. You're the woman who left me the cryptic message about Anne Paxton, aren't you?" Nik said, now recalling the voice mail message and his missed appointment.

"Mm-hmm. Figured it out, did ya?"

"Where are you calling from?"

"Twisp."

"What's Twisp?"

"It's a town."

"It sounds like a speech impediment, or a pastry."

Leza chuckled. "It's neither, but we do have an excellent bakery. I'll treat you to breakfast when you're here."

"When I'm there? I don't even know where Twisp is."

"It's in the Cascade mountains in northeast Washington, and if you want to find out how I know about Anne Paxton and Project Black Bird, you're going to have to come out here, because I'm sure as hell not going to Washington, DC," she said, and then added, "and I'm not having this conversation over the phone. Only in person."

Nik didn't respond immediately. He was considering if he should tell Leza that he had been suspended from his job and wasn't, officially, working for *Newshound*. Similarly, he wrestled with the ethics of not telling his editors about Leza's call. He pondered these questions for a second and then decided on a course of action.

Fuck 'em if they can't take a joke, he thought, channeling Mo.

When Nik returned to his deserted condo later that day, he scrounged around for his battered United States road atlas until he found it under a pile of old *New Yorker* magazines in the front hall closet.

He was having a hard time adjusting to the solitude of his new living arrangement. He had taken for granted the joy Sam and the baby had brought to his life. He missed them. He missed the daily commotion and bustle. He missed the little things. Naps with Isobel and morning coffee with Sam. She wasn't returning his calls or responding to his text messages. Eventually he stopped trying.

After Maggie, Nik had vowed not to make the same mistakes in a relationship again, but here he was, adrift once more. *What did Mark Twain say? There's nothing to be learned from the second kick of a mule. Wonder what Twain would say about the fourth or fifth kick?*

Nik sighed and opened the atlas on the kitchen island and started to look for Twisp on the map. He searched for ten minutes before giving up and plugging the name into Google Earth.

After consulting airline schedules, Nik determined he could fly into Seattle and drive for four-plus hours, over a couple of treacherous mountain passes, or he could fly into Spokane, with a long layover in either Denver or Seattle, and drive for three and a half hours.

Either way, Twisp, population 980, was out in the middle of Bumfuck, but, then again, he had nothing but time on his hands and nowhere in particular to be.

CHAPTER 41

"What do you know about zoonoses?"

It was midafternoon, and Nik and Leza were getting acquainted at the Twisp Bakery. Nik had arrived fifteen minutes earlier after a white-knuckle drive over icy mountain passes. For most of the trip from Seattle, he had been driving through either rainstorms in the lowlands or snow squalls in the mountains. By the time he had reached Twisp, Nik was bleary-eyed and exhausted but relieved to be off the road. The pair had ordered beverages—Nik coffee, Leza tea—when she asked about zoonoses.

"What?"

"Zoonoses," Leza repeated.

"Never heard of it." Nik shook his head. "What is it?"

"It's . . . You know what"—Leza paused, giving Nik a sympathetic look—"forget about that for now. You look beat. We'll talk about it later, after the caffeine has had a chance to do its job. How's that sound?"

"Fine by me. So what do you want to talk about in the meantime?" Nik yawned and looked around.

There were only a couple of other customers in the small bakery, and out front on Glover Street, vehicles, mostly trucks and large SUVs, rolled slowly past on the snow-packed road. Merchants had cleared the sidewalks in front of their establishments and created large mounds of snow at either end of the street. It was late November, and many of the retail businesses had bright Christmas decorations displayed in their windows or outside of their shops.

The weather was sunny but cold, and Nik wished he had packed warmer clothing. Leza was wearing jeans, a tangerine-colored down vest with a gray wool sweater underneath, and hiking boots. An orange stocking hat and a matching scarf and mittens rested on the table next to her tea.

Leza dipped below out of sight and scooped up a stack of colorful notebooks from her bag on the floor and dropped them in the middle of the table. "These," she said.

"Okay," Nik said, examining the pile. "And what are those?"

"Anne's journals," Leza said. "But not here. Get yourself a refill, and we'll talk while I finish making my rounds."

"What, wait, where are we going?" Nik said. "I just got here."

"I know, but it'll give you a chance to see the beautiful countryside while we still have some daylight left. I'll drive and you can read."

"I've been traveling for nine hours, Leza," Nik protested. "First a five-hour flight and then a harrowing car ride. I've seen plenty of the Pacific Northwest already, thank you."

"Come on. Fresh air will do you good, get the juices flowing."

Nik didn't have the strength to argue further and shambled over to the counter and ordered a large Americano to go. He grabbed his coat, satchel, and the journals from the table and followed Leza out the door to the parking lot.

"So you really are a large-animal veterinarian," he said when he saw her truck with the stenciling on the door.

"Yup. Took over the local vet's practice when he retired a couple years ago. Ever seen a branding operation, Nik?"

"Only in Western movies. They still do that?"

"Oh, sure, though more and more ranchers are tagging their cattle with RFID chips or using freeze branding instead of hot iron. I just have to look in to make sure it's being conducted in accordance with state regulations. Shouldn't take long."

As Nik approached the truck, a howl came from inside the cab.

"Say hello to Otto," Leza said as she opened the driver's side door and stepped up into the truck. "Hop on in, Nik. Scoot over, Otto."

"How you doing, boy," Nik said and rubbed the dog behind his ears as Leza wheeled her candy-apple-red Ford F-250 out of the lot and onto Glover Street, past the ice rink, and out onto Twisp-Winthrop Road.

He read in silence as Leza pointed out area landmarks that they passed by on the route. She had placed colored stickers to mark passages in Anne's journals that she thought were important. Nik read those first.

He had made it through two of the journals and started on a third when he paused to ask, "Can I take these with me when I leave? I'll return them when I'm done." Off in the distance, he could see a ski slope. "What's that?"

"You can make copies," Leza said. "I'm not parting with them. I already feel like I'm violating Anne's privacy by letting you read the journals. And that's Loup Loup, our local downhill mountain. It's not very big, but it's fun. Most people around here prefer to cross-country ski."

Nik picked up another journal, and when he finished reading the highlighted pages, he glanced over at Leza. "Okay," he said, "if I'm reading this right—and to be honest, the details are a little sketchy—the government contracted with Xion to rebuild the nation's vaccine stockpile, and as part of that deal, they also had a separate program mandate to research man-made viruses in the lab. The project was code-named Black Bird, and Anne's lab was tasked with spearheading the program."

"Yup, that's my interpretation, too," Leza said. "And it's my guess Anne was intentionally vague in the journals because she didn't want to violate her nondisclosure agreements.

"Somewhere along the line, Anne became suspicious of the government's aims, and she and her boss confronted Xion and government officials about her suspicions. The officials denied any ulterior motives and, shortly afterward, terminated Black Bird, disbanded Anne's lab, and fired the researchers involved in the project.

"And that brings us to zoonoses," Leza said. "I think you're awake enough now to follow the conversation."

Nik buzzed down his window to let the cold air revive him. It was like a slap in the face, and it helped. A little. Otto took the opportunity to stick his muzzle out the window. "Okay," Nik said after a few moments, "zoonoses. Can't wait to hear all about it."

"As I started to tell you in the bakery, they're infectious diseases that jump from animals to humans. It's estimated that six out of every ten infectious diseases in people are zoonotic, meaning they originated in animals first," Leza explained.

"Lyme disease?" Nik said.

"Yup, that's one. Some others that are of particular concern to US researchers are rabies, SARS, MERS, and the West Nile virus."

"They teach you this in vet school?" Nik asked and felt himself starting to nod off.

"No, or if they did, I wasn't paying attention, but I recently got a refresher course from my former faculty advisor, the dean, who also happens to be a veterinary virologist. In 2019, the CDC, the US Department of Agriculture, and the Department of the Interior joined forces for the first time to identify the top eight zoonotic diseases in the United States."

"This is fascinating and all," Nik said, fighting to stay awake. The heat in the truck's cabin was making him drowsy. "But what's it got to do with Xion?"

"I'm getting to that. When I was going through Anne's journals, I came across a newspaper clipping about the administration's chief health preparedness officer—a guy named Lance Craine who Anne briefly mentions—visiting an animal research facility in the Southwest. There was an outbreak of a hantavirus from deer mice in New Mexico several years ago, and he was there, allegedly to receive an updated report on the progress of tracking the disease."

Nik's eyes drooped and his chin gently bobbed off his chest. "I'm sorry," he said, "but I'm still not following."

"In one passage in the journals you just read, Anne mentions her fear that the government was trying to weaponize her research. I don't think Craine was in New Mexico to get a report. I think he was there to oversee experiments to find out whether animals could be used to spread the virus."

Nik's head snapped off his chest.

"We're here," Leza said and pulled off the road onto a rutted lane. "Let me pop in and check to see if they've started branding yet. You can stay in the truck with Otto if you'd like."

"If what you say is true," he began.

"I can't prove it, Nik," Leza said as she opened the door. "That's your job. You're the reporter."

Nik looked over at her and nodded, thinking, *Well, sorta.*

CHAPTER 42

Lance Craine had been cooling his heels for forty-five minutes in a small vestibule outside the hotel room, waiting to see President Warfield, and had just about given up his vigil when the door to the room whooshed open and a middle-aged redhead rushed out, tugging at her skirt, and flew past him. Craine recognized the woman. He had seen her before in the company of her husband at a charity auction hosted by Mrs. Warfield, the First Lady. He thought her name was Rae, or maybe Rhonda. What he did remember was that she had a sultry southern accent.

"Craine, get your fat ass in here," the president barked through the open door. "You got some explaining to do."

Craine waddled in and closed the door behind him. A musky scent hung in the air. The president was standing next to a large lavender sofa, his tie off, shirt collar unbuttoned, the zipper on his fly at half-mast. On the wall opposite from Warfield, a television set was tuned to CNN, and over his shoulder, Craine could see an unmade bed through partially open French doors. A tray with half-eaten sandwiches and french fries rested on a side table.

"Mr. President, if this is about those two men," Craine started in.

"Well, it sure the fuck is, Lance," Warfield said and opened a bottle of sparkling water and picked up a handful of fries from the tray, dipped them in ketchup, and started nibbling on them. "What do you mean you lost contact with them? You assured me these men were professionals. The very best we had, you said. 'Simple operation' were your exact words, I believe."

"Quite frankly, sir, I'm at a loss to explain what happened. We've interviewed the helicopter pilot, and he said they located the woman's transponder signal coming from a remote cabin. He set down in a clearing about a mile from the cabin. The men worked their way to the site, where they made contact with its occupant, and that's the last we heard from them. The pilot, as instructed, returned to base at a prearranged time."

"For fuck's sake, Lance, you got four people in those mountains, any one of whom could cause untold damage to this administration, and we don't know if they're dead or alive. And now you tell me there's a cabin with someone living in it. Is that right?"

"Yes, the occupant is a male, African American. They spotted him when the helicopter passed over the cabin."

"What do you know about this Black Jeremiah Johnson? Who is he? What's he doing living in the mountains in the middle of winter? Is he one of those survivalist kooks?"

"Not a whole lot, sir. We're trying to ascertain that now. He's off the grid. No phone, electricity. Information is a little hard to come by, but we think we may have a solid lead that we're pursuing."

"Jesus, could this be any more fucked up?"

"It'll be okay, Mr. President. I have other reinforcements ready to go."

"Have you lost your fucking mind, man?" the president said, choking on a french fry. He took a drink of water to wash it down and sputtered some more. "You go sending another team in there and lose it, too, then what?"

"Well, sir, it wouldn't be right to leave those other two men behind if they're up there and still alive," Craine pushed back.

Warfield gave him a sideways look. "You've put three trained killers into those mountains to hunt down a twenty-something-year-old girl, and none of them have come back. Don't you think it's time to change tactics?"

"I don't think—"

"That's your problem, Lance, you don't fucking think," the president cut him off. "Now shut up and listen."

"Yes, sir."

"You say that this cabin is in a remote area?"

"That's my understanding, yes. Nothing around for miles and miles."

"And the woman's transponder signal was coming from the cabin? You're sure about that?"

"One hundred percent certain."

"So there's a good chance she's in there. Maybe the girl, too."

"More than likely."

"Okay, then, here's what you're gonna do once you find out who that mountain man is."

Lance Craine picked up the photo from his desk and studied it. A man with tobacco-colored skin, a sharp nose, high cheekbones, and lidded eyes stared back at him.

"His name is Clifford R. Samson, DOB 1-20-64, sir. No known fixed address. He has applied for a trapping permit from the North Carolina Wildlife Resources Commission every year for several decades now, going back to the early nineties. He was cited once for using an illegal leg-hold trap, fined two hundred and fifty-six dollars, and his license was temporarily suspended."

"Any immediate family members?" Craine asked.

"Wife and young daughter, deceased. Other than that, none that we can find. He's a veteran, a Ranger, sir, two tours of duty in Afghanistan, awarded a Purple Heart and Silver Star Medal. Honorably discharged from the army."

"What about the cabin, what do we know about it?"

"It appears it sits on public lands under a ninety-nine-year lease from the federal government. Based on records, it looks like it was built by his grandfather and passed down through the generations. There's about forty years left on the lease, give or take."

"So we got an African American man living up in the mountains subsisting on trapping wild animals?" Craine said.

"Not exactly African American, or at least that's not all, sir. His military records indicate he's part Native American—Cherokee, to be exact."

Craine held the photo up to his face to examine it closer. "Well, Cochise," he uttered, "you shoulda kept your nose out of other people's business, 'cause now I'm gonna have to fuckin' cut it off."

CHAPTER 43

Leza and Nik met at the Twisp Bakery the next morning before he departed, and she bought him breakfast as promised. It was fifteen degrees at eight a.m., and the high that day was forecast to be twenty-two. Nik had bought a bright-purple down parka and was now wearing it. Leza ordered a large chocolate croissant, coffee, and orange juice; Nik, a coffee and a cup of oatmeal. One upside to his personal and professional troubles was that Nik had lost his appetite, and the weight he had gained during Covid and after the birth of Isobel had started to melt away.

"You got the appetite of a sparrow," Leza said and bit into the croissant, gooey chocolate squirting out the sides.

"It's only a recent development," Nik said and sprinkled a couple of walnuts and dried cranberries on his oatmeal. He skipped the brown sugar. Anne's journals were stacked on the table next to him. He had spent most of the night going through them, cover to cover.

"So what do you think now that you've had a chance to read everything?" Leza asked.

Nik wasn't quite sure what he thought. A closer reading of Anne's words revealed mixed messages, a woman who was, at turns, enthusiastic and conflicted about her research.

She was suspicious of management's motives but also saw the benefit of the project. She was in awe of Rothschild's intellect and experience but chaffed at his penchant to micromanage her and her team. And nowhere in her writings did she draw a direct line from "weaponizing" the research to experimenting with animals as a delivery vehicle to spread the virus. That appeared to be all Leza's idea, based on a single newspaper clipping.

Nik sipped his coffee and chose his words carefully. "Umm, interesting," he said.

"That it?"

"I thought it inconclusive, if you want to know the truth."

Leza bristled. "'Inconclusive'? What did you expect, a signed affidavit?"

"Not sure what I expected. Something more definitive, I guess."

"Her journals verify the government had a secret virus program and code-named it Black Bird," Leza pointed out.

"They do, but she also says that Xion management and a White House official, this guy Craine, told her and Rothschild the government never intended to go to full-scale trials and said they disbanded the program before it was operational. I think she even said they called it hypothetical."

Leza folded her arms and glared at Nik. "Well, that's disappointing. What about the fact that everyone connected to Black Bird has ended up dead?"

"Believe me, I think there's a story here, maybe even an important story, or I wouldn't have traveled all the way across the country, but it can't be based on your hunches about zoonoses and slivers of information from Anne's journals. Can you think of anything else Anne might have said or written down somewhere?"

"I've given you all her journals. I'm not hiding anything from you, Nik, if that's what you're implying," Leza said testily. They had raised their voices, and customers in the small bakery were starting to stare at the pair.

"I'm not accusing you of holding anything back," Nik said, lowering his voice. "I'm just asking if there's perhaps some other evidence that you might have overlooked."

Leza rocked back in her chair, bit her lower lip, and thought for a moment. "I scoured her phone for clues—voice mails, photos, text messages—nothing."

"And her computer?" Nik asked.

"Same."

"Okay," Nik said. "I guess that's it, then. I'm packed and checked out of my motel. I'll get back on the road as soon as we finish breakfast. Not looking forward to crossing those mountain passes again."

"There is the GoPro," Leza said offhandedly.

"What?"

"GoPro, it's a small . . ."

"I know what a GoPro is, Leza. What about it?"

"I gave one to Anne for her birthday. A lot of skiers use them now, but the few times Anne tried to use it, the videos were either out of focus, pointed skyward, or of her feet. She hated the damn thing and insisted I return it and get my money back."

"Where is it now?"

"Back at my place. It was in her backpack when they found her. I never looked at it because, well, because it was in her backpack and she never used it. I didn't think there would be anything to see, and besides, it would only make me sad."

"How 'bout we go take a look?" Nik said. "Before I leave town."

They had to wait a half hour while the GoPro's batteries recharged, and when they turned it on, Leza was right. The videos, for the most part, were jumpy, out of focus, and uninteresting. Anne could be heard cussing as she experimented, trying to mount the device on different parts of her equipment, helmet, poles, and skis, obviously growing more frustrated with each effort before powering down the camera.

"See," Leza said as the screen went blank. "She never got the hang of it."

They sat there looking at the white screen when they heard Anne's recorded voice say, "I have Goat Mountain all to myself. It's a glorious day."

An untracked snowfield appeared on the screen. Judging from the angle of the shot, it looked as if Anne had attached the camera to the top of her ski pole.

The camera was pointed upslope, and Anne started to gradually pan across the face of the mountain before turning downhill.

"Who can that be?" they could hear her say under her breath.

The camera came up abruptly, and they could see another skier poling and striding toward Anne. The skier gradually came into focus, and they could make out sunglasses and a candy-cane-colored stocking hat, and then the camera's screen filled with white and abruptly stopped filming. "Ah, shit," they heard Anne say. "The hell with it." And there was a rustling sound and the audio also stopped.

"Looks like it fell into the snow," Leza said. She was staring down at the GoPro, face frozen.

Nik lifted his head and looked at her. "Who discovered Anne's body?" he asked.

"Search and Rescue. She had activated her avalanche beacon, and they homed in on the signal."

"So, it wasn't another skier, then?"

"No, no mention at all of another skier."

"She said on the video that she had the mountain all to herself that day, and then this other skier shows up. You'd think that person would have heard about Anne's death and at least contacted the authorities and reported seeing her."

"Uh-huh. It's big news when a skier dies out here. No way does a local not report that. It had to be an outsider."

"Let me ask you . . . ," Nik began to say.

Leza turned toward Nik and nodded her head before he could finish. "Yeah," she said slowly. "I do. I think that person knows something about Anne's death."

The pair visited a handful of motels, showing the clerks an image of the skier they had pulled from the video. It wasn't a very sharp image, and no one was able to identify the person. They weren't even certain whether it was a man or a woman.

"There is one other place I want to try," Leza said as they walked out of the lobby of a Quality Inn. She could see Otto through the truck's windshield, sitting in the driver's seat and gnawing on the steering wheel. "Otto, stop that," she shouted as she neared the vehicle, and the dog slunk down into the seat.

"Where's that?" Nik asked.

"The Mountain Lodge. It's an upscale resort about twenty minutes out of town. It's worth a shot."

"Your call," Nik said.

"Bad dog," Leza scolded when she opened the truck door. "I'm going to leave you at home if you do that again." The dog crawled over the console and into the back of the cab and lay down on the floorboards.

The Mountain Lodge was aptly named. It sat on the crown of a mountaintop with territorial views of the Methow Valley floor below. It was constructed out of stone and massive lodgepole pines and felt like a large, elegant Swiss chalet.

Neither the clerk at the front desk nor the concierge recognized the person in the photo. Nik showed the image to some members of the housekeeping staff, but they, too, were of no help.

The woman running the lodge's gift shop slid on a pair of reading glasses and examined the image. "Nope, sorry," she said. "You might try the ski shop."

"I just started this job last week," Nina, the girl tending the counter in the ski shop, said when Leza showed her the image. "Maybe our shop manager knows something. He's also a part-time ski instructor. Hey, Robby, you want to come and take a look at this," she called out.

A young man with shoulder-length hair and a bronze complexion ambled out of the back of the shop, a screwdriver in one hand and a ski boot in the other. He glanced at Leza's phone when she held it up to his face.

"Waldo," he said.

"Excuse me? Waldo?" Leza replied.

"Well, that wasn't her name," Robby said. "That's just what I called her because of the red-and-white-striped beanie she wore with the red pom-pom. You know, like in *Where's Waldo.*"

"And?" Nik said.

"No clue. She disappeared."

CHAPTER 44

The fortified steel door squeaked open, and a shaft of yellow light knifed through the darkness, silhouetting a figure standing in the shadows. "Nik?" a hushed voice called out.

"Yeah," Nik said, sounding tired, "over here," and stepped fully into the light. After taking the red-eye from Seattle, he had returned to DC jet-lagged but hopeful that he had stumbled upon a solid lead.

DC Detective Jason Goetz threw open the door and beckoned to him. "Get inside before you freeze to death out there."

Nik climbed a set of precast concrete steps and followed Goetz into a narrow hallway and then down a long corridor past darkened offices, a break room that smelled of sour milk, and a janitor's closet that reeked of bleach. At the end of the passageway, Goetz turned right and led Nik through a doorway and up a flight of stairs. At the top of the stairs, he unlocked an office door and ushered Nik inside.

It was two a.m., and the Seventh District precinct in Anacostia, Goetz's home for the past six months, was quiet and the second floor that housed the detective unit all but deserted.

"Really appreciate this, Detective Goetz," Nik said after Goetz had closed and locked the door. "I'm grateful."

Goetz flipped on a light switch to reveal a cramped office. A swivel chair was tucked behind a gray metal desk that was wedged into one corner of the room. Two oak chairs were stationed in front of the desk, and a computer monitor rested on top of it. Opposite the desk, a whiteboard with large lettering that read "Unsolved Homicides" hung on the wall. There were ten rows of color-coded names on the board that represented more than fifty individuals. DC's murder rate had remained depressingly intractable.

"It's the least I could do after the pounding you took over the death of that Lopes woman. I felt bad for you, Nik," Goetz said. "Not how I would have handled it."

Nik nodded but didn't respond. He figured Detective Jenks had intentionally led the media to believe he was a suspect in the case to settle an old score. Jenks had been hostile toward Nik ever since she had accused him of withholding evidence in a murder investigation. His only hope now was that the score had been settled once and for all, but he wasn't going to hold his breath.

Goetz turned on the computer, and Nik dropped down into one of the oak chairs and looked around the office. A window with wire mesh embedded in the glass let in light from a streetlamp in the alleyway, and a half dozen picture frames lined the window frame below. Goetz glanced up from the computer and saw Nik staring at the pictures.

"That's Phillip, my husband, and our son, Theo," Goetz said.

"How old?"

"Twelve going on eighteen."

Nik laughed.

"Nice coat. Where'd you get it?" Goetz asked.

Nik was wearing the purple down parka he had purchased when he visited Leza. "I got it in a little town out west called

Twisp. It's in Washington State," he said. "Warmest coat I've ever owned. I might never take it off again."

Nik liked Goetz. He reminded him of a number of police sources he had cultivated over the years—decent, hardworking, dedicated. Nik knew there were dirty cops, plenty of 'em, and they made Goetz's job, and the jobs of men and women like him, all the more difficult. Still, the relationship between a reporter and a cop was tricky and filled with land mines. Reporters needed confidential police sources to do their jobs, but get too close, or put too much trust in them, and you could wind up regretting it.

Observing Goetz, Nik wondered again why the DC police department had paired him with Detective Jenks. Was it to toughen Goetz up, or was it the other way around, and Goetz's role was to sand down Jenks's sharp edges? If the latter, it wasn't working, as far as Nik could tell. Or was there some other reason? He made a mental note to ask Goetz at some point.

"Okay, let's see what you got," Goetz said, and Nik slid his chair around the desk and withdrew his mobile phone from his coat pocket. He clicked on the camera icon and opened up a photo album.

Robby, the ski instructor at the Mountain Lodge, had tapped into the resort's video surveillance server and downloaded images of Waldo after Nik had offered him two hundred bucks. Either purposely or by happenstance, Waldo never looked directly into the video cameras. Her head was either dipped down or turned to the side. Consequently, Nik had images of the top of her head and her left and right profiles.

"You don't have a full-on facial?" Goetz asked when Nik showed him the photo album. "The facial recognition software works best that way."

"Sorry, this is all I got, and I'm lucky to have these."

"Text me those three," Goetz said and pointed out which pictures he wanted. He dropped the photos into the software program and hit Enter. "This will take a bit. What name did she go by?" he asked.

"The guy who gave me the photos called her Waldo because, well, never mind. It's not important."

"It might help if you told me what this is related to?" Goetz said, staring intently at his computer screen.

Nik took a moment to think about that. He was instinctively leery about sharing story information with colleagues, let alone law enforcement.

"Promise this will remain between us?" he said.

"I can't believe you'd even ask me that, Nik. I'm taking a big risk here. I could lose my job over this," Goetz said.

That wasn't exactly the answer Nik was looking for, but he said, "Okay, I think she could have information related to the Xion story I'm working on."

"Really, what makes you think that?" Goetz asked, looking up at Nik.

"I can't share that right now, and I may be way off base," Nik said, retreating. "I don't want to incriminate someone needlessly. I've got some experience with that and would like for others to avoid it if possible. You understand."

"Of course. Detective Jenks, she has her own way of doing things," Goetz said. "She doesn't always consult me or ask for my approval."

"I'm shocked," Nik said.

"Coffee?" Goetz asked and boosted himself out of his chair. "It's from a vending machine. It's halfway decent, though."

"Sure," Nik said and dug into his pocket for some money.

"It's on me," Goetz said and waved him off. "I'll be back in a minute."

Nik watched the computer screen as the facial-recognition program cycled through hundreds of images, occasionally slowing down, stuttering, and then reviving and moving on.

He wondered what the machine would produce if he uploaded his own photo.

Goetz reentered the office and placed a white paper cup in front of Nik, who took a sip. "Mmm, not bad. So how does this program work, in layman's terms?"

Goetz sat on the corner of his desk while the computer program worked in the background. "There are more than a half-billion facial photos from databases that the FACE program scans. FACE is the FBI's internal system and it stands for Facial Analysis, Comparison, and Evaluation."

"Bet the ACLU loves that," Nik said.

"Don't get me started. The photos generate a face print that tracks an individual's key facial landmarks—the distance between pupils, the width of the forehead, or the angle of the chin. I've set this search to pull two hundred matches. We'll start there and broaden the search if we don't get what we're looking for."

The computer program stopped whirling, and Goetz squeezed back behind the desk. "Let's see what we got," he said.

Nik watched as the detective scrolled through the images, slowly at first, then quicker, his head moving side to side as if he were watching a tennis match. He paused briefly before continuing to page through the results.

At image 173, he exclaimed, "Bingo."

Nik leaned in. He was staring at Narda Hertzog, thirty-four, from San Diego. She had pale-gray eyes and a pronounced V-shaped face.

"I'll be damned." Nik whistled. "Looks like an identical match."

"Damn close, that's for certain," Goetz said. "You sure you can't tell me a little more what this is about? I might be able to help."

"Thanks, but you've done more than enough already, Detective. Can you forward that picture to my phone?"

"Done," Goetz said as he hit Enter. Seconds later, a ping announced the photo's arrival. "What are you going to do now?"

"I'll send the photo to my source and ask him to verify it."

"And then?"

"And then, find Waldo."

CHAPTER 45

The dry cleaning got dropped off on Thursdays like clockwork. The only question was who would be making the run to the cleaners that morning, Sam or Karsen. Nik parked his vehicle so he had a view of both the front and side entrances of the store in the small strip shopping center. He had rehearsed what he planned to say to Sam and was going over it in his head when he saw the car pull out front and park. The driver's side door swung open, and Sam stepped out onto the pavement, a bundle of laundry in her arms.

She disappeared inside the store and a few minutes later reemerged carrying several garments wrapped in plastic bags. She was glancing down at her phone and hadn't noticed Nik standing next to her car until she was three-quarters of the way across the parking lot.

"What are the odds of bumping into you?" Nik said with a halfway grin.

"Uh-huh," Sam replied, not breaking stride. "What are you doing here, Nik?"

"I'd like to buy you coffee as a peace offering."

"Can't, I'm late for a meeting. Where'd you get that coat?"

"In the other Washington. I was out there doing research on the Xion story."

"It makes you look like a giant grape, and I thought you were suspended from *Newshound.* Why are you still working on the story?"

"It's only temporary. I was moonlighting."

"You have to be working in order to moonlight," Sam said. "Well, nice seeing you."

"Come on, Sam, you can spare fifteen minutes."

She opened the back door, tossed the dry cleaning inside, and looked down at her wristwatch. "Nope."

"Sam, be reasonable," he coaxed.

"No, we're not getting coffee. If you have something to say, you can say it in the car. It's unlocked. I don't want a public scene, and I sure as hell don't want to give you the false impression I've forgiven you because we go to a quaint little bistro like old times," she said.

"Message received, loud and clear."

"Okay, start talking," Sam said when Nik got in and closed the door. She drove a late-model Honda, and Nik rarely rode in the car. When Sam sold her MINI Cooper and purchased the Honda after Isobel was born, Nik had tried to convince her to get a larger car but she had refused. He felt cramped in the car after driving his SUV and twisted around to face her. She remained rigid, staring straight ahead.

"Sam, will you please look at me?"

She swiveled around in her seat, leaned back against the driver's door to put as much physical distance between her and Nik as possible, and folded her arms across her chest. "Better?"

"Yes, thank you. Listen, I just want to tell you in person how sorry I am for what happened, and I apologize. I never intended to jeopardize your career or embarrass you in any way. That's the last thing in the world I'd want to do, but how was I to know Lizzy was going to spike my drink?"

"So, you can prove that?"

"No, I can't, but what else could it be? I'll admit I was pissed after Senator Summers blew me off and you didn't seem to care. I probably drank more than I should have that night, but nowhere near enough to make me do the things I did and then not remember them. That's never happened before in my life."

Sam gave him a skeptical look. "What do you want from me, Nik? Sympathy?"

"I'll tell you what I want, since you asked. I want you and Isobel to move back in with me."

"Not happening." She shook her head. "Nik, you're reckless. I've known that about you from the start, and maybe it's what drew me to you in the first place. Since we've been together, you've been threatened multiple times, beaten, nearly drowned, and hospitalized. I was willing to overlook it before, but not any longer, not now that I have a child who needs me."

"*We* have a child, Sam. Isobel is our daughter."

"Sorry, of course, she's our daughter. I didn't mean to suggest otherwise."

"What is it that *you* want, Sam? What do you expect from me?"

"I'll tell you. I need to trust that I can depend on you, Nik, that you will do the right thing for this family, or this isn't going to work. It's as simple as that."

Nik grew irritated and squirmed in his seat. He felt he had always been reliable and that he had acquiesced to every demand Sam had ever made of him. Agreeing to marry, start a family, support her decision to take on the spokesperson's role for Senator Summers in the midst of everything else going on in their lives. But instead of lashing out, he took several deep breaths to clear his head. "I'll look for another job," he offered. "How's that?"

"What? You're missing the point, Nik. I don't want you to quit your job. That's not what this is about. You love your work, and you're good at it, at least most of the time. I just need you to take your responsibilities more seriously."

"Okay, I hear you and I promise to do better. From now on, you and Isobel will always come first. You have my word. Okay?"

Sam was noncommittal. "We'll see," she said.

"Speaking of Isobel, how's the little Tasmanian devil doing?" Nik asked.

"She's great," Sam said and smiled for the first time.

"And Gyp?"

"Gyp's a pain in the ass, if you really want to know, but he makes me feel safe just having him around."

"Sounds like Gyp."

"Look," Sam said, "we're not going to settle this here, and I really do need to get to work."

"Sure," Nik said and reached for the door handle. He pushed the door open and stepped out of the car. He stood for a moment next to the open door and then bent down and ducked his head back in. "Sam, you know I love you."

She exhaled. "I gotta go, Nik."

Nik closed the door and headed toward his vehicle as Sam pulled away. She stopped and lowered her window. "Tell you what, let's have dinner at my place and we can talk some more. Call me later, and we'll figure out a day that will work for both of us."

Nik watched Sam drive off and wondered if he had just received a reprieve or if he was a condemned man being offered a last meal before the gallows.

CHAPTER 46

In theory, the transmission chain of the Black Bird virus was easy to chart: Lab to crows. Crows to biting insects like mosquitoes. Insects to humans. Human to human. Vaccinating a large percentage of a population severs the link in that chain by providing what's referred to as herd immunity.

But envisioning a virus chain and establishing one in the real world was proving to be anything but easy.

The experiment with the Shepherd's Staff followers in Idaho had clearly demonstrated that the Black Bird virus was lethal to humans and capable of quickly spreading between individuals. Indeed, three of the four transmission steps in the process had been validated—lab to crows, crows to mosquitoes, and human to human.

Only one critical component remained stubbornly unfulfilled: the transmission of the disease from the animal kingdom to humans.

The mink farm trial in Utah had proved to be a complete failure, as were two other minor tests Lance Craine and his people had run.

After taking a few days to reflect on the lessons of the mink farm experiment, Craine had concluded that the failure was partially the result of the small sample size with limited human exposure.

He was determined not to make that mistake again. He needed to go bigger.

Unlike Rome, no roads lead to Nome. The small Alaskan village on the Norton Sound of the Bering Sea has no ferry or train service, either, and is only reachable by plane. The roads leading out of Nome terminate seventy miles from town and are open for just a short duration in the summertime.

The 3,800 souls who inhabit Nome are, for the most part, a rugged, individualistic lot who prize their independence. Nome is perhaps best known for two events—the discovery of large deposits of gold in 1899 and the Iditarod dogsled race, which has its finish line in Nome.

"Alaska, where men are men and women win the Iditarod" is a popular refrain among natives.

Legend has it that a diphtheria epidemic in 1925 was the genesis of the famous dogsled race. The disease ravaged the indigenous population in the Nome area, but a violent winter storm had prevented planes from delivering life-saving serum from Anchorage to the remote village. Faced with a deepening humanitarian crisis, Alaskans organized a harrowing dogsled relay to Nome to transport the medicine. The Iditarod racecourse follows roughly that same route today.

While not totally inaccessible, Nome is perhaps more isolated from the outside world than any town of its size in America, particularly in the brutal wintertime.

That was Lance Craine's primary motivation for selecting Nome for his next Black Bird experiment. The other was the Anvil Mountain Correctional Center.

Anvil Mountain is a regional prison facility for sentenced and unsentenced adult felons, both male and female, and could house up to 115 inmates at full capacity.

Craine reasoned that introducing the Black Bird virus among incarcerated prisoners in the Nome facility would be the safest way to contain the spread of the disease to the outside world while at the same time providing an opportunity to validate the transmission chain of the pathogen to humans from animals.

"No one's going to notice or give a fuck if some dirtbag felons in a godforsaken Alaska outpost die," Craine told Xion's CEO, Bauer.

"Jesus, Lance, I don't know," a nervous Bauer replied. "It could get out of hand pretty damn fast."

"We have to establish that the virus is transmissible, or all of the rest of this is for shit. And besides, we'll be standing by with enough vaccine to inoculate the local population three times over once we have confirmation. There is an infinitesimal chance of an outbreak."

"Is the president on board?" Bauer asked.

Craine hesitated before answering and leaned back in his chair and reached into his pocket for a pair of nail clippers. "More or less."

"What's that supposed to mean?"

Craine started trimming his nails, sending the clippings onto Bauer's desk. "He knows as much as he needs to know, is what it means."

"You think that's wise?"

"Believe me," he said, continuing to clip away, "I know it is."

CHAPTER 47

Fire had driven Clifford Samson into the mountains. It was his guilt that had kept him there. He had lost track of time and couldn't remember how many seasons had passed since he had moved into the isolated cabin or exactly what year he had arrived, for that matter. He didn't run into folks often. Just the occasional park ranger or wayward hiker, and he preferred it that way.

The girl, Puck, was the first real visitor he'd had in years, if you could even call her a visitor. *Puck, who names their child that? Must be a family name,* he thought, *or some kinda joke.*

He looked over at the iron bed where she was resting, peacefully for once. The antibiotics and pain medication he had lifted from the dead men's packs seemed to be working, but he'd seen enough gunshot wounds and injuries in the military to know it might not last. She still needed medical attention. He'd managed to buy some time, that was all.

Whoever had set those killers on the girl would come calling again, of that he was certain, and now that they knew where he lived, and with the weather clearing, he wouldn't stand a chance. Instead of a two-man team, they might send half a dozen armed mercenaries. It'd be over in a matter of minutes.

He nipped at a jug of moonshine and thought about how they might carry off the next assault. *Will they try the same approach, touch down with a helicopter and dispatch a team?* Maybe, but doubtful. Didn't work the first time. He'd bet they'd go for the sure thing the next round.

What might that be? he pondered as he took another pull from the jug. The hooch was making him feel good. He had to be careful. It was a mighty thin line between feeling high and feeling morose and suicidal.

He'd spent many a night alone, stoned, with thoughts of killing himself running around in his head. He had never followed through. Not because he was afraid of dying—he wasn't—but because it would dishonor them.

Maybe that was the reason he was so protective of the girl. His daughter would have been about Puck's age by now had she lived, had he been there to save her and her mother. But he wasn't. He was out tomcatting around, and when he finally made it home that night, the house had burned to the ground, their charred bodies still in bed.

The fire marshal had told him he was lucky. Had he been in the house, he likely would have died, too, when the old boiler down in the basement exploded. He never considered himself lucky. If anything, he thought he was extremely unlucky that he hadn't been killed in the fire. He had made up his mind that when he died, that was the way he was going to go, to experience the same pain they had lived through.

He drifted for a time after that, living on the streets, ignoring pleas from his family to come stay with them, to get help, to ease his pain. He didn't want to hear it.

It was just by chance that Cliff had run into a fellow Army Ranger who was working at a shelter for homeless veterans when Cliff got into a fight with another man over a bunk bed.

A lot of the men in the shelter had drug addictions. Not Cliff. He never touched anything stronger than aspirin. He was your garden-variety drunk. His army buddy got him into a program, and he dried out, though he never did stop drinking altogether, and eventually Cliff moved in with his sister and her family. One Sunday after church, his sister told him if he was interested, he could use the mountain cabin their daddy had left her. She'd not been there since she was a little girl and had no need for it but didn't know what kind of condition it was in. Two weeks later, Cliff packed up what few belongings he owned and set off into the mountains, and that's where he'd been ever since.

"What are you thinking about?" It was Puck. She was awake and sitting up in bed. The coloring had slowly returned to her face, and her voice was growing stronger. She still had a limp and limited range of motion in the shoulder where she had been shot, but she felt more and more like her old self with every passing day.

Cliff twisted around. "How you feelin'?"

"Much better. Those antibiotics seem to have done the trick."

"That's good. You still cold?"

"No. Fact, I'm too hot now," she said and tossed off the layers of blankets and pelts covering her and popped out of bed. Puck looked around the small but tidy cabin and wondered if she hadn't imagined it all. The fact was, it had only been a little more than a year since she was a carefree student attending classes at the University of North Carolina and playing varsity volleyball. Now she was snowbound in a mountain hut after narrowly escaping death. No one would believe the ordeal she had been through. Hell, *she* hardly believed it.

The cabin's floor was ice-cold, and Puck slipped her feet into her boots and picked up one of the furs she had dropped on the floor and draped it around her shoulders like a cape. She often wondered what life would have been like had she followed her boyfriend to Texas like she had originally planned after graduation—until she caught him making out with another girl at a local bar—or if she had pursued that academic fellowship at Berkeley. She was certain of one thing: her life wouldn't be anything like this.

It was growing dark outside, and she walked over to the window above the kitchen sink and looked at her reflection in the pane. She was stunned by the image staring back at her. Dark lines, like small furrows in a plowed field, were carved under her eyes, and her close-cropped hair was matted to one side of her head where she slept on the pillow. She looked ten years older and no longer youthful. Puck took her powder-blue stocking hat from her pocket and pulled it over her head. She glanced back at her reflection and was reminded of one of those refugees you see on television fleeing a war zone. She wasn't at all convinced that even her own mother could pick her out of a lineup at the moment.

Puck imagined her mother was sick with worry and maybe by now had even given up hope that her daughter would be found alive. Losing her husband had been painful and shattering enough, but losing a child, it would be unbearable for her. Puck knew her mother well enough to know she blamed herself for allowing Puck to hike the Appalachian Trail alone. They had talked about her partnering with a companion, but since the trip was so last minute, Puck hadn't been able to find a friend to accompany her.

After her father was killed in the car accident, Puck had assumed she and her mother would grow closer, bond, but the opposite was actually true. Her mother withdrew, and Puck, a sixteen-year-old girl, felt twice abandoned. It seemed they were always struggling to bridge the divide.

"I'm going to wash up," Puck said to Cliff and started walking toward the bathroom, the fur cape flowing behind her.

"Okay. How's your appetite?" he asked.

"I'm starving. I could eat a horse."

"Good. I'll fix us some dinner and then we can talk."

"Venison stew again?"

"No, not tonight. Braised rabbit with morel mushrooms."

"Yum. You're quite the chef."

"I try my best. Something to look forward to anyways."

"What is it you want to talk about?"

Cliff took another drink from the jug. "Surviving."

CHAPTER 48

"You're sure I won't get in trouble for doing this?"

"Absolutely not," Nik said, downplaying Zach's concerns.

"Okay," Zach said and logged on to his computer at *Newshound.* He was talking to Nik on his cell phone in a low voice with his earbuds in so Doria Miller, sitting two desks over, couldn't eavesdrop on his conversation. Besides Zach and Doria, the only other people in the newsroom that evening were a sports editor, a clerk, and a cop shop reporter who had been called in because of a hostage standoff with police near the White House. Mo Morgan was said to be on his way in but hadn't yet arrived.

"All right, I'm signed in. What is it you want me to do?"

"I need you to run a name check through *Newshound*'s private databases. I've accessed all the public databases I can think of and have come up empty so far. I'd do it myself, but the company pulled my permissions when I was suspended."

"And Mo approved this?" Zach hesitated.

"Yeah, yeah. It's fine."

"What's the name you want me to look up?"

"Narda Hertzog. Spelling, *N-A-R-D-A H-E-R-T-Z-O-G.*"

"Got it," Zach said as he keyed in the name. "What databases do you want me to run it against?"

"Military, tax records, court filings, driver's license, arrest records, birth and death certificates. Any and all you can possibly think of. We're looking for a woman in her early to midthirties."

"That's a lot. It's going to take me most of the night."

"Text me when you're done, no matter what time it is. I'll be up."

"Uh, okay, but what if someone asks me what I'm doing?"

"Tell 'em the truth. Tell 'em that you're working on a story."

Nik was asleep when the text from Zach arrived at 5:05 a.m. and set off an alarm that woke Nik. He had placed the phone next to his pillow when he lay down to close his eyes for five minutes. He looked at the time and realized he had been asleep for nearly three hours.

Zach's first text was lengthy and was immediately followed by a string of similarly long messages, which read, in part:

Nik—Sorry for not getting this to you sooner. I was pulled away to lend a hand on a breaking news story and the database search turned out to be more complicated than I anticipated. There are, believe it or not, several women with that name in the US but only two who ultimately matched your description—one a freelance consultant in S. Calif. and the other a grade school teacher in Upstate NY. The consultant I believe is the woman you're looking for. I've attached her address and phone numbers below. But there's a catch. Narda only exists on paper. Judging from the records I was able to access, it looks like she stole the identity of a 6-year-old Minnesota girl who died in a drowning accident in 1995. I think your woman's real name is Jane Atwood, or at least that's the person who registered the mailbox where duplicates of the girl's birth and death certificates were sent by the Minnesota Department of Health. I wasn't able to find a whole lot of useful information on Jane Atwood. One fact that may interest you. It appears she's a contract employee for the federal government and has a top security clearance. I'm beat and heading home. Let's talk later today.

CHAPTER 49

The receptionist for Woodward, Stallworth and Moran knew Nik and liked him. She gave him a warm smile when she saw him step off the elevator outside the reception area. "Want me to buzz Maggie," she asked, "and let her know you're here?"

"No need," Nik said with a shake of the head as he waltzed through the lobby. "She's expecting me."

"Love the jacket," she complimented him. "Purple's one of my favorite colors."

When Nik arrived outside Maggie's office, she was concentrating on a document, a hand to her forehead to keep her hair from falling in her eyes, and didn't notice him standing at her door until he cleared his throat. She tilted her head, a puzzled look on her face. "Nik, what are you doing here?"

"I had a lunch meeting down the street and a few minutes to kill so I thought I'd check in with you about the Xion litigation. I haven't heard anything since we last met."

"I've been busy, and you can't just drop in unannounced like this, Nik. How'd you get past the receptionist?"

Nik shrugged. "She likes my coat. Purple is one of her favorite colors. One of yours, too, apparently," he said, pointing to the periwinkle blouse Maggie was wearing.

There was a rap on the doorframe, and Nik turned around to see a tall, athletic-looking man in his early forties with caramel-colored skin wearing tortoiseshell glasses and dressed in a light-charcoal-gray suit hovering behind him. Nik felt woefully underdressed in his puffy jacket and khakis.

"Sorry to interrupt. Margaret, are we still on to go over that brief this afternoon?"

"Yes. I'm just making a few last-minute revisions to it now, Paul. I should be done shortly."

"Excellent. See you at two thirty, then, and, again, apologies for the interruption."

"None needed. You weren't interrupting. This is Nik Byron, my ex. Nik, this is Paul Robinson, head of litigation."

Robinson extended his hand and said, "Nik Byron? Where have I heard that name before? Aren't you the reporter who the police said didn't kill that woman?"

Nik winced. "Yeah, that's me. Nice of you to mention it," he said and dropped Robinson's hand. Robinson took a step back, sized Nik up, and let out a soft chuckle. "You reporters certainly lead interesting lives, I'll give you that. Well, good meeting you, and, Margaret, see you soon," he said before he dashed off down the corridor.

Nik turned back toward Maggie with a furrowed brow after Robinson departed. "'Margaret'?" he said quizzically. "I haven't heard anyone call you that since your great-aunt Rose made a toast at our wedding."

Maggie waved her hand dismissively. "That's just what he likes to call me."

"Uh-huh. He married? Didn't notice a ring."

"Leave it alone, Nik."

"Sure, Margaret."

Maggie had decorated her office with white leather couches from Italy, a handcrafted Baker writing desk, and a set of colorful original prints she had found in a Charleston art gallery. Maggie always had a keen eye for style. She had decorated their modest home artfully with inexpensive estate sale items and thrift-shop castoffs when they couldn't afford any better as newlyweds, but now that she was a partner with one of DC's most prestigious law firms, she could more thoroughly indulge her expensive tastes.

Nik remained standing on the threshold, waiting to either be invited in or physically thrown out of the building. "I can give you five minutes," Maggie said finally, "but that's all. Close the door."

He stepped in and took a seat on one of the couches.

"Don't get comfortable," she advised. "You've cleaned yourself up."

"Yeah, figured it was time to ditch the lumberjack look. You going to offer me something to drink?"

"Help yourself," she said and pointed to a gleaming round conference table tucked in one corner of the office. "There's water and fresh coffee over there."

Nik retrieved a bottle of water and retook his seat.

"The reason you haven't heard from me is because of all of that business with that Lopes woman. What the hell was that all about, Nik?"

"Short answer, I was set up."

"Oh, yeah, by whom?"

"I'm pretty certain Lizzy Blake. I think she spiked my drink while we were at a press reception together that night, and then a DC detective who has a grudge against me took her sweet time clearing my name."

"You got it all straightened out now?"

"More or less. *Newshound* temporarily suspended me."

"What? If you're suspended, why are you here asking about Xion?"

"The operative word is 'temporary.' I anticipate the suspension will be lifted in a day or two."

"You're unbelievable."

"I think the word you're searching for is 'remarkable.'"

"Don't be an ass, Nik," Maggie said sternly.

"Sorry, I didn't mean to be flip. I really do expect to be reinstated pretty soon, and I don't want the leads I've been pursuing to go cold. And if you're not comfortable sharing information with me, I get it. It's fine."

Maggie contemplatively tapped her fingernails on her desktop as she quietly considered Nik. For a divorced couple with no children to bind them together, their lives seemed to have become more intertwined in some respects after their separation than when they were together. She wasn't quite sure what to make of that. It wasn't a bad thing necessarily, but it probably wasn't altogether healthy, either. They had even had sex a few times after they separated, but that was a while ago. She wasn't about to go down that foolish, if not dangerous, road again. If she was being honest, she liked having Nik in her life. He was a link to her past that, without him, she feared might be erased.

"There is one thing," she said, breaking the silence.

Nik scooted up to the edge of the couch. "And what's that?"

"Well, when the lawyer handling the class-action lawsuit was deposing a Xion employee yesterday, she apparently volunteered that a couple of DC detectives had paid a visit to her at her home the day before."

"That's not surprising," Nik said and slid back on the couch, a disappointed look on his face. "They're investigating Greta Lopes's murder. It's to be expected."

"I agree, had they asked her about Lopes, but they didn't. They said they were investigating the murder of Bernard

Rothschild—you know, the guy whose notebook you showed me with all the bird sketches."

"Wait, Rothschild's *murder*? The woman must have been confused. He committed suicide."

"Apparently it's been reclassified."

"You're certain about this?"

"The woman was under oath, and, like I said, she volunteered the information. There was no reason for her to make it up. She also said she got the impression the detectives were looking into the deaths of the other scientists. Showed her a picture of a potential suspect, a woman. She didn't recognize her."

Nik stiffened. "You get the name of the detectives that she spoke with, by any chance?" he asked.

"Nope, but one was supposedly this tough Black chick and the other a white guy. She called him Mr. Rogers because he was so nice."

Nik let out a low moan, a stunned look on his face.

"What's wrong?" Maggie asked. "You okay?"

"Nothing. I'm fine," Nik said, but he was thinking, *I'm such a dope. That fucking Goetz, he was playing me all along.*

CHAPTER 50

From their vantage point on a ridge above the cabin, the pair could see curlicues of white smoke rising lazily from the rooftop chimney and hear the growl of a diesel generator down below. A translucent moon was rising, and there was barely a breath of wind. The two spotters, one with a snow-caked beard, the other wearing a camouflage balaclava, waited for clouds to obscure the moon before maneuvering lower through the trees and around to the side of the cabin with the window. A faint light was coming from inside, and the bearded spotter held up a scope and adjusted the eyepiece to zoom in on the cabin's interior. He could readily make out two figures seated at a small table in the main room.

"Targets acquired," he said over his shoulder, holding up two fingers. "Call it in."

The second spotter keyed his radio. "We got visual confirmation. Two ducks on the pond. Open season."

"Copy that," came the reply. Then, moments later, "The bird has flown the coop."

"Let's haul ass," the radioman said, and they scrambled up the mountainside through the snow.

The Predator drone came in low and fast and fired its missile a half mile from the target. The projectile skimmed over the treetops, kicking up blooms of snow before diving and slamming full on into the log structure. There was a deafening roar followed by an orange fireball that lit up the sky.

"Direct hit," the spotter radioed.

"Want us to unload the second barrel?" a voice asked in his earpiece.

"Negative. Keep it holstered. We'll do a reconnaissance at daybreak and report back."

"Copy that. Bird returning to the roost. Over and out."

The next morning, the duo made their way down the mountain to the bombed-out cabin and combed through the smoldering debris. The silhouettes of two cindered bodies lay side by side, their charcoaled remains covered in ash and snow. The missile and the fire's aftermath had incinerated everything to a crisp, the only exceptions being the skeleton of the iron bed and the cast-iron potbelly stove. The stove squatted in the center of the cabin's shell, its door blown off, its mouth yawning open like that of a hippopotamus.

"We need to look for identifying evidence. Don't expect we'll find much, if anything," the radioman said as he sifted through the ashes. "I'll take the front, you take the back. Be quick."

His partner walked to what were once the cabin's back rooms, stirring the ashes with a stick as he went. A wet snow had begun to fall, and the ash was turning into slurry and was sticking to his boots. He uncovered melted silverware, disfigured animal traps, a crowbar, the head of an axe, and some nails. He turned back toward the front of the cabin and stepped on something hard. He kicked at it with his toe, and it skittered through the ash. He bent and picked it up.

He spit on it, rubbed it against the sleeve of his coat to clean it, and then held it up to his face to examine it more closely. It was a Leatherman. Turning it over in his hands, he could make out a name etched on the side, "Puck Hall."

"It's the girl, all right," he called out to his partner and held up the versatile tool that Puck's father had given her and that she always carried. "Found her engraved Leatherman."

His partner was bending over the corpses, then stood and spun around, a chain dangling between his fingers.

"Samson's dog tags," he announced triumphantly, swinging them back and forth. "I'll see if I can scrape enough DNA from what's left of these bodies to get some samples, and then let's get the fuck out of here."

"Roger that," his partner said and dropped the Leatherman into an evidence bag, sealed it, and stuffed it into his pocket.

CHAPTER 51

All five of them—Nik, Mo, *Newshound*'s publisher, the company's in-house attorney, and the head of HR—shuffled into Mo's cramped office on a cold, drizzly Sunday morning. No one particularly wanted to be there, but they had agreed to meet to discuss Nik's job status out of sight and earshot of the daily newsroom staff. All were dressed casually, except for the attorney. He wore a blue blazer, a collared shirt, and a tie. Mo sat in one corner loudly cracking his knuckles while the publisher scrolled through emails on his laptop, the HR woman fidgeted in her chair, the attorney listened in on a phone call, and Nik stared out the window at a gray sky.

Mo's office was littered with empty coffee cups, discarded ramen-noodle packages, paperback books, and newspapers. A pile of workout clothes was stacked in one corner, and a set of dumbbells nosed out from under his desk. He had pinned posters of Matt Drudge on one wall and a young Arnold Schwarzenegger on the back of his door.

Nik looked around and resisted the urge to make a joke thanking everyone for skipping church to meet with him.

Instead, he remained silent until the attorney, Barry Clouser, hung up his call and announced, "That was Xion's corporate counsel. The company has agreed not to press charges against Nik for criminal trespass. They are sending over a document to that effect right now."

"Well done," the publisher said. "I'm not convinced anything would have come of it in the long run, but it would have kept the story alive for those jackals on television to continue to feast on us."

"Great," Mo added. "I always thought it was overblown. Now we can get back to work."

"I don't agree," the HR woman pushed back. "Mr. Byron's behavior was inexcusable. *Newshound*'s employee manual explicitly forbids entering private property without permission. I don't think we can afford to look the other way. It would send the wrong message to the other staffers."

The woman, Delores Trumbo, had recently joined *Newshound* from the health-care industry and was appalled by the general disregard of company policies exhibited by its journalists. Had Nik worked at any of the other companies where she had been previously employed, he would have been summarily fired for his behavior. She was determined to make him an example for other wayward employees.

"What do you suggest we do, Delores?" the publisher asked.

"I suggest Mr. Byron remain suspended without pay."

"For how long?" Mo wanted to know.

"For however long it takes," the woman said defiantly.

"I'm sorry, what's that supposed to mean?" Nik asked.

"For you to show the proper remorse for your actions and the embarrassment you caused this company," Trumbo said.

"Delores," the publisher said gently, "I hear where you're coming from, but if the other side is willing to be reasonable and put this matter behind them, I think we should follow their lead. What do you think, Barry?"

The attorney was busy scribbling notes on a legal pad and looked up only when he heard his name mentioned. "Legally," he said, removing his glasses and polishing the lenses on his tie, "*Newshound* and Nik are out of the woods and no longer have any exposure. It's purely an internal personnel matter at this point. My advice would be to place a note in his file and move on."

"Well," Trumbo had started to say when the publisher spoke up.

"I agree. Nik, welcome back," he said, stood, and shook Nik's hand. "And don't ever do something stupid like that again, or next time, I will fire your ass on the spot. Understood?"

"Perfectly," Nik said.

"In the meantime," the publisher added, "you're on probation for, aah, a month."

Mo slapped Nik on the back as the frustrated HR woman gathered up her notes and stormed out of the meeting.

After everyone else had cleared out of the office, Nik quickly brought Mo up to speed on his activities since the suspension. He told him about his trip to Twisp, Washington, to meet with Leza Burdock, Anne Paxton's partner; the discovery of the GoPro video; the clandestine meeting with Detective Goetz; and his conversation with Maggie.

"Damn," Mo said when Nik finished, "I should have agreed with the HR lady to keep you suspended. You're a helluva lot more productive when you're not working than when you are."

"Yeah, for all the good it's done me," Nik said. "I practically handed—no, I did hand—Goetz my best lead."

"So, what do you know about this woman—what did you say her name was again?"

"Take your pick. Waldo, Narda Hertzog, or Jane Atwood. We believe her real identity is Atwood. And we don't know much about her at this point," Nik said.

Mo was seated behind his desk. He tilted his head to one side and scratched the side of his face with the back of his hand. "I see," he said, "and who's 'we'?"

Nik looked sheepish. "Well, I've been meaning to talk to you about that. I just didn't have the right opportunity."

"Uh-huh. Now might be a good time."

"I kinda roped Zach in to help out."

"Kinda?"

"He conducted a couple searches on *Newshound*'s databases for me while I was, mmm, away."

"While you were suspended, you mean? Barred from the office and your network permissions canceled?"

"That's right, though I might characterize it differently."

"How so?"

"A mini-sabbatical."

"You know you could have royally screwed the kid's career even before it got off the ground?"

"It wasn't his fault. I told him it was okay."

Mo held up his hand. "Stop. Don't say another word, or it'll be my head that HR lady wants to put on a pike. So what's next?"

"We've got a plan."

"By 'we,' you mean you and Zach?" Mo said. "Does Zach know about this plan? And please tell me it doesn't include hacking some company's computer network."

"Why don't you ask him yourself?" Nik said and motioned to the other end of the newsroom, where Zach was standing by his desk. "It was his idea."

Nik drove across town to his condo, and Zach followed in the late-model dog-turd-brown Volvo station wagon that had been passed down to him from his parents his junior year in college after he moved off campus and started commuting to classes.

The car was as safe as a Sherman tank, but Zach rightfully thought it made him look like a soccer mom. He was mortified to be seen driving it. He pulled up outside Nik's building and parked on the street.

"Let me guess," Nik said when Zach stepped out of the car, "you're picking the kids up from Little League practice after school."

"Funny," Zach said, "and not very original."

"Love the paint job. You don't see that color much these days," Nik said. "Bet the coeds dig it."

Zach screwed up his face. "Oh, yeah, it's a real chick magnet. Gotta beat 'em off with a stick."

"Well, come on in," Nik said and pushed open the door to his building.

The pair set up shop in Nik's dining room and spread out their computers, notebooks, and files on the dining room table. Nik changed into shorts and a Grateful Dead T-shirt, offered Zach a bottle of water, and they got to work.

Despite Mo's concerns, Zach's plan didn't involve cyber-snooping, hacking into secure networks, or any other high-tech assault, for that matter. Instead, it relied on plain old-fashioned shoe-leather-type reporting, and it started with Greta Lopes's simple command to Nik: "Follow the money."

The bookkeeper had told Nik that Xion's government contract was valued at $3.5 billion and that Xion, in addition to creating vaccines for the US stockpile, had agreed to serve as a central clearinghouse for other vaccine producers, distributing the federal money as instructed by the White House to anonymous numbered accounts. That made the money almost impossible to trace.

Zach had researched the US biotech companies that were enrolled in the government's vaccine program and discovered that all of them were publicly held. That meant they were required to disclose government payments as revenue in filings with the Securities and Exchange Commission. The companies could no longer hide behind numbered bank accounts, and, at that point, it was just a matter of pulling SEC records for the dozen or so companies and calculating who got what.

The two reporters worked around the clock scrutinizing thousands of pages of SEC filings while sitting at Nik's dining room table. The pair did their final tabulation just as the sun outside the apartment's window crawled above the horizon. They were able to account for all but $250 million of the $3.5 billion contract.

"Tell you what," Nik said as he stood and stretched, "how about we grab a couple hours of sleep, clean up, and then head back into the office and start calling these companies."

"Split 'em down the middle?" Zach said.

"Sure," Nik said, "why not. That way, it should only take a couple hours to reach all of them for a comment."

"And what exactly is it that we want to ask them?" Zach asked.

"After we verify that they received government funding, we want to ask them two questions: Have they ever heard of the Black Bird project, and do they know a woman named Jane Atwood, also known as Narda Hertzog?" Nik said. "Let's start there and see where that gets us."

CHAPTER 52

Nik and Zach hadn't been at their reporting long when the phones at Xion's headquarters started ringing off the hook. Angry biotech executives were calling to complain that journalists from *Newshound* were peppering them with questions about some purportedly secret research program Xion was carrying out for the US government. "I don't know what kind of shit you've stepped in, Glenn, but if this is some cheap trick to suck us into Xion's legal mess, it's not going to fucking work," one pharmaceutical executive berated Glenn Bauer, echoing similar messages he had already received that day.

"What did you tell them?" a flustered Bauer finally asked when the executive briefly paused from screaming at him.

"That I hadn't a fucking clue what they were talking about. They wanted to know why Xion had wired our payments to numbered bank accounts instead of directly to the company. Made it all sound like we were part of some grand conspiracy. Hinted at a massive cover-up of some sort."

"Jesus Christ, reporters. Bunch of fucking animals. You can't trust 'em," Bauer said. "Was it that fucking Byron? He tried to break into our offices, you know. It was all over the news. The guy's a known drunk and a loser and has been totally discredited. We should have prosecuted his ass when we had the chance."

"What's Black Bird, Glenn?" the executive asked.

"Blackboard?"

"No. *Black Bird.* They asked about Project Black Bird at Xion. What is it?"

"Oh, right, Black Bird. It's nothing. It was just some hare-brained idea that one of our scientists proposed. I can't even remember what it was about now, to be honest. It never got off the ground. Can't imagine why they'd be interested in that," Bauer said.

"They also mentioned Jane Atwood, who apparently also goes by the name of Narda Hertzog. Name ring a bell?"

"Never heard of her. Who's she supposed to be?"

"I don't know, Glenn, thought maybe you could tell me that."

"Sorry, drawing a blank."

"I see. They also said they weren't able to account for two hundred and fifty million of the government's contract. You holding out on us, Glenn?"

"No, of course not. We paid out every penny. The White House told us where to wire the money, and we sent it on its way as instructed. The account has a zero balance."

"There's some weird shit happening over at your shop, Glenn, and, speaking on behalf of the rest of the companies enrolled in the government's vaccine program, we don't want any of it splattering on us. Understood?"

"There's nothing to be concerned about," Bauer reassured the executive. "I'll have our lawyers call *Newshound* and put a stop to this harassment bullshit immediately. You have my word."

"You do that, Glenn, and, just so we're clear, I don't believe a fucking word you say."

CHAPTER 53

They heard the blast, saw the flash of light in the nighttime sky, felt a rumble in the ground below their feet, and looked back up the mountain in dread as an avalanche roared down a chute toward them at a terrifying speed, snapping trees and obliterating everything in its path. In the blink of an eye, a billowing cloud of snow, like a giant sandstorm, advanced upon them ahead of the surge and enveloped the surroundings, obscuring sky, ground, and horizon. The sound was deafening. They became disoriented and momentarily separated. He called out her name, and she lurched toward his voice. He grabbed an arm, pulled her close, and screamed in her ear, *"Ruuun."*

Puck took a step, stumbled, fell to one knee, and got bogged down in the snow, unable to move. Cliff's hand found her and lifted her free, and he dragged her the last twenty-five yards along the cat track. They reached the mouth of the cave just as the full force of the avalanche rolled over the top, burying them alive in the hollowed-out side of the mountain.

There they lay, panting heavily, hearts thundering, eyes fighting to adjust to the blackness. "You okay?" Cliff asked.

"I think so," Puck said, gasping. "What just happened?"

"Not certain, but my guess is they blew up the cabin and the explosion triggered that avalanche."

"Where are we?"

"It's the cave I mentioned. Watch your eyes," Cliff said and reached up and flicked on the headlamp he was wearing. The lamp's light cast a yellow halo around the pair and temporarily blinded Puck. "Can't make out much of anything. The snow blocked the opening."

"I'm sorry about your cabin," Puck said. "I really liked it."

"Mmm," Cliff grunted.

"And your pelts. All that hard work, gone."

Cliff stood and brushed the snow off his coat and stamped his feet to keep the blood circulating, the thuds bouncing off the cavern's walls. "Market for fur had pretty much dried up anyhow," he said matter-of-factly.

Puck sat up and shrugged off Narda's old backpack and started pawing through her belongings. She fished out a flashlight and shined its beam around the cave. The entrance was about five feet high and four feet wide, and the walls and ceiling were solid granite. A massive mound of snow plugged the mouth of the cave. She twisted around and trained the light on the back end of their shelter. "Where's that lead?" she asked Cliff.

"Dunno. Never had any call to find out. There are a couple side channels that branch off from this main chamber we're sittin' in, a little ways back. That's all I know. You should douse that light and save your batteries," Cliff said and turned off his headlamp.

Puck swung the flashlight's beam around the cave once more before turning it off. "How long do you think it will take them to figure out those bodies aren't us?" she asked.

"Not long, if there's anything left of 'em. You feel like eatin'? I've got some jerky."

"Sure, thanks," Puck said. "It's cold. I miss your cast-iron stove already."

Cliff toggled on his headlamp to locate the food in his pack and handed a piece of jerky to Puck. "I laid in some wood awhile back just in case," he said. "Give me a minute and I'll get us a fire goin'."

Puck tore off a piece of the cured meat with her teeth and slowly chewed it while Cliff gathered an armful of kindling. He teepeed the wood and set it ablaze. "Don't want too big a fire or it'll smoke us out," he said as he blew on the embers.

She edged up to the fire and stretched out. She rested her head against her backpack and glanced over at Cliff. The flames illuminated one side of his face, his skin shiny and polished in the firelight. "I've been thinking about what we talked about back at the cabin," Puck said, "and the only reason I can remotely come up with why anyone would be after me is because of the job I had at the research lab where I used to work."

"What sorta work you do that someone would set professional killers on a young girl?" Cliff asked.

"Well, that's just it, nothing much, really. I was a junior researcher, or, at least, that was my title, but, in actuality, I was more or less a glorified gofer. Sure, I pitched in on writing papers, gathered data, filed government reports, but I also ordered lunch for the staff and helped the older researchers with technology challenges. I mean, I was a peon, if you want to know the truth. It was a great first job out of college, and I worked crazy hours, but no one would confuse me with a decision maker or someone remotely important."

"Gov'ment reports? What kind of reports you talking about?" Cliff asked.

"During the pandemic, Xion—that was the company I worked for—received a large government contract to produce vaccines to replenish the federal stockpile. That's a line of business Xion has been in for a number of years. The contract also called for the company to do some experimental research creating man-made viruses in the lab in order to produce vaccines to combat potential future outbreaks. I had to file status reports with the government on the lab's progress. It was a very secretive project, but in the end, it got canceled before it was fully operational."

"Why'd they cancel it?"

"They said the government withdrew the funding, but the gossip was my boss and Xion's chief scientist protested when they learned government officials had this plan to infect humans with the virus to test the effectiveness of the vaccine."

"Huh, maybe they only claimed to kill the program," Cliff said. "Maybe they actually carried out those experiments and now want to get rid of anyone who might know what they were up to."

"No way. Our country wouldn't do something like that."

"Girl, where you been?" Cliff said. "Gov'ment's been pulling that crap forever. You study your history, you'd know about the syphilis experiments they conducted on Black folk at Tuskegee, illiterate sharecroppers mostly. Doctors intentionally misled those poor people about their condition and treatment. They let them remain infected with the disease, suffer, and die terrible deaths."

"I didn't know."

"Yeah, and don't fool yourself, they'd do it all over again if they thought they could get away with it. Who's running the country now anyhow?" Cliff said.

"You mean, who's the president of the United States?"

"Yeah, I don't follow politics. Haven't for years."

"Ronald Warfield's the president."

"Why does that name sound familiar?"

Puck shrugged. "You know," she said, "I'm not supposed to discuss my work with anyone outside of the lab. I had to get a government security clearance and sign nondisclosure agreements before being allowed to even join the project. I could go to prison if they found out what I told you."

Cliff snorted and laughed out loud, startling Puck. It was the first she had heard him laugh in all the time they had been together.

"What's so funny?" she asked.

"You," he said.

"Why's that?"

"If you live."

"What? What's that supposed to mean?"

"You mean you could go to prison *if you live*."

"Oh," Puck said, and sat up and hugged her knees close to her chest and rocked back and forth on her haunches as she stared into the fire. "I get it. Ha, ha."

The fire had all but died out when Puck woke, cold and stiff from sleeping on the cave's floor. She could make out the lumpy shape of Cliff's body just a few feet away and could hear his heavy breathing. He had stacked a pile of wood nearby, and she picked out a few small pieces and laid them atop the fading embers. She bent close to the ashes and blew. A flame flickered to life, and the dried wood crackled as the fire slowly spread.

She pushed her hand close to the firelight and dipped her head low to look at her watch. It was two forty-five a.m. She had been asleep for only a couple hours. She carefully stacked larger pieces of wood on the fire and watched as saw-toothed shadows cast by the flames danced on the cave's walls.

Puck let the heat from the fire warm her before she started stuffing her belongings into her backpack. When she had finished, she stretched out her leg and nudged Cliff with the toe of her boot. "Cliff," she said, "wake up."

He ignored her and edged closer to the fire, where he curled up into a tight ball like a caterpillar. Puck stood and stepped over the fire toward him and kicked at him. "Cliff, get up," she demanded.

Cliff stirred and raised his head. "What time is it?" he asked.

"Almost three o'clock."

"In the mornin'?"

"Yeah. We need to get going," Puck said.

"Goin'? Goin' where?"

"Out of here. I know a way out."

"Yeah, me, too. Start diggin', and when you get tired, wake me and I'll spell you. It'll probably take a couple days without shovels."

"No, we're not going to tunnel our way out. The snow would probably cave in on us if we tried. There's another route."

"What are you talkin' 'bout? You're not making any sense."

"I know how to get us out of here, Cliff," Puck said.

"And how you know that?"

"Because it came to me in a dream."

"Don't say. A dream? That's what you woke me up to tell me?"

"That's right, a dream, with my father. He showed me the way out."

"Your daddy?"

"He's often in my dreams. We're wasting time, Cliff."

Cliff looked sleepily at Puck, yawned, and scratched his head. "Be a minute," he said. "I need to pack."

"Okay," Puck said, "but hurry. We don't have a lot of time. They'll be looking for us."

"Your daddy, he tell you that, too, in this dream?"

"Mm-hmm, he did."

CHAPTER 54

Jason Goetz felt lousy betraying Nik, but he didn't argue when Detective Jenks suggested the idea. "Help him, if you must, but only if we can get our hands on what we want," his partner instructed Goetz. "And if your conscience bothers you, don't make any promises about keeping the information confidential." While Goetz might have harbored personal doubts about the deceit, he did as Jenks asked because he owed his career to her. It was Jenks who had plucked a demoralized Goetz from DC's sex-crime unit when he was on the verge of quitting the force. There was no chance he was going to tell her no.

Goetz had steadily built a file on the woman the facial-recognition program had identified as Narda Hertzog. It didn't take him long to discover that Hertzog was an alias and the woman's real name was Jane Atwood. Goetz still didn't understand how Atwood tied into the Xion investigation, but he believed that her role would eventually be revealed the more information he gathered. He picked up the file from his desk. It wasn't exhaustive, but it was a good start, and it was getting thicker by the day. He decided to read through it once more before sharing it with Jenks:

Jane Austen Atwood, aka Narda Hertzog, aka Waldo, was born out of wedlock in Wheeling, West Virginia, in 1986 to a 16-year-old academically gifted high school student and part-time waitress who named her daughter after her favorite novelist. The girl's father, Randy Atwood, was a 22-year-old auto mechanic who quit his job and joined the US Navy shortly after he learned of the pregnancy. He was never heard from again. The girl's mother, Amanda Draper, dropped out of high school to have the baby but got her GED a year later and moved to Cincinnati, where she went to work for the US Postal Service.

Atwood attended an all-girls Catholic school in a Cincinnati suburb and graduated with honors and received several scholarship offers from East Coast schools to play women's lacrosse. She enrolled in the US Military Academy at West Point after receiving a nomination from her congressional representative, and excelled at marksmanship, self-defense, and combat skills. She was expelled from the academy in her junior year after being accused of supplying drugs to fellow cadets.

After bouncing around in various menial jobs, Atwood landed a position as an entry-level analyst at Lighthouse Defense, a private-security, risk-management, and military-contracting company located in the Washington, DC, area. The company eventually deployed Atwood overseas to work on US security operations, where she trained under former US Special Forces personnel. Her work was classified.

After stints in Europe and Central America, Atwood returned to the US and was assigned to a Lighthouse division that supported law enforcement agencies in combatting terrorism, narcotics smuggling, organized crime, and human trafficking. Atwood earned a reputation for provoking violent confrontations and gunfights with suspected criminals and is known to have fatally wounded at least three individuals during her tenure.

Atwood left Lighthouse for unspecified reasons and became a freelance security contractor working primarily for the US Department of Defense, Homeland Security, and the US Secret Service. In the role of a freelancer, she appears to have adopted several different aliases and false identities in addition to Narda Hertzog.

Her last known address was a beachside community in San Diego. Her current whereabouts are unknown.

Goetz made two additional copies of the file before walking one down to Jenks's office. After he had finished, he weighed the files in his hands and recalled Jenks's instructions: "Don't make any promises about keeping the information confidential."

Goetz locked the original file in his desk drawer and tucked a copy inside his coat pocket.

CHAPTER 55

Dark veins of lightning torched the nighttime sky outside the White House while inside President Warfield sat alone in front of the fireplace in the Oval Office, a drink in one hand, lost in his thoughts. An aide slipped in from a side door to stoke the fire and when he was through retraced his steps to leave.

Warfield hardly took notice. He finished the drink in one swallow and refilled his glass and continued to brood over the news he had received.

The DNA test results had come back, and the bodies in the cabin belonged to the two soldiers of fortune they had dispatched to the mountains, not the recluse, Samson, or the young research assistant, Hall. That could mean only one thing. They were still alive and on the loose somewhere up in those mountains. There was no trace of the Atwood woman.

As troubling as that was, even more disturbing was the news that reporters were asking questions about the Black Bird project, Atwood, and a missing $250 million in government funds that were supposed to have gone to vaccine production. Warfield had also gotten wind of Lance Craine's plan to conduct a Black Bird experiment at a prison facility in Nome, Alaska.

"Nome *fucking* Alaska," the president muttered, shaking his head.

Warfield looked down at his drink and was surprised to find the glass empty again. He swirled the cubes and debated having another. He'd already had three drinks. Or was it four?

"What the hell. Why not?" he said and pushed up from the chair. Warfield gave himself a healthy pour and plopped back down and took a sip. He'd be sure to nurse it slowly this time.

He made up his mind. It was time he took control of the Black Bird operation. If he didn't, he might be looking at spending the rest of his life in the Big House instead of another four years in the White House. No way in hell he was going to let that happen.

Amateur hour is over starting right fucking now, he told himself as he sucked on an ice cube. *Don't they get it? It's never been about China, really. Of course, you can't trust the cocksuckers, but who can you trust? Hell, I halfway admire the Chinese, tough sons o' bitches. It's about political power, for Christ's sake. And political power is about money. End of fucking story. Can't have one without the other, I don't give a shit what anyone else says.*

Warfield nipped at his drink and smacked his lips. He picked up a poker and jabbed at the fire, launching a cloud of sparks that landed in his lap. He yelped and jumped out of the chair, and when he did, he spilled his drink. "What the fuck," he cursed.

The door to the Oval Office sprang open, and a Secret Service agent rushed in, her hand on the butt of her gun. "Everything all right in here, sir? I thought I heard you cry out?"

"Fine, fine, Leticia. Just some sparks from the fire is all," an embarrassed Warfield said and brushed off the front of his trousers with the back of his hand.

"Very good, sir," the agent said, turned, and exited the room.

Nice ass, Warfield thought and let out a small belch as he refilled his glass. *Wonder who she's boning?*

He punched the phone on the table next to his chair and told the operator to get Lance Craine.

"Mr. President, how are you this evening, sir?" Craine said when he came on the line moments later.

"Looks like the mountain man and girl have given us the slip again," the president said.

Craine had become accustomed to late-night harangues from the president, particularly after Warfield had been hitting the bottle. "We'll get 'em, Mr. President."

"That's what you keep saying, Lance, but that's not why I'm calling."

"Oh?"

"Heard about your little Nome experiment."

"Mr. President, I hope you don't think I was trying to hide something from you."

"No, no, not at all, Lance. Perfectly understandable, and I appreciate that you want to insulate this office from, um, the fallout in case it doesn't go as drawn up."

"Exactly, sir," Craine responded.

"Fact is, it's a brilliant idea. Wish I had thought of it myself."

"Well, thank you, Mr. President."

"I don't need to know the details, but tell me, have you moved the product yet?"

"No, sir. That's the next step. Should happen in a day or two. We had to get our systems in place first. Took a little longer than I had hoped. It's Alaska."

"Good. I want you to personally deliver it and take that fellow from Xion with you."

"Sir?"

"You heard me."

"I'm not sure that's such a good idea, Mr. President."

"Nonsense. If we're going to pull this off, I need the two of you working side by side. Can't afford any more fuckups."

"Sir, I, um—"

"It's settled. I've made my decision. You'll take a government jet. I'll have one standing by for you. You like flying those Gulfstreams, right?"

"Yes, but—"

"Perfect. Have a good trip," Warfield said and hung up.

CHAPTER 56

Puck poked her head out and squinted. After spending hours trapped in darkness, the light stung her eyes and they filled with tears. She peered through watery slits and could just make out the sun edging above the treetops.

"Whatcha see?" Cliff asked.

"Sky, clouds," Puck whispered. "Boost me up so I can get a better look."

He wrapped his arms around her legs and heaved, shoving her shoulders and upper body through a crevice they had discovered in the rocks. Puck flinched in pain from the bullet wound in her shoulder but didn't make a sound, fearing someone might be nearby and hear. She twisted to the right and then back to the left, scanning the terrain. Trees and snow, as far as the eye could see. "Coast is clear," she said and wiggled free. "Come on out."

Cliff wedged his body through the opening and, a moment later, was standing alongside Puck. He rolled his stiff shoulders and rotated his neck to work out a kink. "I'll be damned," he said, "dreams do come true."

After walking hunched over or crawling on their hands and knees along the cave floor, they had finally seen a shaft of light coming through the rocks. They had made their way to it and found a gap big enough to squeeze through.

"Know where we are?" Puck asked.

"Yeah, think so," Cliff said and studied the landscape. "Couple miles below the cabin, or at least where the cabin used to be." He stretched out his arm and pointed a finger. "See that boulder down there in the distance?"

Puck stared where Cliff was pointing. "Yeah. Looks familiar."

"It should. That's where I found you. Well, not right there exactly, but around the bend from there. The river is off to the left of that."

Puck nodded her head, slowly recalling her struggle with Narda, getting shot, and the spot where Narda had died. "Seems like a long time ago," she said. "You think her body's still there, under the snow?"

"'Magine so. How's the leg?"

Puck bent over and rolled up her pants. Her knee was bleeding, and a button-size patch of flesh hung by a few threads of skin. "All that crawling didn't help any," she said.

Cliff slid the pack off his back and took out a roll of tape and rewrapped the wound. "Best I can do for now. You have any penicillin or pain pills left?"

Puck shook her head no. "Just ibuprofen."

Cliff nodded. "Okay. With luck, we'll be out of here late today. Think you can make it?"

"You kidding? I've come this far. I'll be damned if I'm not going to cross the finish line. Let's go."

They started down toward the river, Cliff in the lead, carving a path in the snow for Puck to follow. They were about fifty yards from the boulder when he stopped and cocked an ear.

"What?" she said.

"Shhh," Cliff said and remained rigid, listening. He finally shook his head and started walking again. "Thought I heard something. Guess not." He went another twenty-five yards and stopped again.

"I heard it, too, this time," Puck said. "What is it?"

He swiveled his head, trying to locate exactly where the sound was coming from. "Snowmobile."

Puck peered up at Cliff, her face a mask of anxiety. "How we gonna outrun it?"

Cliff glanced back up the mountain and shook his head. "We can't."

Standing only a few feet from where Narda's frozen and partially exposed body lay in the snow, the ground around the corpse packed down by the paw prints of wild animals scavenging for food, the whine of the snowmobile growing closer, Cliff calmly instructed Puck, "Once you cross to the other side, look for the game trail. Think you can find it?"

Puck nodded. "That's what I followed to get away the first time."

"Good. Snow will be fairly trampled down by now. You're going to head downstream. Stay on the trail for a couple miles until you come to the waterfalls. Follow me so far?"

Puck nodded again.

"Okay. There's a spot about two hundred yards below the falls where the river's slow and shallow. Should be frozen solid. That's where you cross back over to the other side, but be careful," Cliff said and reached inside his backpack. "Once you're on the other side, the trail dies. You're going to have to bushwhack. Here, take this," he said and shoved a compass into her hands. "Head due east from that point. You'll cut the Appalachian Trail in a couple hours if you make good time. From there, you're home free."

"Where are you going?" Puck asked, the growl of the snowmobile's engine nearly on top of them now.

"I'm going to try to draw them away from you best I can. You need to get out of here so you can tell your story. Now go."

Puck looked back over her shoulder when she was standing in the trees on the other side and saw Cliff, about fifty yards away, skidding down the middle of the frozen, snow-covered riverbed, a snowmobile bearing down on him.

CHAPTER 57

Nik held the envelope at arm's length and studied it before cautiously tearing it open. *Newshound* reporters had received mail laced with all matter of suspicious substances in the past—some toxic, most harmless—and he wasn't taking any chances. He peeked inside, and when he didn't see anything alarming, he turned the envelope upside down and shook it. A one-page letter floated to his desk.

Nik unfurled the page and quickly read it over. He checked the postmark. The envelope had been mailed from Arlington, Virginia, just across the river. There was no note attached explaining why he had received the letter or who had sent it. He held it up to the light to see if there were any identifying marks on the stationery but didn't find any.

He laid the paper on his desk, smoothed it out, and read it once again, more slowly this time. Jane Atwood was the subject of the letter. Some of the information contained in the letter was new; much of it confirmed what he and Zach had uncovered through their own reporting. The cadence of the letter suggested it was part of an official report, probably written by a government employee, not something dashed off by a civilian.

Only a few people—ten or twelve at the most—knew of Nik's interest in the woman. He could think of just a handful who worked in government—a Pentagon official Nik had cultivated over the years, an IRS source, and DC Detectives Jason Goetz and Yevette Jenks. He ruled out Jenks immediately. That left the military officials, Goetz, and the IRS source.

Then again, maybe Zach had talked to government sources who were familiar with Atwood, but, if that were the case, the letter would be addressed to Zach, not Nik.

If it was Goetz, was this his attempt to extend an olive branch to Nik for deceiving him about the Atwood photo in the first place, or was the detective setting him up like Jenks had, by issuing a "no comment" when asked if Nik was a suspect in the Lopes murder?

Nik's impression of Goetz had changed. He no longer viewed him as Jenks's bubbly, slightly empty-headed junior partner. Goetz was far more calculating than he had given the man credit for.

Nik had arrived at the office early to catch up on emails and let his officemates see him at work now that his suspension had been lifted. He opened the contact list on his phone and tapped on Goetz's phone number. He got the detective's voice mail. "Jason, it's Nik. We need to talk. Call me," he said cryptically and hung up.

Next, Nik walked down to *Newshound*'s podcast operations in the building's basement, looking for Mia, but instead found Mia's producer, Teo Mezos.

"What do you want?" Teo snarled when he saw Nik standing in the hallway. Nik and Teo had fought constantly when the pair had worked together on podcasts, and what little relationship they had permanently ruptured when Teo leaked Nik's story notes to Lizzy Blake. Mia had forgiven Teo and given him a second chance. Nik never would.

"Well, if it isn't Benedict Arnold," Nik said. "Where's Mia?"

Mia stuck her head out of her office door and held up a finger. "Hey, Nik, give me a second to wrap up a segment."

Mia had built a successful podcast empire for *Newshound*, and the company had rewarded her by significantly upgrading the operation since Nik had worked there, expanding the studio, adding new recording booths and equipment, and hiring additional staff. Nik felt she had more than earned the chance to be in the running for *Newshound*'s chief editor job.

"What's up?" Mia asked and steered Nik into her office. When the door was closed and Teo couldn't overhear the conversation, Nik said, "You remember that private security outfit you talked to a couple of years ago when we were working on the OmniSoft story?"

"Yeah, I think so. What about 'em?"

"I might need to get in touch with your source, but I can't remember the company's name or whom you talked to."

Mia spun around and tapped the keys on her computer. Mia's office had also received a makeover. Gone was the castoff office furniture, desk, chairs, and stained couch, replaced by sleek chrome-and-glass tables, a customized stand-up desk, and abstract paintings. "Company's name is Yellow Jacket Defense. The guy I talked to was Robert Churchill. I'll email you his contact info, and check with Mo. He also had a source there."

"Thanks, I will."

"What's this about?"

"Xion. We're getting closer. We have a solid lead on a woman who saw Anne Paxton just before she died, perhaps witnessed her death, maybe even had a hand in it. We've been able to trace a large portion of the money the government spent on its no-bid vaccine program, and we've confirmed there was a secret research program at Xion."

"Sounds promising, Nik, if you're able to confirm it."

"I'll admit we don't have it all nailed down, especially the research piece, and there's the little matter of two hundred and fifty million in government funds that we can't account for. And it's not just me. A lot of credit goes to Zach."

"What about the girl?"

"Not good. They've given up the search. She's presumed dead."

"Shit." Mia exhaled. "She wasn't much older than Zach."

"Yeah, I know," Nik said and opened the office door. "Anyway, thanks for the info."

"Sure. Let me know if there's anything else I can do to help."

"Will do."

Nik stepped out into the hallway and noticed Teo sneering at him from behind his desk. "Saw you on TV, Byron," Teo said as Nik started walking away. "You looked guilty as hell to me."

Nik ignored Teo and took the back stairway to the newsroom six floors above to get some exercise. He was in the stairwell when his phone vibrated. It was Jason Goetz. He answered, but even before he could say hello, Goetz said, "This is about the photo of the woman, isn't it?"

"No, Detective, it's not," Nik replied. "But I'm happy to talk about that if you'd like."

"Not particularly. What, then?"

"Bernard Rothschild."

"Oh, so you've heard?"

"Yeah, I did. You've reclassified his death. It's now a murder investigation, I'm told."

"News travels fast."

"How 'bout you fill in the details, Detective. Believe you owe me that."

"Off the record?"

"Okay."

"What would you like to know?"

"Who killed him, obviously?"

"We dunno, yet. Current thinking is it was a professional job made to look like a suicide, and we think whoever killed him also killed Greta Lopes."

"What made you change your mind?"

"We were finally able to get our hands on the evidence, piece together his movements, talk to a motel guest who was in the adjoining room. Said before he left to go out for the evening, he heard two men's voices coming from Rothschild's room. Then there was the knot."

"The knot?"

"Yeah, both victims died of strangulation—Rothschild by a rope; Lopes, a scarf. In both instances, the killer used a simple Hoxton knot around their necks."

"Guess this means you believe the suicide note was a fake and that Rothschild wasn't obsessed with the young research assistant after all? Somebody fed that bullshit to Lizzy Blake, Jason, just like they told her that I was a suspect in the Lopes killing."

"I know, Nik, but it wasn't us."

"Uh-huh, if you say so. Why'd they kill Rothschild and Lopes?"

"I was hoping you'd have a theory on that," Goetz said, "since all ours seem to be going nowhere."

CHAPTER 58

Zach and a few of his college buddies were at a bar in Adams Morgan taking advantage of free happy hour appetizers and cheap beer, and he didn't hear his cell phone's ringtone over the crowd noise. It was only later when he'd stepped outside to search for some extra money in his car that the phone began ringing again. He pulled it out of his pocket and looked at the screen. He had missed two calls. Both from the same number, the number that the call was coming from now. He didn't recognize it.

"Hello?" Zach said, a little buzzed from the beers he had gulped down.

"Zach?"

"Yeah."

"My name's Billy Clayton."

The name meant nothing to Zach. "Uh-huh," he said and pressed the speaker button on the phone and set it on the passenger seat. He started rummaging through the car's console and glove box and under the driver's seat for spare change.

"Lauren Kline from the Park Service said I was to get hold of you."

Zach's head snapped up, and he banged it hard against the steering column. "Fuck."

"Everything all right?" the caller asked.

"Yeah, yeah. Lauren told you to call?"

"She did. They found her."

"Found her? Found who, the girl?"

"Yup."

"Alive?"

"Yup. Alive."

"Holy shit. When?"

"Few hours ago."

"How is she?"

"Pretty rough shape, from what I gather."

"Is she conscious?"

"Dunno. That's all I was told about her condition. Sorry I can't be of more help."

"Where is she?"

"Being airlifted to a trauma center hospital in Charlotte as we speak."

"Who found her?"

"Apparently she walked out. A park employee came across her in a shelter."

"Jesus, that's incredible."

"Sure is. Lauren thought you'd want to know."

"Tell Lauren thanks for me, Billy. It's Billy, right?"

"It is, and I'll do that," Billy said and hung up.

"Fucking A," Zach shouted and pounded his fist on the dashboard and cranked over the car's engine. "Fucking A," he said again and peeled away from the curb as fast as the lumbering Volvo station wagon would go. His buddies would have to find another way home.

CHAPTER 59

Later that evening after Zach had filed his story about the missing hiker being found alive and was racing to the airport to catch a flight to Charlotte, Nik was manning the night desk at *Newshound* when an Associated Press story out of Anchorage moved across the wire:

A pair of F-35A Lightning IIs from Eielson Air Force Base in Fairbanks, Alaska, was diverted from a routine training mission today to intercept and follow an uncontrolled government jet racing across the northern Pacific Ocean. The fighter pilots tailed the aircraft for nearly two hours before it crashed into the sea, killing all aboard, including a Warfield administration official and a biotech executive.

The Federal Aviation Administration reported air traffic controllers lost contact with the Gulfstream G550 after clearing the twin-engine jet to climb to 40,000 feet northwest of Anchorage at 11:20 a.m. An FAA spokesperson said air controllers reported significant changes in altitude by the plane, but the flight crew did not respond to multiple radio calls from ground control.

A Pentagon official said the military began pursuit of the government aircraft at 12:12 p.m. and intercepted it at 1:05 p.m. over the Aleutian Islands. The Air Force pilots reported its occupants appeared to be unconscious and the plane's cabin windows frosted over, leading aviation experts to speculate that the aircraft had lost pressurization.

The pilots trailed the plane on a steady northwest heading as it repeatedly dipped and climbed between 22,000 to 52,000 feet. The pilots only broke off pursuit when the passenger jet began to wobble and then plunged nose first into the Pacific Ocean, apparently having run out of fuel.

According to the flight's manifest, Lance Craine, chief health preparedness officer to United States President Ronald Warfield and a retired Air Force pilot, was captaining the two-man crew. The copilot was identified as Randal Tompkins, a US Navy major. The only passenger on board the 16-seat jet was Glenn Bauer, the chief executive officer of Xion Labs, a biotech company based in Rockville, Maryland.

The flight's final destination was listed as Nome, Alaska, and the manifest reported the plane was transporting two crates, measuring six feet by four feet, consisting of medical supplies.

News of the jet crash sent shares of Xion Labs into a free fall in after-hours markets. The White House issued a press release saying the president was monitoring the situation but declined to comment on Craine's mission to Nome, or precisely what types of medical supplies the plane was transporting. City officials in Nome said they had not been alerted to a shipment of medical goods from the federal government and were at a loss to explain what the crates contained.

An investigation is underway by the FAA, but efforts to recover the plane's wreckage and black box appear unlikely given the location where the aircraft went down, a government source, who requested anonymity, told reporters.

The following day, President Warfield held an impromptu news conference on the south lawn of the White House before departing to Camp David. As the blades of Marine One whirled in the background, Warfield told reporters that a preliminary investigation indicated that Lance Craine, in concert with Xion CEO Glenn Bauer, had created a phony bioweapon research project to siphon hundreds of millions of dollars from the government's vaccine program.

"The First Lady and I got down on our knees last night and prayed that some good would come from this tragic accident," the president said, a catch in his voice, "and our prayers have been answered. Had the plane crash not happened, we might never have uncovered this betrayal of the public's trust. My pledge to the American people is that I will get to the bottom of this, and to that end, I've assembled an independent panel made up of distinguished public servants to conduct a thorough investigation into the nation's vaccine stockpile program. I've given explicit instructions to the panel to leave no stone unturned, and I expect them to work night and day to deliver a full report to my desk in three months."

Reporters shouted questions at the president after his brief remarks, but the helicopter's churning rotors drowned out their voices, and Warfield glided away from the pack. As the helicopter lifted off, Courtney Sachs, Warfield's director of communications, peered across the president's seat and out the window at the throng of reporters below, their upturned faces filled with impotent, confused expressions, and asked, "Have you really appointed an independent panel already? That was fast."

"If you want to call party loyalists and hacks who will report directly to the attorney general an independent panel, then, yeah, I have," said Warfield, who smiled and waved to the reporters and White House staff gathered on the lawn to see him off. "Oh, I'll add one or two toothless do-gooders to round out the group to make it appear balanced."

"That was a nice touch about you and the First Lady praying together," Sachs complimented her boss.

Warfield chuckled. "Hell, I haven't seen Mrs. Warfield in nearly two weeks, and she hasn't spoken a word to me in over a month, ever since that little incident with the ambassador's wife, but whatever."

"Do you really think the panel will be able to produce a report in three months' time?"

"Fuck no, but it'll buy me some time. I told the attorney general to slow-walk the goddamned thing until after the election. By then, people will have forgotten, and even if they haven't, it'll be too late to do much about it. Oh, the liberals and the press will piss and moan, but let 'em."

"You watching this?"

"Yeah, Mo, I am," Nik said, standing in his kitchen in boxers and a T-shirt drinking bitter, warmed-over coffee. President Warfield had just mounted the steps of Marine One, turned, and saluted the military honor guard before ducking his head and disappearing inside the helicopter. "Warfield just threw Craine and Xion's CEO under the bus. He's going to pin everything on them, claim Craine went rogue, that he had no idea what was going on," Nik said.

"Probably," Mo said.

"And that independent panel, that'll be a total fuckin' whitewash."

"Mm-hmm. So, where's this leave your story?"

"All depends," Nik said.

"On what?"

"On what the girl's able to tell us."

"And what if she doesn't know anything?"

"That could be a problem."

CHAPTER 60

Puck wasn't talking to anyone. She was dead.

Shortly after she arrived at Carolinas Medical Center in Charlotte, unconscious, severely frostbitten, dehydrated, and with barely a pulse, she went into cardiac arrest and her heart stopped.

"She died while she was on the gurney in the emergency room," the attending physician would later report.

But by dying where and when she had, Hall had provided the medical team with the rare chance to save her life.

She remained clinically dead for nearly an hour while staff administered CPR and rushed to hook her up to an extracorporeal membrane oxygenation machine, which pumps blood outside of the body to a heart-lung machine that removes carbon dioxide and delivers oxygen-filled blood back to tissues in the body.

"It's the most advanced life-support system in the world," her doctor would say later, "and it allows us to keep the patient viable by bypassing the heart and lungs."

After doctors restarted Hall's heart, staff remained at her side and monitored her for twenty-four hours until she stabilized. Initially, her heart labored to circulate blood throughout her body and her kidneys weren't functioning properly, but eventually her vital organs returned to working at near capacity.

"While we've been able to stabilize the patient, I'm afraid she has a steep hill to climb to full recovery and may yet suffer some long-term neurological and physiological damage," her doctor said. "In addition to the health issues we've described, she also lost a good deal of blood from a severely lacerated knee and what appears to be a gunshot wound to her shoulder. I've never seen a patient with such a strong will to live. It's a miracle she's survived for as long as she has, to be honest."

Four days after they disconnected her from the machine, Puck opened her eyes.

It would be months before she fully recovered her memory and motor skills.

CHAPTER 61

President Warfield's political enemies screamed for his scalp and demanded public accountability into what they referred to as Vaccinegate. Warfield ignored the uproar and maintained that he knew nothing about the scandal or the missing government funds. He claimed Lance Craine had gone behind his back, and insisted his handpicked panel was in the best position to conduct a proper investigation. In a series of town hall meetings across midwestern and southern states designed to get the president out of Washington, not a single participant raised the vaccine topic with Warfield during question-and-answer sessions.

"The American people couldn't give a rat's ass about Vaccinegate and congressional hearings," Warfield confided to a group of influential donors at a private luncheon in Phoenix.

"As our good friends south of the border like to say, '*Es a nada burrito, amigo,*'" Warfield deadpanned, drawing guffaws and nods from the wealthy crowd at the president's play on words to his standard "it's a nothing burger" reply.

As was often the case, Warfield's political instincts proved correct.

Senator Eva Summers, whose presidential campaign was starting to gain traction, commissioned a series of polls around the president's handling of the vaccine stockpile program. Only 7 percent of respondents rated the issue somewhat important, far down the list from the economy, climate change, health care, immigration, and crime.

The senator's polling also revealed that, if the election were held in the next month, Warfield would win in a landslide with more than 60 percent of the vote.

"I just don't get it," Summers complained to Samantha Whyte as the two pored over the poll results one evening in the senator's office. "It's as if the pandemic never happened."

"People want to move on with their lives now that things are finally returning to normal," Sam said, "and, as luck would have it, Warfield has found the perfect scapegoats—two dead guys lying at the bottom of the Pacific Ocean."

"Pretty damn convenient, wouldn't you say?" Summers lamented.

Over at *Newshound,* Nik was locked in heated discussions with editors and management about the fate of his Xion story. It wasn't going particularly well.

"I hate to be the bearer of bad news, Nik," Mo said, "but I think we're going to have to sit on the story at least until we see if one of these congressional investigations turns up anything."

"You can't be serious," Nik said and turned to Mia, who Mo had asked to attend the meeting in the hope that her presence would soften the blow. "Mia, tell him he doesn't know what he's talking about."

"I would, Nik, if I thought so, but I happen to agree with Mo on this one."

"I don't believe what I'm hearing," Nik said. "The story practically writes itself. What am I missing?"

"What's the lede, Nik?" Mo asked.

"That the government spent hundreds of millions of dollars conducting secret bioweapons research at Xion under the guise of the vaccine stockpile program. How's that grab you?"

"*Alleged* research program. According to Warfield, that was just a front Craine and Bauer used to plunder the Treasury," Mo countered. "Besides, it's not exactly news, is it? That's what his so-called independent panel is investigating."

"It wasn't phony research. That's a smoke screen. That's what Warfield wants people to believe. The bioweapons program was real."

"If what you say is true, Nik, and I'm not doubting it, why did Craine and Bauer conduct the research in the first place?" Mia continued. "What was the end goal? What were they trying to accomplish? I guess that's never been clear to me."

"We don't know precisely," Nik said, exasperated. "All we can do at this point is offer informed speculation and, oh, by the way, all the people who do know are dead. Tell me you don't see the connection."

Barry Clouser, *Newshound*'s corporate attorney, who had been sitting off to the side quietly taking notes, interjected, "Nik, you do understand that our critics will claim any story that isn't one hundred percent verifiable, with on-the-record sources, is merely an attempt by *Newshound* to strike back at Xion for embarrassing us by releasing the video of you trying to break into their facilities."

"That's bullshit," Nik said, "and you know it."

"Perhaps, but that's what they'll say."

"What about the woman, Jane Atwood? Have you located her?" Mia asked.

"No. There's been no sign of her. We even sent someone to stake out her apartment in California."

"And Rothschild and Lopes, what are the DC cops saying about their deaths?" Mo asked.

"I got some stuff, but it's all off the record. I can't use it."

Mo asked, "Has Zach had any luck getting the girl to talk?"

"She's not refusing to talk, Mo," Nik said, the frustration rising in his voice. "She can't fucking talk. She suffered neurological damage of some sort."

"Sorry, Nik, but the story has too damn many holes," Mo said, "and until they're plugged, I wouldn't be comfortable recommending we publish."

"This is un-fucking-believable!" Nik shouted. "So you're just going to let the story die, accept the administration's whitewash?"

"Come on, Nik, calm down. You know us better than that. It just needs more time, s'all we're saying," Mo said.

"Don't fucking tell me to calm down. I am calm. And, yeah, I did think I knew the two of you better, but clearly I was wrong. Shame on me," Nik said, gathering up his notes and storming out of the office.

"That went over well," Mia said.

"Yeah," said Mo, staring up at the ceiling, hands resting on top of his head, fingers interlaced. "Like a lead fuckin' balloon."

CHAPTER 62

Three Months Later

Nik carefully lifted the bottle out of the roiling water and squirted half a dozen drops of liquid onto his wrist. The milky substance stung and raised little red welts on his skin, and he unscrewed the cap to allow the formula to air cool. Next, he would check the temperature with a thermometer before offering the bottle to Isobel for her nighttime feeding. He knew his method was old school, but it was what he preferred.

In the past a less patient Nik would have skimmed over the preparations, but now that Sam and Isobel were living with him again, he was more exacting and took care to do the small things properly. Sam had remained lukewarm to the idea of moving back in and only agreed to reunite on a trial basis in order to gauge Nik's willingness to take the relationship's responsibilities more seriously.

She never doubted that he loved her and Isobel unconditionally, but she was aware that there was a side of Nik that viewed commitments not as obligations, necessarily, but as something more akin to aspirations, nice to have but not critical. That didn't work for her, but Sam now had to admit Nik had changed and he appeared to be all in. They'd even talked about rescheduling their long-delayed wedding.

There were several factors that had influenced his metamorphosis. Nik had come to realize just how much he stood to lose and perhaps never regain if Sam walked away. Then, too, Maggie, his ex-wife, announced her engagement to her partner at the law firm, Paul Robinson, bringing that chapter in his life to a close once and for all.

And lastly, Nik had lost interest in work after the Xion story fizzled.

He had patched up his differences with Mo and Mia as best he could and had moved back to the daytime shift, which allowed him to have a more normal home life. Fellow staffers embraced Nik's return to the newsroom, and for a time, the new routine energized him. But it was short-lived, and before long, he tired of the assignments and became unmotivated.

He found himself daydreaming about quitting his job to become a stay-at-home dad and about writing a novel. Nik was financially well off after *Newshound* had gone public and, with Sam's income, didn't need to work.

"What are you doing in there, milking the cow?" Sam called out to Nik from a back bedroom that she had converted into an office. "She's fussing and needs to eat before we can put her down for the night."

"Be there in a second, babe," Nik said and screwed the cap back on the baby bottle and hustled out of the kitchen and down the hallway. He found Sam seated at her desk, her hair up, dressed in her favorite crewneck sweater and faded jeans, two laptops propped open, cans of Diet Coke perched on corners, and the floor littered with thick printouts.

Isobel was standing in her playpen and started squealing when she saw Nik with the bottle. He offered it to her, and she reached out two chubby hands that she clamped around the bottle and then started guzzling.

"You almost done?" Nik asked and surveyed the pile of reports on the floor. "There's something I'd like to talk to you about."

"Nowhere near, but I can take a break for a bit after we put her to bed."

Nik glanced over at Isobel. She had drained half the bottle and was still chugging away.

"Shouldn't be long now," he said. "What are you working on?"

"Revising a speech Senator Summers is giving to a medical association next week about the Affordable Care Act."

"Riveting," Nik said and yawned.

"It's important."

"I have no doubt."

There was a clank, and they both turned to see the baby bottle skidding across the floor and Isobel lying flat on her back in the playpen, asleep.

"What did you put in her formula?" Sam asked.

"A shot of brandy. Why, don't you?"

"No, but I like the way you think. I'll have to give it a try," she said and lifted Isobel from the playpen. "You want to make a pot of coffee and I'll put her to bed?"

"Deal," Nik said.

"So, what do you want to talk about?" Sam asked when she was back at her desk, cradling the warm coffee mug in her hands.

"I'm thinking about quitting *Newshound*."

"*Really*. To do what?"

"The daddy-day-care thing while working on a book idea I have. Plus, the intramural baseball season is starting up. I'll have plenty to keep me busy, and with the money I made on the

Newshound IPO, we can live more than comfortably on your salary, I figure."

"This isn't about the Xion story, is it? Because if it is, stories get spiked all the time in the news business, Nik. You of all people should know that."

"I'd be lying to say it didn't play a part, but it's not just that. It feels like it's time. Past time, actually. So, what do you think?"

"It's not a crazy idea. If the senator's presidential campaign really takes off, I'll be on the road constantly. It'd be comforting to know you were here holding down the fort. And you'd be good at it."

"Well, that's high praise coming from you."

"I mean it. You've really stepped up, Nik. When are you thinking about letting them know?"

"Thought I'd wait until the end of the month. Give me a little more time to think things through."

"Sounds reasonable."

"I appreciate you not throwing cold water on the idea immediately. I wasn't sure how you'd react."

"Of course."

"So, what's all this stuff?" Nik said and nudged one of the printouts on the floor with his toe.

"Federal campaign contribution reports, both ours and Warfield's. I swear to God, the man mints money. He's outraising us three-to-one. And his super PACs, they're a gusher of dark money. Hundreds of millions of dollars pouring in, and we're blind to where it's coming from or from whom."

"How do they manage that? I thought PACs had to disclose their donors?"

"They get around it by first routing donations through dark-money nonprofits—501(c) entities—which do not have to disclose who the donors are."

"Mind if I take a look?"

"Be my guest. Trying to figure out where the money is coming from is a Rubik's Cube."

Nik picked up Warfield's personal campaign report and started flipping through it. Donor names and the amount they contributed were listed alphabetically. Nik recognized many of the names, a who's who of Washington lobbyists and the politically connected.

He dropped the Warfield report back on the floor and plucked out a filing labeled "Super PACs." The printout, again arranged alphabetically, listed the name of the PAC, its treasurer, where it was incorporated, how much money it had raised, and, if required, donor names and amounts. Nik noticed most of the big donations were from LLCs, limited liability corporations, that were able to sidestep the disclosure requirement.

Nik leafed through the listing. It was standard fare—Americans for Free Enterprise, $156 million; American Patriots, $12 million; Businesses for Tax Overhaul, $25 million; Better Government Choices, $6 million; Coalition for Families, $2 million; Conservatives to Re-Elect Warfield, $275 million; Defenders of Democracy, $8 million; Friends of Freedom, $31 million; and so on.

Nik's eyes glazed over and the report hit the floor with a thwack. "I've seen enough. Think I'm going to bed to read."

"Don't blame you. I still have an hour or more left here. I'll try not to wake you. Good night," Sam said and tilted her chin up toward Nik, who leaned down and gave her a lingering kiss and ran his hand over her thighs.

"Wake me," he said. "I insist."

Sam winked. "Sure thing, Romeo."

After brushing his teeth and admiring his slimmed-down physique in the mirror, Nik climbed into bed with a biography of Ben Franklin. It was a door stopper, and he'd been struggling to get through it for several months. Within minutes, his eyelids drooped, and the book slid out of his hands.

In the middle of the night, long after he had made love to Sam, Nik's eyes flashed open and suddenly he was wide awake. *"Crew,"* he said softly to himself and then quietly spelled out the letters: "*C-R-E-W.* Fuck me. That's gotta be it."

Nik tumbled out of bed, his heart thundering in his chest, and fumbled around in the dark before he found his glasses on the nightstand, slipped them on, and then rushed out of the bedroom to Sam's office, nearly tripping over Gyp, curled up on the floor.

CHAPTER 63

Had Zach not known differently, he never would have suspected that Puck Hall had survived multiple near-death experiences. Looking at her now, sitting in a chair in her cheery, sun-filled apartment, she was a picture of health, clear-eyed, rosy-cheeked, her chestnut hair thick and shoulder length. It was only when she spoke that it was apparent there was something wrong. She talked haltingly, if at all, and struggled to complete her thoughts. She would start describing an event, stop, start again, then stop before giving up altogether in frustration. And because of this, she had only been able to provide fragments of her ordeal to examiners.

Her doctors believed that Puck's condition had more to do with the trauma she had endured in the wilderness, rather than the cardiac arrest, and speculated it was possible she could snap out of it at any time given the right stimuli. What that might be, they couldn't say.

When Nik tracked Zach down at the college bookstore where he worked after his internship ended to ask him to temporarily return to *Newshound*, he warned Zach that Puck was still undergoing intensive speech therapy and that he shouldn't expect a whole lot from an interview but that they had to try.

Now, Zach smiled at Puck as she sat cross-legged in the chair opposite him. A giant, colorful get-well card, the size of a big-screen television, hung on the wall behind her and read, "Don't Fuck with Puck." It was from her former college volleyball teammates and coaches.

Zach started out the conversation by recounting the stories *Newshound* had published about Puck's disappearance, the search-and-rescue operation, and her discovery. He told her that he had remained in contact with her mother and the National Park Service throughout the ordeal and that he had a sixth sense that she would be found alive despite the odds. Puck listened intently to Zach and followed along with her eyes but didn't offer a comment.

When Zach would gently ask a question, Puck responded by either shrugging her shoulders, shaking her head, or widening her expressive eyes, but not once did she attempt to speak.

Seeing any hope fade that Puck would be able to assist in their reporting, Zach quickly skimmed over the details of the rest of the Xion story. He concluded by telling her that *Newshound* editors had initially declined to publish the story because they felt it was too speculative but now were reconsidering, based on new information. Nothing Zach said elicited the slightest verbal response from Puck.

It was only when Zach mentioned Anne Paxton's name in passing as he was packing up his things to leave that Puck finally spoke.

"Hhh . . . hhhow'd she die?" she huffed.

"Skiing accident," Zach said, then paused before adding, "allegedly. We haven't been able to prove it, but we think foul play might have been involved. Can I show you something, Puck?"

She nodded.

Zach pulled his phone out of his pocket and started swiping through screens. When he found what he was looking for, he turned the phone toward Puck and held it up for her to see.

Puck's head jerked sideways as if she had been backhanded. Her body stiffened, her eyes flared, and her breathing intensified. She remained rigid and drew up fully in the chair, a dark expression carved on her face, mechanically working her jaws like a steam shovel, as if she were chewing on a strand of barbed wire. Something inside of her appeared to have ruptured.

"You know her?" Zach asked and waited.

Puck continued to exercise her jaws. "I know her," she said, her speech returning, the voice flat, clear, strong, the warble gone. "Narda."

"That's right," Zach said, startled by the sudden change that had come over Puck. "She went by the name Narda. Narda Hertzog. Her real name is Jane Atwood. We've been trying to find her."

"You won't," Puck said.

"Why's that?"

"She's gone."

"Gone?"

"Dead."

"Dead? You sure?"

"Yeah, I killed her."

Narda's photo was apparently the jolt that Puck's senses needed to break free of the chains imprisoning her mind. Her voice and speech returned, not in a rush, but slowly, and it took several hours for her to relate her tale to Zach.

She told Zach about first meeting Narda at Sassafras Gap on the Appalachian Trail, the ambush two days later, then the second attack where she was shot and Narda killed. She told him about Cliff, the fur trapper, finding her half frozen in the snow and taking her in and caring for her, and the two attempts by armed men to kill her and Cliff, and getting trapped in a cave by an avalanche. She didn't know what had become of Cliff. The last she saw, he was luring a man on a snowmobile away from her so she could make her escape.

The retelling of the events exhausted Puck, and later, after Zach had left, she went to bed and slept for eleven solid hours. She woke fresh and called Zach the next day and arranged to meet again. She wanted to relay the information she had discovered on Narda's phone.

CHAPTER 64

Ronald Warfield was leaning against the railing of the presidential yacht, smiling warmly at the busty cocktail waitresses and collection of NRA executives and gun-rights advocates he was hosting for an evening cruise on the Potomac River. Courtney Sachs sidled up next to him and held her phone in his face so he could privately read the headline: "'Federal vaccine funds secretly ended up in coffers of Warfield's political supporters,'" the president mouthed silently.

Warfield spit out the crab cake he was eating, and his face turned the color of mayonnaise that had been left out in the sun too long.

"Y'all right?" asked Mindy, a perky redhead from Texas, one of a half dozen young female servers all dressed identically in cowgirl getups with matching six-shooters, low-cut vests, and chaps.

"Seasick," his communications director responded and steered the queasy commander in chief belowdecks.

The story swept through Washington like wildfire. It had taken some digging, but Nik was eventually able to confirm his late-night hunch—that the super PAC Conservatives to

Re-Elect Warfield had been the recipient of the wire transfers Greta Lopes had made to an account with the same four identifying initials—CREW.

Nik's story traced how $250 million in vaccine funds had hopscotched around the globe before it wound up in the bank account of the innocuous-sounding "For a Better America," a dark-money nonprofit that then funneled the proceeds to Conservatives to Re-Elect Warfield. Coincidentally, the two entities shared many of the same board members, a number of whom were either former Warfield political appointees or donors.

Over the next several weeks, the news only got worse for the president.

A friendly FAA bureaucrat had leaked Nik a detailed manifest from the Gulfstream jet that had crashed in the Pacific Ocean. It disclosed the contents of the two crates the plane was carrying in its cargo hold. One crate held vials of a manmade virus and its accompanying vaccine, the other crate cages of crows.

Nik shared the flight manifest, Bernard Rothschild's notebook, Anne Paxton's journals, and internal Xion documents he pried loose using Freedom of Information Act requests with a panel of internationally recognized virologists. The panel blasted the Warfield administration and the late Lance Craine for conducting what it concluded was an illegal attempt to create a bioweapons program with the sole purpose of introducing the virus to human populations through contact with infected crows. The panel said it did not find any evidence that the program had succeeded and believed that all traces of the virus lay buried at the bottom of the Pacific Ocean.

The reporters were also able to paint a compelling picture of Jane Atwood as a mercenary and for-hire assassin sent to kill Anne Paxton and Puck Hall, and linked her, through phone records, to Lance Craine.

President Warfield disappeared from public view and only briefly surfaced to do a sit-down interview with Fox's Lizzy Blake in which he maintained his innocence, claimed he had no control over outside PACs, cursed Lance Craine, and attacked Nik Byron as a tool for his political opponent Senator Eva Summers, calling his reporting nothing more than a "political hatchet job."

"And a drunk," Lizzy reminded him.

"Right, that, too," Warfield concurred.

The Speaker of the House of Representatives, a member of Warfield's own political party, felt Warfield had left him no choice and reluctantly initiated impeachment proceedings against the president of the United States.

EPILOGUE

To avoid a certain trial and conviction in the US Senate, Ronald Warfield resigned his presidency. His vice president was sworn in and immediately became his party's leader and shoo-in nominee. Despite assurances to the contrary, he refused to pardon Warfield.

"You promised a full fucking pardon," Warfield protested. "Otherwise, I would never have resigned."

"My advice, cop a plea, Ron, and I'll grant clemency. Pardon wouldn't be prudent with an election coming up and all. You understand," his former running mate said.

"You cocksucking little weasel, you'll pay for this," Warfield threatened as he was led away by Secret Service agents.

"My, my. What a nasty temper," the new president said, shaking his head, "and the language. I'm only glad Mother wasn't here to witness that," he said of his wife, now the First Lady.

"Not a good look, sir," Courtney Sachs said and slid a piece of paper across the presidential desk. "I've taken the liberty to line up interviews for you with all the major news talk shows on Sunday to lay out your agenda to the American people. Hope you don't mind."

Senator Eva Summers, after losing the Iowa caucuses and New Hampshire primary, had a strong showing in the Super Tuesday primaries and appeared to be a legitimate contender for her party's nomination to be its presidential candidate in the fall.

A search party found Jane Atwood's badly mauled and nearly decapitated body in an abandoned wolf's den. They also recovered the charred bodies of two men in a burned-out cabin and a partially submerged snowmobile in a river swollen with snowmelt.

Searchers could find no trace of Clifford Samson, the former Army Ranger and fur trapper.

Puck Hall staged a full recovery, and except for some stiffness in her wounded shoulder when it rained, she had no lingering health effects. Zach graduated from college and accepted a reporting position at *Newshound,* where Mo and Mia had been named co-chief editors of the organization.

Investigations into the deaths of the former Xion employees remained ongoing.

As for Nik, he finished the first draft of his novel, *When the Stars Came Out*, a fictionalized account of the 1942 World Series between the New York Yankees and the Kansas City Monarchs of the Negro League, and was preparing to submit it to agents. He loved being at home with Isobel and didn't regret his decision to leave *Newshound.* Sam, as she predicted, was living out of a suitcase as her boss crisscrossed the country campaigning. She slept peacefully, when she found the time to sleep, knowing Nik was at home tending the fires.

SNEAK PEEK FROM THE NEXT BOOK IN THE NIK BYRON INVESTIGATION SERIES

RENDEZVOUS

by Mark Pawlosky

PROLOGUE

Rural Virginia

Nik Byron's chin trampolined off his chest, jolting him awake, just moments before his vehicle was about to slam into a telephone pole. He jerked the steering wheel hard, veered left, shook his head, cracked open the driver's window, and decelerated, gliding the restored Ford Bronco onto a darkened off-ramp. He gulped down mouthfuls of cool air to settle his jangled nerves and coasted to the bottom of the exit, depressed the clutch, stopped, and looked around. It was unfamiliar terrain, and a heavy mist hung in the air. He had relied on Waze to navigate to the rural crossroads, and the disembodied female voice was now instructing him to turn south. Nik slowly let out the clutch and nosed the Bronco onto the access road. The vehicle's front end had just crossed the centerline when a loud roar shattered the predawn calm. He snapped his head toward the sound and instantly was blinded by onrushing lights. He felt a violent impact, glass shards stabbing at his face, neck, and hands, his body whipsawing, and heard the high-pitched screech of metal on metal, like a runaway train applying its brakes. Then . . . silence.

"Mister." A faint cry came from nowhere, like a whisper over open water. "You awright?"

Nik's eyes fluttered open.

He lay motionless, the space around him as dark and impenetrable as the bottom of the ocean, the air damp and smelling faintly of clover. He thought he was awake, but then again, maybe it was a dream. When he passed his hand in front of his face, he couldn't see it, and when he reached up to touch his cheek, he couldn't feel it.

Struggling, he propped himself up on his elbows, and that's when he realized the vintage US Navy flight jacket he was wearing had gotten wound around his head like a cloak. He slowly unwrapped the garment and looked about. It was nighttime and his vision blurred. He groped in the darkness for his wire-rimmed glasses, found the twisted frames nearby, and slid them on, the lenses smeared with blood. He could make out stars and a crescent moon overhead.

"You hear me?" the voice said, now closer. Nik swiveled to locate the source, and when he did, an electric bolt ripped down his neck and spine and a searing pain exploded in his skull. He dropped his head between his legs, gagged, and nearly blacked out. When he looked up, a frog-eyed old man with a rubbery face was bent low over him, peering down, his breath like sour milk.

"Where . . . where am I?" Nik croaked.

"Be still," the old man advised. "I called 9-1-1. Ambulance should be here shortly. What are you doing out here at this hour?"

Hazily, Nik began to recall events. He was on his way to rendezvous with a source, a woman, about a story. "M-my v-vehicle?" he stammered.

The old man jerked his chin back over his shoulder, toward the road. Nik's eyes followed the gesture. He could see an orange glow in the near distance.

"On fire?" Nik asked.

The old man nodded. "Not much left, to be honest. Just a burned-out husk, mostly."

"B-b-but how?"

The old man shook his head. "Damned if I know. It was that way when I arrived. Looks as if you were broadsided and thrown from your vehicle and landed in this hayfield."

"Where's the car that hit me?"

"No sign of it, but it must have been one helluva big rig, by the looks of things. Practically seared off the front end of your vehicle. Miracle you weren't killed."

"I remember now. I was turning and didn't see it until it was nearly on top of me," Nik said, and added absentmindedly, "I wasn't wearing my seat belt. My dog, Gyp, chewed through it a couple weeks ago."

"Lucky thing for you, too," the old man said. "You'd have been roasted alive if you were strapped in."

Nik asked, "You see a blue SUV, woman driver?"

The old man shook his head again.

Nik heard the wail of sirens.

The old man cocked his head. "That'd be the ambulance," he said. "Sheriff, too, I s'pect."

"Help me up," Nik said, and attempted to stand. His legs quivered and his knees buckled. The old man caught Nik under his arms just before he toppled over. The effort exhausted Nik and he blanched and started to retch.

"You shouldn't try to move, son. From what I can tell, you're fairly busted up and lost a good deal of blood," the old man said and gently lowered Nik back to the ground. "Is there anybody you want me to call, let them know what happened?"

Nik's eyes clouded over and he struggled to form words. "Yeah," he finally managed to utter. "The White House."

ABOUT THE AUTHOR

© 2022 Evan McGlinn

Mark Pawlosky is an award-winning author and journalist. A former reporter for the *Wall Street Journal,* editor in chief of CNBC on MSN, and editorial director for American City Business Journals (ACBJ), he oversaw financial news channels in the US, London, Munich, Paris, Tokyo, and Hong Kong. He successfully helped launch several media operations nationwide, including MSNBC and ACBJ. A graduate of the University of Missouri's School of Journalism, he is the author of the Nik Byron book series. *Black Bird* is the third novel in the series, preceded by *Hack* and *Friendly Fire.* He is at work on the next book, *Rendezvous.* You can learn more about the author and series at www.markpawlosky.com.

Printed in the USA
CPSIA information can be obtained
at www.ICGtesting.com
CBHW031519070524
8184CB00006B/52

9 798218 330033